CH00779804

ISBN: 9798840699584

Cover design by: Erelis Design
Library of Congress Control Number: 2018675309
Printed in the United States of America

KING OF WAR

Part Four in the Viking
Blood and Blade Saga

Peter Gibbons

In Memory of Bryan. Swa hi bylde forð

A PASSAGE FROM THE WANDERER, A 10TH CENTURY ANGLO SAXON POEM

þonne won cymeð,
nipeð nihtscua,
norþan onsendeð
hreo hæglfare
hæleþum on andan.
Eall is earfoðlic
eorþan rice,
onwendeð wyrda gesceaft
weoruld under heofonum

Then dark comes,
nightshadows deepen,
from the north there comes
a rough hailstorm
in malice against men.
All is troublesome
in this earthly kingdom,
the turn of events changes
the world under the heavens.

ONE

874AD.

The Lords of the north were viciously brutal and notoriously wealthy men. Sea Lords and Viking Jarls hoarded the proceeds of countless raids up and down the coasts of Saxon England, along the east coast of Ireland, across the wild lands of Strath Clota, and west in fertile Frankia. Hundr ran across a wind-whipped hilltop. The ice in the air made his eyes water, and his hands were red and raw from the cold where he clutched a coil of seal hide rope. He glanced over his shoulder, and his men loped through the bracken behind him, lean and hungry. He knew the risk was worth the reward. His fleet of five warships was moored in a secluded bay west of the island, a high-sided rock-encircled inlet with no beach and nowhere for ships to dock. Its inhospitableness meant that the inlet was unwatched by the island's Lord, Ketil Flatnose, Jarl of the Orkney Islands. Therefore, Hundr had been able to clamber up the treacherous cliffs along with his men—hard men, killers, and warriors all.

"Firelight, there," called Einar the Brawler, shouting above the howling wind. Einar pointed into the belly of a valley curling away to the north, where the orange glow of firelight danced and flickered from buildings and halls.

"That's the stronghold," said Hundr, and he paused, dropping to one knee. Einar came alongside him, his hard, slab-like face set against the cold.

"The wall doesn't look too high from here," Einar remarked, and he shook his head as bare-chested warriors ran past him clutching long-handled war axes. "Madmen. Wearing no breastplate or brynjar is one thing, but they must be colder than an ice bear's tit." He pulled his cloak around him against the cutting gusts.

"When we get down there, we need to get over that wall quickly. I'll go up after Ragnhild and tie the rope. Make sure you send two men after me." Hundr clapped his friend on the shoulder, and they set off at a run again, sprinting just behind his berserkers. The cold air burned in his chest, his breath coming in quick gasps. The stronghold loomed out of the darkness, its torchlight illuminating pockets of timber and thatch. It was a wolf moon, full and bright, giving just enough light for Hundr to see where he put his feet. Too little moonlight would have made such an attack impossible. A man could put his foot in a divot or slip on a turd, and a scream would give them up to any sentries on the walls. Hundr let the slope quicken his pace, breaking into an all-out run as the hill flattened out, and he came within thirty paces of the walls. In the darkness, the tree trunks looked like a giant's under-bite, shadowed timber chopped to spikes rearing from the earth in a jagged growl.

"Ragnhild, are you ready?" he shouted as loud as he dared without waking the warriors within the fortress, for there would be warriors in there. This was the stronghold of Ketil Flatnose, a Norse Jarl who had forged a reputation for raiding and ruthlessness. Ketil had taken the Orkney Isles by his sword and created his own jarldom, or earldom, held strong by his fleet of warships and the strength of his warriors' blades.

"Just get me up there," Ragnhild called back as she ran. The night obscured her scarred face, except for the whiteness of her teeth as she flashed a grin at him.

Hundr ran hard for the wall, ignoring the chance that a sentry on the walls might spy him and his warriors as they descended upon the fortress. Orkney was an island, and if any man landed a ship of bloodthirsty Vikings on its ports

3

or beaches, then Ketil would hear of it in no time, and his warriors would be ready to meet that enemy with steel. Hundr, however, had taken the treacherous route, scaling the rock face and risking death to seize the element of surprise. He slammed his back into the timber posts of the stronghold's wall, the smell of smoke drifting out of it like a stamped-out campfire. Hundr knelt and cupped his hands, and without pause, Ragnhild ran towards him. When she was two paces away, she leapt at him, placing a muddy boot in his cupped palms and launching herself with a grunt. Hundr spun around and caught her feet just as she grasped the outside of the timber spike above. He pushed her heels up, and then she was gone, up and over the walls like a rat scurrying along a mooring rope. Ten heartbeats later, her face appeared over the parapet, and Hundr took the seal hide rope from his shoulder and threw it up to her. Another ten heartbeats, and he had scaled the wall, climbing hand over hand up the rope where Ragnhild had secured it. Hundr clambered around the sharpened point of the walls' stakes and crouched on the fighting platform atop the walls. He scanned the inside of the stronghold. It was deep into the second watch, and sputtering torches cast a dim light along a mud-churned path that ran across the length of the town. On either side of the pathway were stone-built houses with thatched roofs, and rising from the darkness was Ketil's hall, high gabled and with smoke billowing from its central smoke hole like a sleeping dragon. A grunt below caused Hundr to peer over the parapet, and he saw Ragnhild wrenching her axe from the skull of a gate guard. It was she who had grunted with the effort of tugging her blade from the bone and brains of the dead warrior. Sleeping on duty had cost him his life, and Ragnhild was a pitiless killer.

The planking beneath Hundr's feet shuddered as two warriors slunk over the wall to drop either side of him—wild men stripped to the waist, their torsos glistening with sweat. They were both berserkers, men who had joined Hundr's crew from the ashes of defeat. Facing death, they had sworn oaths to Hundr and now brought their maddened battle fury to his banner. Hundr leapt from the fighting platform to drop into the belly of the sleeping fortress, and the two berserkers followed. They ran to where a heavy wooden beam barred high twin gates of oak, as thick around as a man's waist. The three raiders braced their shoulders underneath the beam and heaved. Then, just as the beam shifted out of its iron crutches, a door opened from a building ahead to spill laughter, torchlight, and a stumbling drunk into the moonlit pathway. Hundr paused, his shoulders trembling under the weight of the beam. He held his breath as the drunken man scratched his beard and let out a mighty belch. Ragnhild knelt before the door and carefully removed her recurved bow from her back. It was an eastern weapon of horn and wood with the power of a mule's kick in its crafting. Hundr wanted to shout to her to wait, not shoot at the man until the gate was open and his warriors were within the fortress. But she took a white-feathered arrow from the quiver at her waist and nocked it to the string. The bow creaked in the quiet of the night as she drew it back to her ear. The bow thrummed, and the arrow whistled as it flew in a low, flat line to slam into the drunk man's chest, throwing him backwards and into the pathway's filth.

"Shit!" gasped Hundr as he let his breath out. "Get the gate open, now." Visions of Ketil Flatnose marching from his hall, backed by scores of warriors, flashed in Hundr's mind. He heaved again, and his berserkers heaved with him. The beam groaned and scraped and moved a handsbreadth. More men tumbled through the steaming doorway and immediately saw the man dead in the dirt. They turned with shadowed faces to see that their island stronghold was under attack, that the sea raiders themselves were being raided. One of those men died with a wicked arrow shot thudding into his face, dropping instantly, but the other man roared the alarm and awakened the fortress.

The beam rose free of its callipers and

dropped to the earth with a dull thud. Hundr drew his axe from its loop at his belt and reached behind his back to draw his broken-back bladed seax. He left the two berserkers to haul open the gates, the heavy timber creaking on its iron hinges, and Hundr strode forward to stand with Ragnhild. Bodies poured from other buildings, gathering like gulls on a fresh catch. More torches spat into flame, and shouts of alarm became replaced by howls of defiance as the warriors of Ketil Flatnose came to kill the raiders. Ragnhild continued to loose her shafts, and the deadly arrows forced bodies out of the pathway, back to the fringes of the houses and into cover. Hundr heard a roar behind him, and his men came flooding in, hungry for blood and silver. He watched as the brave warriors formed a makeshift shield wall at the centre of the pathway ahead of him. It was only three shields wide, but it covered most of the pathway and would present a formidable barrier to the onrushing Vikings. Hundr felt his anxiety wash away. He wiped away a drip of fluid where it leaked from his dead eye to run down a ravaged cheek.

"Gorm," Hundr said as he grabbed the brawny arm of a raven-haired berserker about to dash past him. "Take your men and destroy that shield wall. Then, cut a pathway to Flatnose's hall. That's where the silver will be." The baleful figure of the berserker captain nodded, and he bellowed to his bloodthirsty warriors to follow him into the slaughter.

"Einar, take a crew left, Ragnhild right. Come to the hall from the north." There was no need for a response. Ragnhild and Einar had fought with Hundr in countless skirmishes, raids, and battles. They had scaled walls, sacked cities, and killed kings. They were the sea wolves, masters of war, and they knew their business. Hundr trusted his berserkers would cut their way through the enemy shield wall. Then, they would use their brutal strength and fury to drive their way up the stronghold's central pathway and onward to Ketil's hall. Hundr ran to his left and then darted into a ginnel running between two rows of stone houses. He pounded up the narrow laneway, leaping over piles of broken wood and bales of rancid hay. His breath still came ragged and fast from the run across Orkney's stark hills. The walls closed in, and Hundr had to turn sideways to squeeze his frame through the space, his axe blade scraping on the roughly dressed stone.

For a terrifying moment, he wondered what would happen if he was trapped there and captured by Ketil. What sort of horrifying torture would the sea Jarl conjure to punish the impudence of a man who attacked his fortress? But then he squeezed free and tumbled out of the pressing walls to trip into the pathway, falling on his elbows into the mud, still clutching his weapons. He glanced to his right, where men roared, weapons clashed, and his berserkers fought Ketil's warriors in the torch-lit darkness. He looked to his left, and there was Ketil's Hall. Now that Hundr was closer, he could see the skull of a monstrous bull hung over the doorway, the pale bone almost glowing in the moonlight.

"Bastard!" he heard a gruff voice shout. Hundr looked up to see two warriors approaching him from a building opposite. One charged with a spear held two-handed, looking to skewer Hundr whilst he was on his knees. The other came on with an axe above his head, poised to strike a heavy blow. Hundr's foot slipped in the mud as he tried to stand. He could smell sweat and ale on his attackers, and they were too close for him to have enough time to stand and defend himself. Hundr launched forwards between the legs of the advancing foes. He rolled and slammed his axe into the hamstring of the spearman and rose to drive his seax into the spine of the axeman. He felt warm blood on his hand and let the seax go. The spearman had fallen to his knees, and Hundr swung the blade of his axe across his face with an audible crack. The axeman was on the ground, whimpering and clawing to reach the seax buried up to its hilt in the meat of his back. Hundr grabbed it and wrenched it free, the wound making a sucking sound like a boot in a bog. He kicked the warrior over and saw the man was old. He was bald, and his beard was grizzled and grey.

"Where is Ketil?" asked Hundr. The fortress should have been swarming with warriors by now, spear and axe warriors of equal, if not greater number than Hundr's crews. However, despite the fighting in the streets, the force Hundr had expected to fight had not yet materialised. The fallen warrior groaned and grimaced as his life blood eked out into the earth. Hundr ripped the man's axe from his hand. "Tell me where Ketil and his warriors are, and I'll give you the blade." To die without his axe would rob the old warrior of his chance at a glorious afterlife, either in Odin's mighty hall in Valhalla or Thor's hall, Thruthvangar.

"At sea, gone this last week. Please, my axe..." said the man weakly, and Hundr gave him the blade.

"Go, friend, to Valhalla. Find a bench, drink with the heroes, and save a place for me." Hundr left him and ran to the hall. He almost laughed at his luck—Ketil away, and the wealth of his hall lay virtually unprotected. Hundr was certainly due some luck, and his men needed silver. He had fought a brutal campaign in Ireland, and his men had come away with no silver to show for the dangers they had faced. If there was one thing they expected a Lord to do for his men, it was to provide silver and warrior rings.

Hundr had taken the quick route of the alleyway to get to Ketil's hall because he wanted to see the trappings of the famous sea Jarl before his men ravaged and plundered it. He reached the great hall and leant his weight on the doors, pushing them open and leaving a smear on the wood with his blood-soaked hands. A wave of warm air and the smell of roasted meat and fresh bread greeted him. In the hall, women and children screamed and fled to the shadowy corners, out of the torchlight and away from the one-eyed warrior who'd brought death to their island. He stalked inside—fresh floor rushes crunching underfoot as he went. Before a crackling fire at the central hearth, four warriors came towards him. Again, they were old. White hair and shaking hands advancing, blue-veined hands clutching heavy axes. Hundr lowered his weapons and sighed as Einar, and his men came thundering past him, cannoning into the old warriors and slaughtering them with ruthless efficiency. Hundr strode to the fire and saw a long table at the rear of the hall with chairs draped in furs.

"Where is Ketil's silver?" Hundr called, his voice echoing around the high rafters. He could hear the sobs of women in the shadows, but there was no reply. "Tell me where Ketil keeps his silver, or I will burn this hall and leave you all inside to roast in the flames."

"Set me free, and I will help you steal Ketil's horde," came an unseen voice, deep and resonant.

Hundr stepped towards the voice and saw a figure sitting on the stones surrounding the hearth. The figure raised his hands and rattled heavy chains, grinning beneath a pelt of long, matted hair. "Set me free, brother. Bring me with you."

"What is your name?" asked Hundr, inching closer to the strange figure. The man rose to his full height, and Hundr took a step backwards because the man was huge. Hundr himself was taller than most men, but this man was a full head taller than even he.

"Rollo," said the man. "My name is Rollo. Set me free, and I will help you steal Ketil's horde."

"I will set you free, now tell me?"

"Move the table, and you will find a door. Beneath that door is Ketil's hoard."

TWO

Rollo stank as though he had been living in a midden pit. Welts covered his skin from what Hundr thought were burns from hot irons on his neck and arms. His filthy, matted hair hung in long ropes, as did his beard.

"You have already told me the hiding place of Ketil's hoard," said Hundr, stepping back from the man's stench. "Bush, shift that table out of the way and see what's underneath."

"Come on, lads," Bush grinned. He was a short but sturdy man, with a heavy paunch hanging over his belt and bald save for a ring of long hair that ran around below the bottom of his skull but went no higher than his ears. Two crewmen helped him, and the chairs scraped on the hard-packed earth as they dragged them away. The women in the shadows whimpered again as Bush flipped the table over in a crash of tankards and plates, and the men pushed it towards the back of the hall. Bush turned and grinned at Hundr, a gap-toothed grin beneath his greying beard. He knelt and hooked his sea-weathered hand around a rope handle and pulled.

A section of the floor rose as Einar, Ragnhild, and the men poured into the hall. Their breath steamed, and their faces were as feral and hungry as wolves in the dancing torchlight. They strode to Bush and gathered around the hole he had found on Ketil's floor.

"Well?" said Hundr.

"We are as rich as Frankish lords," Bush announced and cackled to himself, slapping his shipmates on the shoulders and dancing a jig in the floor rushes. The men laughed along with him and hauled four chests of dark oak. Einar turned out those chests, and the ring and clank of silver and gold echoed around the rafters in a glorious song.

"Einar, Ragnhild, divide it up and make a share for each man. It is long overdue," said Hundr, which was true. It had been a long year of fighting and dying. Hundr had lost friends and oath men on Ireland's cursed soil, and in the end, his men had left with nothing to show for their bravery. So, he had risked everything to bring them here to the hall of a famous Viking warlord and would now steal Ketil Flatnose's wealth from beneath his floor.

"You said you would set me free, Lord," said the prisoner. Hundr turned to face him again, looking up to meet the tall man's eyes.

"What did you do? Why are you chained so?" asked Hundr.

"I came to Ketil to offer my service, but he suspected me. He thought me a spy," Rollo answered, and he flashed a grin of white teeth behind his dark beard. "I will fight for you if you set me free. I dare say a man like you needs men who can fight."

"A spy for who?" Hundr pressed.

"Ketil is a nervous man. He has made many enemies during his long years of raiding and fighting. He thought one of those men sent me to harm him, but I did not come for that." Rollo shrugged.

"Can you fight?"

"I am sworn to a northern Jarl, and I was his champion before this," the man replied, raising his chained hands.

"We will see about that," said Hundr, and he ordered one of his men to find some tools and get Rollo out of his chains. Hundr walked over to Einar, who was busy sorting the treasure into piles for each crew. Hundr had five ships, and each ship carried between thirty and forty warriors. They had lost men fighting in Ireland, but he still had many men, so for each to get a share of the hoard, there would need to be a lot of silver. "Is there enough?" he asked.

"Enough for a share for each man." Einar smiled, as he held up a fist full of arms rings and coins bearing the strange marks of the mussel-folk from the far south, where the sun burns men's skins dark. "I'll keep this one for Hildr, though." It was a shining silver cloak pin fashioned into the shape of a swan, and though she remained aboard Hundr's ships in Orkney's inhospitable bay, she had earned her reward ten times over. Hildr was Einar's love, and she was a Valkyrie warrior from the band of warrior women Ragnhild had once led. Most of those brave women were dead after years of hard fighting in the lands of the Saxons, in Frankia and Ireland. Only Ragnhild and Hildr remained of that all-female war band.

"She will like that, and let's hope she keeps the ships off the rocks. We need to get away from here quickly," said Hundr. The bay was precarious, hence why Ketil did not guard it. Hundr feared that, as the tide rose, his ships would be driven into the jagged rock faces around the bay and become lost. So, he had trusted Hildr to make sure the vessels remained safe.

"My Lord will kill you all," came a shrill voice

from the shadows.

Hundr had forgotten about the women and children who had scattered to the edges of the hall when he had burst in.

"When Ketil returns and finds cowards have stolen his wealth, he will not rest until he has you under his knife," the voice spoke up again.

A man's whisper shushed it, and Hundr marched towards them, past the throng of his men, where they waited for their share, rubbing hands and talking excitedly amongst themselves.

"Who is it who speaks so, from the shadows?" said Hundr.

A woman stepped forward. Her chin raised and jutting, arms folded across her chest. Hundr stopped mid-stride because the defiant woman emerging from the shadows was beautiful. She had a pile of golden hair braided around her head, her neck was long and slender, and her eyes flashed the ice blue of a frozen mountain tarn. He saw her eyes dart across his ravaged face, and Hundr was suddenly aware of his ugliness. The son of Ivar the Boneless had taken his eye years earlier in Northumbria. A white-hot knife had burned it out and scarred his face, and Hundr knew he was not a fair man to look upon. Ivar's son had died, and Hundr never usually gave his appearance a second thought. He looked just as he was, a fighter who had clawed his way up from bailing the bilge of the warship Seaworm to becoming a warlord and master of five ships. Bush had often chided him because his face put the men off their food, and more than once, he had presented Hundr with a patch to wear over his ravaged, empty eye socket. This was the one time he wished he had taken his old friend's advice.

"I am Sigrid Ketilsdottir," said the woman, as though she had announced that she was Queen of all Denmark and Norway. A small weasel-faced man crept from the shadows, his head bowed and back bent. He raised an apologetic hand to Hundr and tugged at Sigrid's sleeve, but she pulled her arm away and tutted at the fawning man. "Are you brave enough to give us your name, thief?" she demanded.

"My name is Hundr."

"Hundr? A dog's name?" she said, with eyebrows raised. It was not his real name, his name from when he was a boy in the East, but it was the name given to him by Einar's crew when he joined them as a bail-boy. Hundr had served Einar in those days, and he'd been glad to do so.

"My name is Hundr, and I take your father's silver in the same way he took it from other men," said Hundr.

She frowned at that truth. "Nevertheless, he

will hunt you for what you have done here today. What will become of us women at the hands of you and your plunderers?"

"You will not be harmed. We are not wicked men, my lady. We follow drengskapr, the way of the warrior. And a man does not make a reputation by killing women and children."

"So, you have a reputation?" she asked, a smile playing at the corners of her mouth, causing her cheeks to dimple. She teased him, even as his warriors were in her hall armed with axes and spears, dripping with her father's silver. She was stunning, and in Hundr's brutal world of darkness and blood, she shone like the north star.

"Not one to hold up next to the glory of your father," he replied, which commended Ketil. He was a raider, just like any other, but Ketil had settled in his island home and made a fortress out of it. He had a famous name, and Hundr supposed that was no small thing.

"What is it you seek, Hundr? Is it silver or reputation?"

"Both. I want what all men who take to the Whale Road want—to build upon my reputation, be a good ring-giver to my men, and earn my place in Odin's hall. Now, men will know that I have successfully attacked the stronghold of Ketil Flatnose, Jarl of the Orkney Isles."

"The next time we meet, you will probably take the place of your new friend, Rollo, there. My father will cut out your tongue, slice your hamstrings, and use you to empty his slaves' shit pots for food."

"I can only hope that the next time we meet, it is in better circumstances than that, my lady. For it would do me good to see your face again." Hundr surprised himself with his own words. He tore his gaze from hers in embarrassment. He would rather face a shield wall of Spear-Danes than speak soft words to a woman. Her face blushed, and the little man tugged at her sleeve again.

"That little turd is mine," shouted Rollo from across the hall. His chains fell to the floor. One of Hundr's men had found some blacksmith tools and had prised open the shackles. The huge prisoner rubbed at his wrists and nodded his thanks to the man who had freed him. He strode across the hall, and the women in the shadows whimpered. The little weasel-man shuddered and tried to slink away, but Rollo covered the distance in four long strides, grabbed the man by the ear, and dragged him towards him. The little man cried out, reaching towards the hidden women, but none came forth to speak for him. Rollo pulled him close and rammed his thumb suddenly and savagely into the man's eye. He twisted and gouged, and the little man howled as blood and jelly popped onto his cheek. "You are mine now. You like to burn and cut and hurt. Well, now it is my turn," growled Rollo.

"What is this man to you?" asked Hundr.

"He is a thing of Ketil, cunning and wily—not a man for the shield wall, but he likes to hurt those who are chained and cannot fight back. It was he who convinced Ketil I was an assassin when I am simply a warrior looking for a war."

Hundr saw the venom in Rollo and left him to his vengeance. He looked away as Rollo cast the screaming figure to the floor and battered him with his fists. Hundr was about to turn back to Sigrid when the berserkers he had let loose on Ketil's warriors burst into the hall. The blood of the fallen coated their bare chests, and they strode through the hall, axes dripping with gore and their eyes still wide with battle fury. Their leader, Black Gorm, laughed loudly when he saw the treasure, and he raised his long-handled war axe to lead his men in a roar of victory. Gorm saw Hundr and then noticed Sigrid. He marched towards her, a feral and vicious look on his cruel face. Hundr took a step in front of her, and Gorm laughed again, nodding as though he understood Hundr wanted the beauty for himself. So instead, Gorm reached a brawny arm into the shadows, wrenched forth a short, plump serving girl and threw her towards his men. They pushed her between them and tore at her clothing.

"No women and children, Gorm," shouted Hundr. The berserker captain snapped his head towards Hundr and snarled. Hundr stood firm. "You are my oath, man, and I say no women and children. You know that. So let the woman go. Take your fill of whatever weapons and silver you can find in the fortress, but leave the women alone."

"We are the ones who broke the shield wall. This is our reward," said Gorm. He wore his hair long and loose, and a shovel-shaped beard framed his face. Gorm was not as tall as Hundr, but he was broad in the chest and heavily muscled. He bore the whorls and writhing dragon tattoos of all berserkers on his arms and torso, the marks of the wild warriors, the war-crazed men who do not fear death. The rest of the crews, even the hardest of men, trod carefully around Black Gorm and his men. Gorm shuddered and barked at his men to let the girl go. Immediately, a muscled man pushed her to the ground and kicked her savagely.

"Do you want to make the square?" Hundr bellowed at the man, the noise echoing around the smoke-blackened rafters of Ketil's hall. "You and I can fight now, right here. You are sworn to be my man, so you do as I say. Do you want to fight?"

The berserker showed his teeth and looked from Gorm to Hundr. Black Gorm shrugged and looked at Hundr. To be a leader of fighting men, Hundr needed them to respect his authority, and for the berserkers, that meant they had to respect his prowess as a warrior. The man stepped forward, and Hundr sighed. He had hurt the warrior's pride in front of his shipmates, and the man could not back down. Hundr must show his men that he was in command, and any sign of dissent must be put down quickly and with savagery. It was no simple thing to lead five ships' worth of killers, men who took to the seas in search of war and silver and burnish their own reputations bright with blood.

"I'll fight him," piped Rollo cheerfully, and he rubbed his hands together like a child at yule. Hundr looked at the big man; allowing him to fight Gorm's man was a good outcome. If the berserker lost, then there would be bitterness towards Hundr amongst Gorm's men, and if Rollo lost, nobody would mourn his passing, and the berserker would be happy with his victory.

"Not here," said Hundr. "By the ships. Get all of this divided out and make sure the shares are fair. We need to be gone from this place." He looked at Sigrid, and she spat at his feet. "You fought well today, Black Gorm. Your men are savage fighters. But keep them in check," he uttered as he marched out of the hall, resisting the urge to glance back at Sigrid.

THREE

A blustering rain spat across Orkney's hills from the sea. It danced and flew on a chill wind to whip Einar's ears like the breath of a frost giant. He watched as the men lowered chests of coins, rings, torcs and other finely crafted treasures down the sides of Orkney's iron-grey cliffs and onto the decks of the ships below. The raid on Ketil's stronghold had proved successful. Einar nodded with satisfaction to hear the men laugh and joke amongst themselves as they moved their captured horde down the cliff face on ropes and rigging. He leant over the edge of the cliff, searching the deck of the Seaworm for Hildr, his love. He caught a flash of her blonde hair moving between the rigging, which warmed his heart. She looked up and rewarded him with a wave and a smile, and Einar waved back, relieved to see her safe and well. Not so long ago, she had been held as a prisoner inside Dublin's high walls. Einar had fought his way in to set her free, and he and Hundr had fought their way back out again. They had lost friends and oar-mates that day, but she was free and safe, and that was everything.

Above the sound of the men at work, Einar could hear the sigh of the sea below, and he looked out across a calm swell as the sun awoke from her slumber. Sól rose from her sleep to begin her daily race across the sky. She cast a red hue across the horizon as her two horses, Árvakr and Alsviðr, drew her chariot into the heavens to begin their daily flight from the great wolf, Sköll. In the depths of their hearts, all men rejoiced when Sól rose each day. One day, she would not rise, and Sköll will have devoured her, beginning the horror that will be Ragnarök, the doom of the gods and the end of the world.

A boy joined Hildr in the Seaworm's bows and waved up at Einar. Einar smiled and waved back at the lad. It was Finn, son of Ivar the Boneless. Finn had fallen into Einar's care, and he loved him like a son. Perhaps like the son he would never have.

Einar rubbed his stinging eyes and wiped his hand across his face. It was coated with the layer of grease that always comes from a night awake and at work. His knees ached, and old wounds in his shoulder and hip throbbed at him. Too many years at sea, too long at the blade. Men behind him made a basic fighting square. They simply threw down four shields to make its corners, and Einar turned to see the berserkers readying their man for the fight. Einar shook his head. A man would die in that square, and they would miss his axe when Ketil Flatnose caught up with them. He walked to where Hundr stood with Bush, another old friend and one of the few remaining men of the original Seaworm crew from the days when Einar was Jarl and sworn to Ivar.

"We'll be loaded up soon," said Einar. "Best to get this over with quickly." He nodded to the square.

"Aye, before Ketil's fleet comes peeking around the island to trap us in his bay," agreed Bush. He slid the stained leather helmet liner from his head to scratch at his bald pate, which was as white as a goose egg.

"Ketil won't be home for a while," said Rollo, striding across the fighting square towards them. Someone had given him an axe and shield, and he weighed them up as he walked, rolling his shoulders and smiling. "He's gone to Norway. There's a war there, a war to see who will unite the fjords and be the first King of all Norway."

"How is it you know this?" inquired Einar. The prisoner's easy manner rubbed him up the wrong way. He wasn't sure why, but there was just something off about his cocky levity. A man striding along so confidently when he'd been a shackled slave only moments earlier didn't seem right. "I heard that you've been wiping Ketil's arse for a year or more?"

Rollo laughed and leaned his weapons against his legs to strip his filthy jerkin over his head. He tossed the stinking rag onto the dew-topped grass and hefted his weapons once more.

"I listened. Ketil was a fine man for a chat whilst he was shitting."

Bush laughed, and Hundr frowned.

"What else did you learn about Ketil?" asked Hundr.

"King Harald Fairhair wants to be King of all Norway and already is King of most of it. There are a few Jarls who yet oppose him. The leader of that merry band is Kjotve the Rich, and those Jarls meet now to decide how they'll fight Harald. Ketil Flatnose is rumoured to support Harald, but the King eats up land and Jarls like Jörmungandr, the world serpent. So Ketil goes to see if he should ally with Kjotve and if there is a risk that Harald would take Orkney like he has taken so many other lands," said Rollo, and he turned to watch his foe prepare to fight. On the opposite side of the square, Black Gorm and his berserkers were slapping each other's faces, roaring, and whipping each other into a fresh battle-fury as they prepared their man to fight. "Those boys are getting a little too excited," Rollo grinned and chuckled to himself.

"I wouldn't be so sure of myself if I were you," warned Bush. "Like as not, they will be drinking ale from your hollowed-out skull by nightfall."

"If I kill him, do I have a place on your crew?" asked Rollo without turning to look at Hundr, which annoyed Einar. He could at least show some respect to the man he wanted to serve. Rollo knew a lot about Ketil and King Harald and the goings-on in Norway, and Einar hoped Gorm's man put a hole in his guts as a reward for his arrogance.

"If you kill him, you can swear to me and join my crews, yes. Of course, you will have the enmity of the berserkers and their leader, Black Gorm, but you can pull an oar for as long as you survive," said Hundr. "Tell me of Harald Fairhair. How friendly are he and Ketil?"

"Harald is a ruthless king, a warrior king. He's sworn not to cut his hair until he becomes King of all Norway, hence the name and his long hair. He has fought his whole life, starting in Rogaland. His axe and his cunning have made him rich and powerful. Since his father's death, King Halfdan, Harald has killed jarls and kings and expanded his lands. He was bent on war and victory. Ketil fights for Harald, or at least he has in the past. But Ketil is no fool; he worries Harald will take his island as he has taken so much from so many others. So, he goes to see what Kjotve the Rich has to say."

"How is it you know so much, Rollo? Who are you, and how is it you came to be Ketil's arse wiper?" asked Einar.

Before Rollo could answer, Hafthor, the berserker he would fight to the death, appeared at the opposite side of the rudimentary fighting square, entered, and waited in its centre. He clashed his axe on the iron boss of his shield and snarled at Rollo, spittle flying from his mouth as he worked himself into a rage.

"Looks like our friend is eager to die. I'll have to save my story for another time, old one," smirked Rollo, and he turned and winked at Einar.

Einar's hands curled into fists, and his teeth ground like stones in a mill.

"Why is he fighting in your place?" Einar asked. Hundr was the Jarl and never a man to shy away from a fight. Moreover, Einar knew Hundr to be a skilled and savage fighter. Hundr's skill at arms had seen him rise from nothing to his current position.

"Why, Einar? Would you have me die in there under Hafthor's axe?" said Hundr, and he smiled at Einar, or at least he tried to smile, the gesture marred by his ruined face.

"No, but you and I both know that you are punishing Gorm and his men to remind them of their oath to you."

"And that we don't make war on women and children, we are drengr."

"I know, we follow the way of the drengr. But why let this pup fight? We should have left him where he was."

"Let's see if he can fight. If he wins, we add a skilled warrior to our crew, and remind Gorm's men of their oath. But, on the other hand, if he dies, we have lost nothing, and their victory buoys Gorm's men, and they remember their oath, anyway." Hundr smiled.

"Sometimes, your cunning is too deep. It makes my head hurt," said Bush, sliding his helmet liner back into place. "Anyway, he's hardly a pup. The bastard is huge." He nodded towards Rollo, who stalked towards Hafthor.

Einar watched the young man move. He walked on the balls of his feet, was slim of waist and broad of shoulder. Einar was taller than most men, and Rollo topped even him by a full head. He seemed to know a lot of the goings-on of the great and good, and Einar would make sure he found out who the young man was, how he had come to be Ketil's prisoner, and where his knowledge came from. Ketil was not known as a gentle man, and if Rollo was his enemy, the Jarl would have slit his throat without a second thought. So, there was undoubtedly more to Rollo than met the eye.

Hafthor let out a sky-splitting roar and came on at Rollo with a savage sweep of his axe, and Rollo danced away like a girl at the spring feast of Eostre. Hafthor spun around and cut at Rollo's legs and turned that cut into a lunge, which Rollo swayed aside from, and he twirled elaborately away as Hafthor tried to bully him with his shield. Gorm and his men howled in frustration, and the rest of the crews gathered around the edges of the square to watch the two men fight. Rollo looked around at the men and raised his axe to them in salute. Some men cheered, but most were shouting Hafthor's name and bidding him to cut Rollo's head from his high shoulders.

"He moves well," said Hundr, rubbing his beard.

"He's a cocksure bastard," grumbled Einar, and Bush laughed.

Hafthor came on again and swung his axe overhand in a wild attack, all anger in the blow. It was a mistake. A child would have seen the strike coming, and Einar saw the glint in Rollo's eye as he saw it, too. In a heartbeat, Rollo let go of his own axe and shield and stepped in to grab Hafthor's wrist as it came towards him. Then, with his other hand, he grabbed the forearm where Hafthor held his shield. Rollo dropped to one knee and smashed that arm over his thigh, and Einar heard it snap. It was a terrible sound, and even Einar, a veteran of a hundred fights, winced at the wound. Hafthor yelped in pain, and Rollo grunted as he rose to his feet. He kept hold of Hafthor's axe hand, and with his other hand, he grasped his foe around the throat and lifted him from the ground. Hafthor's legs dangled and kicked in the air, and Rollo brought him close, staring deep into the man's eyes as he throttled the life from him. The men around the square, including Gorm and his berserkers, fell quiet. Hafthor's legs stopped kicking as Rollo's mighty grip throttled the life from him. Einar realised his mouth was open, so he put his teeth together. Rollo tossed Hafthor's corpse to the ground, a full man's length, across the square.

"I killed him fair, and he died with his axe in his hand," Rollo called to Gorm. "I am a crewman now, and if any man disputes this fair fight or wants to take issue with me, then now is the time for it. I'll fight any man, here and now." He paused and scanned the warriors, looking into each man's eyes, including Einar's. "I claim this man's weapons and clothing, shield and oar by right of combat." He looked at Gorm and raised his palm in peace. Black Gorm looked at his men and then nodded at Rollo to show he would hold no grudge over his man's death.

"A fine display," said Bush.

"We've wasted enough time here," gruffed Einar. "Let's get back to the Whale Road."

Later at sea, Einar held firm on the Seaworm's tiller. The power of Njorth's waters fought against his strength as Einar kept the ship on its course north. Hundr had ordered them to sail hard for Norway, towards Harald Fairhair and his war for the rule of the North and his battle against Kjotve the Rich. With a name like that, Einar had to admit—the Jarl was to Vikings what flame is to a moth. Since they had left Ireland, the ships had hugged its coastline and then onto Northumbria, up and around the craggy headlands of the Scots until they had reached Orkney. Now, however, they were really on the Whale Road. Einar looked over his shoulder at Hundr's ship, the Windpsear, as her long, sleek hull sliced through the white-topped waves like a blade. Einar had sailed across the vast sea countless times, which was grim work. He felt the dryness on his face from the salt and the cold and looked over at Hildr and his men huddled in the bilge. A sail was tied over the bows to shield them from the worst of the wet. Out here, the sea was black, or the dark green of mould, all roar and danger. Waves could be as high as the largest cliff, and there were no sounds other than the crash and surge of the sea. No birds, nothing but the sea god Njorth and his fury.

Sea spray and rain had soaked Einar through, and he had to close his mouth tight to stop his jaw from chattering. His mail lay wrapped in an oily sheepskin beneath the steerboard, but his jerkin, breeks, and wool cloak were as heavy as stones on him. Einar's wrists and neck burned with their chafing. His belly was empty and sour, sick of the cold, wet meat they had eaten for the last two days. They had stacked the oars in their crutches amidships, and Einar looked at them longingly, dreaming of calmer coastal waters. Out in the deep, every day was danger. A storm could scatter or cast them asunder, and no man would ever learn their fate. He watched Hildr huddled with Finn in her arms, holding him close to give him warmth from her body. Her swan-shaped cloak pin kept her swaddled in a black cloak. Father Darragh, the boy's Christ priest, was also huddled in the bilge. The priest cared for the boy and had come with him from Northumbria.

Despite knowing that Finn was not afraid, Einar recognised the risk in bringing those most precious to him out into the wilds of the deep sea. Their whole way of living was a risk, and it was no way to bring up a boy unless you wanted to bring him up hard. Einar looked across at the surging waves ahead. Soon they would spy land to the east—Norway, the home of the warriors.

No man ruled in Norway but by the strength of his arm. It was the land of the Vikings, where all matters were decided by force of arms. The crew's purses were fat with silver and their arms thick with rings from Ketil Flatnose's hoard. They were happy and content to follow their Jarl Hundr into whatever he had planned in Norway. But as Einar watched Hildr and Finn shuddering in the ice-cold sea spray, he knew he should make a better life for them. A safer life. He had once dreamed of settling down and buying land to farm somewhere. That dream still lived in his heart. To do that, though, he would need more silver and have to find a place to purchase. A safe place.

Bush was shipmaster on the Seaworm, and throughout the journey, he busied himself with his sticks and sun stones. He marked the sun, and when Sól hid herself from view, Bush would use his stones to find the way north and east. The day after the Seaworm crew had eaten the last of the cold mutton stowed in the bilge, Bush shinned up the mast to get a better look ahead with his stone beneath a sky thick with clouds like whey in a butter churn. As he strained, stretched, and cursed the sea and the sky to hel, Finn yelled out from the prow. The boy's high-pitched call captured everyone's attention.

"There, look," shouted Finn. He pointed to the east, and there, sure enough, a solitary seagull wheeled in the wind. It dipped and swooped, let out a caw, and was gone. The crew cheered, and Einar whooped along with them because land was close, and they had survived the treacherous deep of the Whale Road. Everyone aboard was suddenly busy, pulling down the spare sodden wool sail that had served as shelter, stowing blankets and making the ship ready to approach land. They tacked amidst the shifting wind hard east, and before long, Einar could make out the haze of land in the distance.

Hundr's ship banked towards the Seaworm. The Windspear was a long, magnificent warship with a single oak trunk for her hull and a black raven staring out from her sail. Hundr had planned to change that banner to his own sigil of the single eye, but there had been no chance to do that since leaving Ireland. The raven banner belonged to the sons of Ragnar Lothbrok, from whom Hundr had won the Windspear in a great sea battle years earlier. The ships came alongside, and men threw ropes across the bows to bring the hulls carefully together. Einar, Bush, and Hildr leapt over to land on the Windspear's deck, where Hundr and Ragnhild waited for them at the steerboard.

"We should sacrifice to Njorth and thank him for safe passage," said Ragnhild, as she hugged Hildr close in greeting.

"I don't think I'll ever be warm again,"

grumbled Bush.

"So, we have arrived in Norway," said Einar, raising his eyebrows at Hundr, inviting the Jarl to speak.

"Harald Fairhair fights to make himself King of the North," Hundr began, passing a hard-baked biscuit to Einar. "We must pay a tribute to Harald and apologise for our raid on Ketil. We don't want a powerful king as an enemy. Also, he is locked in a fight with the wealthy Jarls of south Norway, and a war is underway."

"If what Rollo says is true," said Einar, casting a sideways glance at the huge warrior who stood watching them at the prow.

Rollo caught Einar's eye and waved to him, a grin splitting his broad face. Einar frowned and spat over the side.

"If what Rollo says is true," Hundr allowed. "Where there is war, there is opportunity. So, we find King Harald and join our men to his. He will pay us for our blades, and there will be silver for us in his victory."

"What if Harald doesn't want our blades? When he hears about our little raid on Ketil Flatnose, won't Harald want to kill us and tell us to stick our tribute up our arses?" asked Ragnhild.

"First, we will apologise to Harald. If he

doesn't accept that or our offer to fight for him, we leave. Then, we go to Kjotve the Rich and make him the same offer. Either way, this year, we fight in Norway. But this time, we fight for silver, reputation, and ourselves."

"If Harald doesn't kill us first..." huffed Bush, "...In it up to our bloody necks again."

Einar liked the idea. They had spent too long fighting for others, and now they would fight to make themselves wealthy—which was, after all, why men took to the Whale Road in the first place. Einar stayed on board the Windspear and enjoyed a meal with Hundr, Hildr, Ragnhild, and Bush. They ate and drank and talked of old battles and rare fights and remembered fallen friends, and then the next day, they met the black sailed ships of Harald Fairhair.

FOUR

Hundr's fleet sailed lazily on a calm sea heading east. The difficulties of the deep Whale Road were behind them, and Hundr had allowed a day of easy sailing whilst they cruised along Norway's coast in search of King Harald and his war. Bush had spied sails earlier that day, and Hundr had followed their course at a distance so as not to look like a threat. The sails ahead had come about slowly, and four warships approached. Each flew dark green sails, and brightly painted shields adorned their flanks. They were fast, sleek drakkars and came to see who approached the coastline with a fleet of five ships. Such a force was not to be taken lightly, and Hundr had expected to be challenged, eventually. He watched them from the Windspear's prow. He curled his arm around the dragon beast's head and leant into the wind, enjoying its freshness in his hair. The first of those ships dropped its sail, and two banks of oars sprang from its sides in impressive unison.

"They know their business," said Ragnhild. She stood next to Hundr, staring at the green ships off Norway's coast. Hundr saw a steep-sided fjord to their east, which looked to be the small fleet's destination before they had spied Hundr's sails.

"They do, and one of them comes to talk." Hundr nodded. The largest ship now had its oars in the water, and they beat towards the Windspear, her snarling beast head glowering at Hundr from across the waves.

"Are you sure about going to Harald?"

"No. But I also don't want a king for an enemy. We have enough enemies."

"With the surviving sons of Ragnar at our back in Northumbria and Dublin, we could do without another powerful enemy. You are right in that. But Ketil is as dangerous as they come, and we just stole his hoard."

"True. Which is why we are here to apologise to his king," Hundr said, and smiled at Ragnhild. She chuckled and shook her head.

"I count thirty benches."

"Aye, could be seventy warriors on board. She's as long as the Windspear."

"Let's hope she's not as fast," quipped

Ragnhild, smiling.

"Let's hope those ships can tell us where Harald is and that they don't belong to some war-hungry Jarl who wants to pick a fight."

"Not that we ever try to pick a fight." Ragnhild smiled again, and the wind whipped her hair back from her face. There were wrinkles amongst the scars, and she had grey hair around her temples, signs of a hard life fought on the front line.

"It's good to see you smile again. Not that you were ever filled with the joys of life, of course."

"We have to put dark times behind us," she said, looking down at the deck. "I miss Kolo and Sten. So many friends gone."

Hundr nodded in agreement. Kolo and Sten had both died in a fierce battle on Dublin's walls. Kolo had been Ragnhild's lover and a skilled warrior from the lands far to the south, beyond the shores of distant Ispania.

"I must return to Upsala one day," she whispered. "The Valkyrie await me there, my old order. All the girls I rode with are dead, save Hildr and me. Thirty of us sailed from Upsala, ordered by our High Priest, Vattnar, to pledge our blades to the vengeance of the sons of Ragnar and to invade Saxon lands. It has been eight long years since I was home—I've been remiss in my vows."

"I will take you there, Ragnhild," said Hundr. "Once we make sure King Harald won't be our enemy, I will take you to Upsala. I give you my oath on it. Your Valkyrie warrior sisters will welcome you home as the hero you are. Even if you have grown older and now carry more scars than a fishing boat's hull."

She laughed and punched him in the arm. Hundr remembered seeing Ragnhild for the first time back in Saxon Northumbria, years earlier. She and her band of Valkyrie warrior women had thundered into battle, serving under the banner of Ivar the Boneless and his brother Sigurd Snake Eye. They had much in common, he and Ragnhild. She, too, had lost an eye in battle, and she too was an abandoned child forced to find her way into the brutal world of warriors and blades.

"The green sails are King Harald's ships," shouted Rollo across the deck.

Hundr turned to him and nodded thanks. He saw the crew exchange nervous glances at the news that the approaching ships belonged to Harald Fairhair, the war-king of Norway.

"We should prepare, brynjars and axes," growled Einar. "If they want to fight, we can kill everyone on that leading ship and be away from here."

"No, stay calm. We might have time to

apologise to King Harald before he knows what we have done. No one can have sailed this far north ahead of us. So, he won't yet know of our raid on Orkney. Also, if what Rollo says is true, Ketil plans to side with Harald's enemies. Either way, we want to join this war and find some silver in it, so we must come in peace," Hundr said.

"What if King Harald doesn't like your apology for sacking his supposed friend's island stronghold?" asked Ragnhild.

"Then we will get to Upsala faster than you thought."

The leading green ship glided through the swell, its clinker-built hull loomed high, and for a heart-stopping moment, Hundr thought they planned to ram him. He was about to follow Einar's advice and call the men to arms when he heard an order barked across the water. One bank of oars rose on the green ship, dripping beads of glistening water, and the other bank pulled to turn the warship alongside the Windspear in a graceful and well-timed manoeuvre.

"Ho, there," came a sonorous voice across the gap between the ships. The accent had the thick burr of the men of Norway. "Whose ships are these in King Harald's waters?"

Hundr looked at Ragnhild and Einar, but they

just shrugged. So, without further delay, Hundr cupped his hand to his mouth. "I am Jarl Hundr, and these five ships are my own," he bellowed.

"What is your business?"

"I come to speak with King Harald."

"With five warships? Who do you serve?"

"I serve no man. Who are you who makes these demands of me?" It was a risk to challenge the King's man, but Hundr had not fought his way from the lands of the Rus and across Britain, Frankia, and Ireland to be challenged by a herald.

"I am Rognvald Eysteinsson, and I speak for King Harald."

"Do you want to shout across the bows or come aboard and talk like men?"

Rognvald was younger than Hundr expected. His blonde hair was long and braided, and he had a smooth face with a sparse beard. He was not a tall man, nor was he broad in the shoulder. He wore a shining brynjar and had a fine sword belted at his waist in a fleece-lined scabbard. His arms were thick with rings, and he wore a thick silver chain doubled about his neck. So, whilst he did not have the battle-hardened look of Hundr and his warriors, Rognvald was a wealthy man, which meant he wielded power and influence.

"Welcome, Rognvald," said Hundr, noting that he had not introduced himself as a Jarl.

"Jarl Hundr," said Rognvald, casting his bright blue eyes about the Windspear and looking up at Einar's slab of a face. "Where is your jarldom?"

"These five ships, my warriors, and their axes are all I own." A famed and powerful warrior-lord named Haesten had made Hundr a Jarl years earlier in Frankia. Hundr had learned many years ago that a man could call himself whatever he wished if he had the strength to back up that claim. A man could call himself King and only own three pigs and a shit-stinking shack until another man forced him to stop and bend the knee.

"A sea Jarl, then?" asked Rognvald. Which Hundr knew meant that Rognvald thought him a marauder. Which, of course, he was. But a marauder with five drakkar warships filled with warriors was a Jarl, if he said so.

"So, you are Harald's man?" Hundr inquired, ignoring the question.

"Yes, I am King Harald's man. What is your business with him?"

"I hear there is a war, and where there is war, there is a need for warriors."

"So, you would swear an oath to the King and pledge your allegiance to him?"

"I will bring my warriors to his banner and fight for silver, but I swore an oath to Odin long ago never to be under the sway of another man."

"So, you want to fight for pay?"

"I want to talk to Harald."

"We have a problem here beyond this fjord," said Rognvald, stroking his thin beard. "A troublesome Jarl who needs bringing into line. He is strong, with many warriors. There might be a fight, so bring your ships and your blades. Then, if you prove you are not an enemy to the King, I will bring you before him."

Hundr frowned.

"I don't need to prove anything beyond the truth of my words."

"These are times of war, Jarl Hundr," said Rognvald, and he raised his hands in peace. "There are those who would do anything to stop the King from unifying all of Norway. Therefore, I must be sure of a man's intentions before bringing him to my lord."

"Very well," said Hundr, frowning and fixing Rognvald with his dead eye. "We will help you with your troublesome Jarl."

Hundr ordered his men to furl the sail and ready their oars. Bush banged his axe on the iron boss of a shield in rhythmic beats, and the men grunted and hauled on their oars. At each beat, they dipped and pulled the wooden blades out of the sea and then dipped again. The rest of Hundr's fleet did the same, and they followed Rognvald's ships into a gap between two sheer cliff faces of black and white rock, which turned to deep green pine where the hill rose to taper away, high into the lands beyond.

"Are you sure you know what you are doing?" asked Ragnhild as Hundr steered the ship between the cliffs.

"This is what we do, Ragnhild. We sail, and we raid, and we fight. This is the life a'viking," he said.

"I know that. I am as much of a drengr as the next warrior. But there is a difference between living a life as a Viking and sailing blindly into a county we don't know, following a man we have just met, based on the word of a man who was cleaning Ketil Flatnose's shit bucket."

"When you put it like that, maybe we are taking a risk. But what better way to further a reputation than winning a war for a king?" He smiled at her, but Ragnhild shook her head. All his life, Hundr had dreamed of becoming a known man, a Viking warrior with a name known across the world.

"You already have a reputation. Men know you killed Ivar the Boneless and Eystein Longaxe. So what more do you want?"

"More, Ragnhild. There will always be more wars to fight, more silver to win. This is what we are. We do the gods' bidding. We fight and hope to build enough fame in our lives to warrant a place in Valhalla. Should we find a port and become traders, or till the soil?"

"No, you know I follow the way of the drengr. I am a Valkyrie, for Odin's sake. It just can't go on forever. Some day we must stop, or we will be old and grey and still sailing the seas looking for a fight. That's all I am saying."

"So maybe we will be lucky, and they will slaughter us in this fjord. Then we can drink and laugh in Valhalla."

Ragnhild laughed at that. She went to get their mail from where it was stowed under a rowing bench. The precious brynjars were wrapped in oily sheep's fleeces to keep out the worst of the seawater, which would rust the metal. Hundr followed Rognvald's ship, and the Windspear snaked along a narrow channel, where the rock faces drew close before widening into an emerald-watered, light-filled span of green and brown. Hundr marvelled at the beauty of the high-sided valley above the clear waters. Ahead, a shingle beach stretched up a slope towards a fringe of gently swaying trees. But before that tree line was a vast, walled town of bright yellow timber.

"Odin, help us," Hundr whispered to himself. He'd noticed a long pier stretching across the fjord, cutting the bay in two. The two walls contained a gap wide enough for two ships to sail through, but it was the only way to approach the town from the water. A pair of towers flanked the gap, and a thick, tautly pulled rope stretched between them, sitting above the waterline. The pier, towers, and rope would prevent any ship from approaching the town unless the thick rope was lowered. And Hundr guessed that the Jarl of this place would not lower his gate-rope for Rognvald and his warriors.

"I hope we don't have to attack this place," said Ragnhild, adjusting the fit of her brynjar and handing Hundr his mail. "It looks like a bastard."

Evidently, they would need to get through the gap between the towers before they could attack the settlement.

"Archers," came a shout from the stern.

Hundr looked to see a stream of riders racing around the edges of the fjord. They surged out from the town like a line of ants in the summer sun. Once they reached the piers, they left their horses and took up positions along the wall.

"That surely cannot be his plan?" scoffed Hundr, watching as one of Rognvald's ships rowed next to the pier and threw up ropes topped with iron hooks over its high wall. Men climbed the ropes until the defending archers appeared above them and poured the shafts into the climbers, then into the ship itself. "Get us closer," Hundr ordered. "Row as close to the gap as you can. Shields to the prow."

"You can't ram the rope," said Ragnhild. "It won't break, and they will trap us for use as target practice."

"Take off your brynjar."

"What? With archers about to turn us into a floating hedgehog?" she said, and then slowly shook her head as she realised what Hundr was planning. "I hope you're not thinking what I think you're thinking."

Hundr pulled off his boots and took his seax from its sheath at his back, where it hung from two thongs. He left everything on the deck apart from his breeks and axe. The men heaved their oars, and the Windspear drew closer to the high wooden walls.

"Be ready to bank away from the walls upon my order," called Hundr. "Ready those shields. Come around in a circle. When you see the rope come down, make for the gap."

An arrow slapped onto the deck at Hundr's bare feet, and he gritted his teeth. His men made a shield wall at the prow, three shields wide, with the front-line crouching to allow two more rows of shields to overlap above them. Hundr handed the tiller to one of the crew and walked carefully down the ship's length, watching his step so as not to trip his bare toes on the ballast stones in the bilge. He could hear the men on the walls roaring and shouting their defiance. Arrows banged and thudded into the makeshift shield wall at the prow, sounding like heavy iron rain. Ragnhild was with him, and Hundr leaned over the side. They were getting close, and shafts splashed into the water around the Windspear. Hundr's heart quickened, and his mouth was dry. He could wait for Rognvald to work out a better way to get through the sea barrier, but Hundr already knew how to do it. He could hold his ships back and watch Rognvald die or break off the attack. But that was not how reputations are made. If there was a fight, then Hundr would fight it.

The Windspear drew close, and Hundr could see the faces of the men on the walls, strained and concentrated as they poured shaft after shaft into the attacking fleet. More of Rognvald's ships pulled alongside the walls, and more ropes went up for brave men to climb into the hail of arrows. Hundr waited for two more strokes.

"Port side, up oars," he shouted. The oars came up, and the ship banked hard. Hundr leapt over the side and splashed into the icy waters of the Norwegian fjord. Its chill snatched his breath, and he came up gasping in sharp bursts, stunned by how cold it was. Hundr moved his axe from his hand to put the haft between his teeth. It was almost too big to fit, and the corners of his lips stretched almost to splitting. Hundr kicked his legs and swam with long, powerful strokes towards the rope. He could hear arrows slapping into the surrounding water, and the iciness stung his dead eye socket. Hundr pulled the water, and as he neared the rope, its thickness surprised him. It was four separate ropes twisted together like a Saxon torc to make one rope as thick around as his body. An arrow whipped the water's surface next to his face, and Hundr cried out in shock. He swam faster and reached up to curl an arm around the monstrous rope. He had made for its leftmost side where it was attached to the timber wall tower by an iron ring. On the opposite side of the gap, the men above were busy killing Rognvald's men, and the tower shielded him from the archers up high. He pulled his axe from his mouth and sawed its sharp, bearded blade back and forth across the rope. A head suddenly burst through the water next to him, and Hundr was surprised to see Rollo grinning at him from the fjord. He had expected Ragnhild to follow him into the water, and he looked back to see that she was four strokes behind Rollo.

Rollo pulled a seax from between his teeth and cut at the rope frantically.

"There's no messing around with you, is there?" quipped Rollo, as he leant into his task, out of breath from the frantic swim.

"This is the only way in, so why wait?" said Hundr, his axe slowly cutting through strands of the rope.

"We have only just met this Rognvald. Why die for him?"

"He is the King's man, and if we help him take this place, the King might overlook our raid on Ketil."

"Or he might kill you anyway," said Rollo, and together they had now cut their way through one of the thick ropes.

"You followed when you could have waited."

"Glory isn't won by waiting," said Rollo, grinning again as he sawed.

"Bloody fools," hissed Ragnhild as she, too, reached the rope and began slicing at it with an axe.

Hundr looked out at the bay to see that the Windpsear had followed his instructions and come about in a wide sweep. The men had her ready to charge through the gap once the rope was down. Rognvald's men were still climbing the walls and still dying there. Abruptly, another strand of the thick rope twanged as Rollo severed it, and they were halfway through. A tremendous splash on his blind side covered Hundr in water, and a warrior burst through the surface to swing an axe at him. The enemy had leapt from the tower above to attack them as they tried to cut the rope. Hundr blocked the cut with his axe and leapt towards his attacker. They grappled each other and dipped below the surface. The enemy had his hand around Hundr's throat, and his hold was strong, crushing Hundr's windpipe. Hundr fought for grip and realised the warrior had dropped his weapon. The man had one hand on Hundr's axe hand and the other around his throat. Hundr slipped his free hand downwards and grabbed his attacker's manhood, twisting and savaging it with all his strength. He could hear the man howl, muffled and strange beneath the water, and the man released his grip on Hundr's throat and axe hand to clutch at his damaged groin. Hundr burst through the surface and, in one motion, brought his axe down with a slap through the water to cleave his attacker's head open and turn the ice-blue fjord crimson.

He turned just in time to see the rope spring apart, hacked through by Rollo and Ragnhild. The men aboard the Windspear roared as they saw the rope sink into the water. Finally, the fjord was free to enter, and Hundr's men would do Harald and Rognvald's work.

FIVE

Ragnhild climbed up the criss-cross timber-log planking of the tower, dripping water onto Hundr and Rollo as they followed her lead. Hundr heard the splash of the Windspear's oars behind him as she approached the gap in the fjord wall. As soon as the rope bridging that gap had snapped, Ragnhild had begun her climb.

"We must clear those archers," she shouted.

"Careful when you reach the top," Hundr said, worried that Ragnhild would hop over the tower's lip to be shot to pieces by the archers within. He quickened his pace, trying desperately to catch up with her. Hundr clambered up two more rungs in no time and reached the tower's summit. They had cut the end of each log square, and as Hundr reached up to grasp the topmost log, he heard Ragnhild let out a bloodcurdling war cry as she landed within the archers' tower. The men up there shouted in alarm, and Hundr pulled himself up by his arms, desperate to get there before they killed Ragnhild. Hundr had lost enough friends. They all knew the risk they took living the Viking life, but that knowledge didn't soothe the pain of a lost friend.

Hundr scrambled over the lip of the tower and fell onto its fighting platform, the timber planks hard under his ribs as he landed on his side. He looked to see two archers pushing at Ragnhild with their bow staves, driving her towards the edge. Hundr took his axe from his mouth and sliced it across the legs of her first attacker, and then he spun on his back to kick the legs of the second. He leapt upon that man, bringing his axe down to thud into his chest. The archer looked at Hundr, eyes wide with surprise as his blood spilt on the golden timbers beneath him. Ragnhild stood over the corpse of the first attacker, but she stared, grimacing, into the space on the tower behind Hundr. The hairs on the back of his neck made him shiver.

Hundr leapt to his feet and spun to see an enemy with his bowstring drawn to his ear and his arrowhead flitting between him and Ragnhild, poised to fire but hesitating to pick who to shoot. One of them must die at so short a distance, and Hundr edged himself between the arrow and Ragnhild. The archer smiled and loosed. Hundr closed his eyes, waiting for the inevitable pain, as he heard the thrum of the bow. But the pain did not come. He opened his eyes just in time to see the arrow fly wildly into the air, and Rollo was at the top of the tower behind the archer. Rollo had the man by the throat, and with his monstrous strength, he lifted the archer from his feet and threw him over the side to plunge, screaming into the water below. Rollo put his hand on the timber posts and leapt on the platform, the timber planking shuddering beneath his weight.

"You thought you were going to die," said Rollo, pointing at Hundr and laughing.

Ragnhild charged past them both, keening her Valkyrie war cry, running beyond Rollo and out onto the wall behind the tower. However, her battle cry was cut short as an arrow thumped into her shoulder, stopping her mid-run. Hundr's heart leapt into his mouth, and Ragnhild fell to her knees. He raced past her and threw his axe at the closest bowman, its shining blade turning in the air before slamming into the enemy's face with a wet slap. Hundr bent to pick up Ragnhild's axe from the fighting platform and charged at them, Rollo following close behind him. The remaining archers fled before his grim, scarred face and his fury. He turned back to Ragnhild, and she leant against the wall, her breathing ragged and her face pale.

"Don't die. Please don't die," Hundr pleaded, taking her hand in his own. It was cold and clammy.

"Your ship is through, and the others follow," said Rollo, peering over the parapet. "Go to them. I will look after the woman."

Hundr looked at Ragnhild. She nodded at him, teeth gritted against the pain. Hundr knew he had to go. If he wanted to make sure Rognvald, and therefore Harald, knew it had been him who had opened the way beyond the fjord, he had to join the attack.

"Keep her alive," he said to Rollo, before kissing Ragnhild's forehead and jumping over the tower's edge, diving into the cold fjord.

He swam through the frigid water until Einar grasped his hand and hauled Hundr aboard the Seaworm, where he collapsed on the deck, shivering and breathing hard.

"That was some gamble you took to help this Rognvald, a man you have only just met," said Einar, as he wrapped Hundr in a thick, warm cloak. Einar helped him stand, and Hundr glanced back up at the tower.

"An arrow wounded Ragnhild," murmured Hundr through chattering teeth. The cold of the fjord felt like it was in his very bones.

"Where is she now?"

"Up there, with Rollo."

"Rollo? I don't trust that bastard. We should send men back for her."

"Do it as soon as we beach the ship," Hundr said. They both strode to the prow, where Hildr stood with her bow, ready to shoot. The Windspear had already landed, her hull driven up onto the shale beach, and her men poured from the bows with whoops and battle cries. Another of Hundr's ships ran into the beach, and Hundr saw Black Gorm and his berserkers leap from the vessel into a mass of waiting warriors.

"Where is this Rognvald?" muttered Einar, peering back towards the gap. "He asked us for help and comes late to the fight."

"His men were dying on the walls, climbing into bowshot," said Hundr, and he cast off the cloak as they raced towards the shore. "Find me an axe and a shield," Hundr called over his shoulder. Moments later, he held the weapons in his hand.

"One more stroke, lads, make it count," shouted Einar to his crew. They heaved at the water, and the ship surged forwards. Hildr loosed arrows from her recurved bow into the mass of men who awaited them on the shore, men who fought frantically to defend their homes and people. "Oars up," Einar ordered, and the oar blades came up in unison. The crew armed themselves, the clink and clank of axe, spear and shield thick in the air, the din of battle growing louder as they drifted at speed into a gap between the already beached ships.

Hundr stumbled forwards as the Seaworm's hull crunched into the shale beach, the scraping of the stones on her keel and clinker-built timbers sounding like the claws of a Loki giant wrenching at her.

"This had better be worth it," gruffed Einar. His face screwed up at the awful sound.

Hundr looked across the bay and saw Rognvald's ships rowing through the gap in the fjord wall.

"If we can capture this Jarl and bring the tale of it back to King Harald, then he might just forgive us for our raid on Ketil," Hundr said, looking at Einar. His broad face was lined, and his hair and beard were greying. "It's time to get rich, Einar, time to fight for ourselves. Let's see if Harald can make us rich; maybe it's time to find some land of our own."

Hundr jumped into the shallows, landing heavily in the shale and stumbling forwards. A spearman came for him, only to be flung backwards by one of Hildr's arrows as it slammed into his chest. Hundr charged forward, out of the water, and crouched on the beach behind his shield.

"Shield wall! Shield wall!" Einar bellowed as he joined Hundr, overlapping their shields together. Hundr saw the enemy beyond. They were in a ragged line, unsure how to deal with the attack storming up their beach. Gorm and his berserkers were tearing into the left flank of their shield wall, and the men from the Windpsear attacked their right. The enemy in the middle looked at each other, needing an order which did not come. Some had charged forward toward Hundr to kill him as he emerged from the water, which was the right thing to do. They should have killed him, as he was off-balance, but they hesitated as more men came ashore and made a shield wall of their own before them.

"They will break. They must have been so confident that no enemy would breach their bridge over the fjord that they never thought to organise themselves within," said Hundr, as more shields overlapped his and formed a line.

"Let's break them then," Einar grunted. He rose from his crouch and urged the men forwards. The sounds of weapons clashing and men dying filled the fjord. Einar quickened his pace, and Hundr kept abreast with him. "Kill, kill, kill!" Einar roared as they smashed into the enemy shield wall.

Hundr braced himself for resistance, but the enemy gave way. Hundr ran straight through their shield wall as though children held it. He turned and saw Black Gorm hacking one man down with his fearsome long-bladed war axe and then hurling another out of the way with his monstrous strength. The enemy shield wall was broken. Hundr's men had first outflanked their lines and then rolled them up. Their warriors raced back towards the town, no doubt looking for their wives and children to offer whatever protection they could in the face of defeat and the terrible prospect of their homes being sacked by the attackers.

Einar whipped his axe across an enemy warrior's face, and the man fell, clutching at the terrible wound. Another warrior charged him, and Einar smashed him backwards with the iron boss of his shield and cut the man's belly open to send him reeling back. They had won the beach, so Hundr turned and ran towards the starched buildings of the town. He pounded along the shale, and past fishing nets hung high to dry out in the sun. He ran up a wide street, flanked on each side by low, single-story buildings with steep thatch. A man came at him from a doorway, but Hundr just dodged away from his wild spear thrust and kept driving forward. Ahead of him, he could see the Jarl's hall; it was a longhouse. The gable was crested by a ship's prow and a beast's head; all painted in bright reds and greens. Two warriors stood at the entrance. They wore fine mail brynjars and were armed with shields and axes. The doors behind them were open, but Hundr could only see a black cavern barred by two warriors. The Jarl's hearth troop must be inside, the chosen men ready to defend his home and family. *They should have been on the beach. It's too late now.*

Hundr stopped running and hefted his shield in front of him. He suddenly felt vulnerable. He had left his precious mail brynjar aboard the Windspear when he had jumped into the fjord. Hundr realised he'd charged recklessly into the town. He wanted to take the Jarl himself as a prize and a story to tell the King, but he found himself alone in his haste. The two men guarding the hall came towards him. They were both big men, wearing shining helmets on their heads, covering half their faces with two large rings encircling their eyes. Hundr braced himself behind his shield and awaited their attack. The warriors came on, axes resting on the iron rim of their shields. They knew their business and would try to pin him between their shields and cut into his soft flesh with their sharp axes. Hundr snarled, the battle joy washing over him. It had been a long winter since the horror of the war in Ireland, and he was thirsty for enemies and their silver. So, he waited, shield braced and ready for their attack. Hundr could smell the leather of their padded shirts beneath their armour and the acrid stench of their sweat. He bunched his shoulders, and at the last moment, just as their shields were about to thunder into his, he twisted away to his left. Hundr crouched as he moved, bringing his axe around in a wide, low arc. The blade sang as it came about and chopped through the tendon of the first warrior's ankle. Hundr dropped his shield and launched himself into the injured enemy, driving him into his comrade and shoving them backwards. His injured mate fouled the second man's shield, and he cursed as he tried to heft it. But it was too late. Hundr swung his axe overhand, and its blade crashed into the man's face. It clanked as it hit the bottom of his helmet, and blood mixed with the pure white of his smashed-out teeth as they flew into the air. The two attackers were writhing in the mud, lying on one another. One was screaming, and the other made a strange mewing sound through his mangled face.

Hundr left them. He picked up one of their axes so that he carried one in each hand and marched towards the Jarl's hall. The longhouse rose above him, the painted eyes of its ship's prow beast glaring at Hundr as he approached. There would be a Jarl beyond the doors, a powerful Earl who had resisted King Harald and now faced defeat. Hundr paused for a moment, wondering at his part in that. Had he not cut the rope barring the fjord, would Rognvald ever have scaled the fjord wall from his ships? Under the hail of arrows, Hundr wasn't so sure. He knew little or nothing of this King Harald, nor if he was a good or bad King. Hundr reminded himself that such things did not matter. A king was a king who owed it to his men to make them rich and burnish their reputations. He strode through the hall's doorway and into the gloom beyond. Gasps and cries of women and children echoed around the rafters, and Hundr blinked his good eye, struggling to adjust to the change from daylight to the smoky darkness of the hall. As his vision cleared, he saw a long strip of hard-packed earth covered in fresh golden straw. They had moved eating benches to the eaves at the sloping sides of the room, and on his right, a fire blazed. Ahead, Hundr saw two lines of warriors, ten men in two rows of five, all finely armed in brynjars and hefting shields.

"Who is this man who raids my home? I am Jarl Rurik," came a deep, commanding voice from the rear of the hall.

Hundr saw a figure there, tall but bent at the shoulder. Grey, stringy hair fell over a bronze circlet on his brow, and his beard was long and of the purest white.

"My name is Hundr," he called back and raised his two axes in salute.

"A dog's name?" asked the Jarl, a mocking tone in his voice. "Are you a thing of King Harald, he who would encircle the entire world like Jörmungandr?"

It was not the first time Hundr had heard this reference to the King. Comparisons with the world serpent were not flattering. Harald was undoubtedly greedy and ambitious. But who was to say this Jarl Rurik was a better man? Maybe he was cruel and murderous, and Harald brought a wicked man to heel? Hundr dismissed such thoughts. He was not here to judge either Harald or Rurik.

"Throw down your arms, and no more men need to die today," said Hundr. The Jarl laughed, and his men came on, grinning at Hundr from behind their shining helmets.

Hundr swallowed. Alone against ten men. He cursed his unwise charge through the town.

"Looks like you need a hand," came a voice over Hundr's shoulder. A voice he knew, the voice of an old friend.

"Just in time, Einar," said Hundr, smiling.

Einar flanked Hundr, and more of his men poured through the hall's entrance to fill the space with blades, shields, and war fury. Black Gorm and his blood-soaked Berserkers forced their way to the front, and Gorm looked down at Hundr, his face and bare chest sheeted by other men's lifeblood.

"Very well, we will lay down our arms," called the Jarl, his old voice cracked and resigned.

"That time has passed. Your men came forward to kill me, and now they must die," said Hundr, and he nodded at Gorm. The berserker howled at the rafters and launched himself into the advancing warriors, and his wild men followed. Hundr stood back, leaning against the oak frame of the open entranceway. He listened to the crash of iron on iron and the screams of dying men. He had denied Gorm his bloodlust on Orkney and knew he could not deny him twice. It was best to satiate the hungry berserkers with warriors' souls now than have to drag them away from women and children later.

"We should send men for Ragnhild. She will still be with Rollo on the fjord wall," he said as Einar approached.

"I already sent Bush up there to get her," replied Einar. "This is a fine place, a place a man could call home."

"It is, I suppose. It's King Harald's now."

"We don't even know its name, this place we have ripped from its Jarl."

"Let's find out then," said Hundr, nodding ahead as the berserkers finished the rest of Rurik's warriors with ruthless brutality.

Hundr stalked through the fallen bodies.

Warriors writhed and moaned in pain, and Hundr stepped over a screaming man whose arm they had severed at the elbow. Einar knelt and cut that man's throat after ensuring the fallen warrior held a knife in his remaining hand—an act of kindness in sending the dying man to Valhalla.

"This place is ours. Let us loose before the others take our spoils," growled Black Gorm. His dark hair and beard dripped gore, and his chest still heaved from the exertion of battle.

"I will reward you for your bravery, Gorm," said Hundr, meeting the berserker's gaze. "As I will your men. We won't butcher these people. That is not the way of the drengr. Odin watches, and you honoured him with the warriors you have killed today."

"Piss on bravery. Let us loose. This place is ours," Gorm grunted, and he took a step closer to Hundr.

"Remember your oath, Gorm. I killed Eystein, your Lord, and you swore to be my man if I let you live. You could have died that day. Do not challenge me now."

Gorm snarled and barked at his men. They stalked from the hall, dripping with malevolence.

The old Jarl came down from his raised eating table, helped by a young man. The Jarl approached Hundr, his hands shaking as he walked. He was tall and must have been a formidable-looking Jarl in his youth.

"So, warrior, you have butchered my men, and Vanylven is yours. This place that has been my home, and my forefathers' home, back to the days beyond reckoning. My son is out there somewhere, fighting. Dead now, no doubt," said the old man. His grey, rheumy eyes were watery, and his skin pale.

"We are drengr, and this is the way of the gods," said Hundr. "We take what we can, and men must protect what they have. So we honour Odin with our victory here today."

"Bring my sword," the old man called, turning back to Hundr. He could feel the old eyes searching the ravages of his face and looking at his mail and axes.

"You do not look like a lord, you who has lain my people low."

"Do you yield to me, Jarl Rurik?"

A woman came from the shadowy edges of the hall. She carried a sword in the crook of her arm, its hilt bright with ivory carvings and its blade sheathed within a red scabbard, crossed with leather wrapping. She was a tall woman with raven hair. Tears stained her cheeks, and she handed the sword to Rurik, never taking her furious gaze off Hundr.

"I yield, and here is the sword of my forefathers. Fenristooth, I named it, for it bites as deep as the fangs of that mighty wolf who will come for Odin at Ragnarök. However, I yield on one condition, fierce young warrior."

"Name it."

"That my people, the wives of my sons and warriors, and my youngest son here next to me, be allowed to sail away from this place with their lives. Spare them your men's wrath."

"That, I fear, is not my decision to make. But I will do all I can for your people."

"The defiant Jarl Rurik, brought to heel," came a shout from the rear of the hall. Rognvald paused at the doorway, his hands on his hips, admiring the longhouse and smiling mirthlessly at Rurik.

"Take the sword," said the old man, pleading in his eyes. Hundr took it from him, and the feel of the hilt sent a shiver through his body. Once, Hundr had owned two fine swords, but he had lost them both in the battle on Dublin's walls. To feel the weight of a sword blade again in his hand brought back memories, painful memories of fallen friends, and unwise decisions. He walked back down the length of the hall and could feel the eyes of the women huddled in the darkness upon him, silently begging him to protect them from the wrathful hunger of his victorious warriors.

"The Jarl has yielded this place. He asked for the women to be spared," Hundr said to Rognvald, looking into his young, smooth face.

"There can be no pity for those who oppose the King," Rognvald uttered, and Hundr saw ruthlessness in his eyes.

"We played our part in the taking of Vanylven."

"You did, and you shall be rewarded. I will bring King Harald to you."

"Einar, bring the men. We will wait on board our ships." Hundr marched from the hall, shouldering his way through Rognvald's warriors, who pushed their way into the Jarl's home. Hundr squeezed his eyes closed as he heard the first screams.

SIX

Einar strolled along the docks of the fishing port—the sun warm on his face and the cawing of gulls cutting through the calls and shouts of fishermen as they unloaded their catch and market stall owners hawked their wares to passers-by. The air was thick with the smell of fresh fish and the familiar salt taste of the Whale Road, stretching away in a grey-green hue to the west. They had followed Rognvald north and arrived at a small coastal village to meet King Harald Fairhair.

"Is Harald a great king?" asked Finn, who walked at his side. The lad spoke with a mouthful of cooked fish, and Einar ruffled his curling locks of brown hair.

"He will be King of all Norway," said Einar. "They say he has not cut his hair since he was a boy, vowing not to cut it until he is King of the

North."

"He must have hair longer than you, Hildr," smiled Finn, and he giggled as Hildr reached down to tickle him. "Does he know my father and my grandfather?"

Hildr looked at Einar and shrugged.

"I would say he knows of them. They are both famed warriors, with reputations known the world over," said Einar. Finn was the son of Ivar the Boneless, and his grandfather was Ragnar Lothbrok. Mighty names, drengr's whom warriors fought to emulate and told stories of their deeds at firesides across the northern lands.

"So, the King will be glad to see me, then?" asked Finn.

"We won't tell him you are Ivar's son. Some things are best kept secret, for now," said Einar.

"But Hildr says we shouldn't tell lies," protested Finn, scowling at Einar. Finn was not a small boy, but neither was he a youth. Such matters were hard to explain, and Einar looked to Hildr for support.

She shook her head, her blonde hair blowing softly in the breeze, her eyes warm and kind.

"We do not tell lies. You are right. Sometimes, however, we say nothing or keep certain matters to ourselves. That is different to telling a lie," she said.

Finn thought about that for a minute.

"Will we practice today?" he asked and put his hand on the haft of the axe in its loop at Einar's belt.

"We shall. Now, look at the fishermen there," Einar pointed to where a crew unloaded shining fish, fresh to sell at the market. "Why don't you see what they have caught?"

Finn nodded, smiling, and he ran to look at the fresh catch. Einar watched him go and sat on a wooden fence, part of a pen which held three goats. The animals were munching a bale of hay on the pen's far side and paid Einar no attention.

"They butchered those people in the fjord," Hildr said as she sat next to Einar. He reached over and held her hand.

"Sometimes, that is how it goes in war. We don't kill women and children, as you know. But others do. You have seen this before."

"True. But it doesn't make it less sickening. They do themselves no honour," she tutted.

"We are still alive, you and me. And we have Finn. That is something to thank the gods for. What news of Ragnhild?"

"She suffers. We had to cut the arrow out. She lies aboard the Windpsear now. We must keep her wound clean. That is the danger, as it is with all wounds."

"I fear for Finn whenever we come to a new place or cross paths with other crews. His name is famous, and his uncle Halvdan in Dublin wants him dead. He is Ivar's son and the heir to the throne in Dublin. Halvdan will not want that hanging over his head."

"I know," Hildr said, smiling as she watched a grizzled fisherman show Finn an enormous crab caught in a wicker trap. "But he must live with the weight of his name, and we must make him strong enough to survive the difficulties which will surely come his way. You do not trust this Rognvald?"

"He's young and ambitious, and his king is powerful." Einar shrugged. "Hundr believes there is wealth and opportunity in King Harald's war. He is probably right. This is what we do. We find places where we can fight, please the gods, and make ourselves rich. But I do not trust Rollo. Something about him doesn't sit right with me."

"He seems fine enough, cocksure and bold, perhaps. But no more so than Hundr was when we fought in Frankia or Northumbria."

"I want to know why he was a prisoner of Ketil Flatnose. He must come from somewhere and be of some value if Ketil kept him alive. If he offended Ketil, why wasn't the sly bastard killed?"

"He fights well. And it was he who led us north

to King Harald. Perhaps you should talk to him and find out what you want to know."

"Maybe I will," said Einar, and he scratched at his beard. Even the thought of talking to the big young warrior irked him. "Let's just hope Hundr was right to follow Rollo's advice and that this King Harald will make us rich."

"You and I have been fighting for a long time. We are not rich yet."

"No, we are not." Einar stretched his waist to relieve the ever-present, dull ache in his back. "I am old now, maybe too old to be sailing the Whale Road with these young adventurers. When I served Ivar, I dreamed I would be a landed Jarl by now with a hall, a warm fire, and some men to farm the land."

"And a good woman?" she teased, elbowing him in the ribs. They laughed together.

"Yes, a good woman. As the years go by, it seems that we sometimes fight for the wrong things. When I was young, like Hundr, Rollo, and Rognvald, reputation was everything. When men called me Einar the Brawler, the name made me proud. I used to crave combat, beg men to challenge me to fight, and I would challenge at the slightest insult. Now, I think that reputation is an empty pisspot. And the wealth we seek seems like a fool's dream. How many men who go a'viking do you know who are rich?"

"Haesten is rich," she said. "Hundr has five ships, which is a fortune in itself. Others are born into wealth. I took my oath to be a Valkyrie warrior and serve Odin, but I had no choice. My father sent me to Upsala when I was a girl."

"Most men who are wealthy lords are born into it. Haesten is different. We fought alongside him in Frankia, and he really has made himself wealthy. He has silver and ships. But more importantly, he has his own land, wife, and child."

"You used to speak of settling down, finding land. You still desire that?"

"For you and me, yes. That fjord we attacked, Vanylven, was a fine place. A man who is Jarl of a place like that could be happy and proud and raise his family in peace."

Hildr smiled at him and brushed a stray golden hair away from her face. "You could see us there, you, Finn, and I? In the hall, a Jarl and his lady?"

"Well, maybe it's ambitious. It was a big place. But I grow too old for all of this. I can't be on the Whale Road with a white beard and no teeth."

Hildr laughed.

"Your beard is already speckled with white. But you are a long way from being too old to fight yet. This is our life, Einar. The sea, the crew. Hundr and Ragnhild. We have lost so many friends. All my Valkyrie sisters are dead, Kolo, Sten, Blink. What would we do, and who would come with us if we settled down? It's a fine dream, and I think all men dream of a long hall with a roaring fire and a hearth troop of warriors to drink ale with and talk of the old days."

"You tease me, my love. But I yearn to have roots, to leave something behind. Maybe it is the longing of all men and a foolish desire. But do not be so quick to trample on my dreams, or maybe I will have to find a new lady for my great hall to sit with me by the roaring fire."

"You should be so lucky," she scoffed, punching him on the arm, and they laughed together. "So, we will feast with a king this evening?"

"Aye. King Harald invites us to his table to celebrate the defeat of Jarl Rurik. He must have ridden overland with his men. His ships are not here if he has a fleet."

"Not at this small place," Hildr said. "Why is he here?"

"To take oaths from more local Jarls, to secure his place as King of all Norway. Only a few Norse Jarls remain opposed to him now."

Rognvald had led them to this place, a port town perched on a steep-sided hillside. It rose sharply from an inlet which faced east, protecting the fishing town from the cruel temper of the sea.

"So, let's see what kind of man this King Harald is then. And let's hope he can give us the riches we search for."

Later that day, as the sun fell behind Norway's peaks to cast a red glow across the sky, Einar sat inside a warm hall. A fire crackled and burned at its centre, and folk filled its feasting benches. Each bench was teeming with fresh fish, shellfish, warm bread, honey, and haunches of roasted lamb and pork. The smell of the food filled Einar's mouth with saliva, and his stomach rumbled and growled at the prospect of it. The people could not eat until the King arrived, so they drank instead, and Einar took a long pull at a horn of frothy ale. He had rubbed his brynjar down with a fistful of sand from the beach, and it shone now like the day it was forged. Hildr had persuaded him to run a comb through his hair and beard, and he looked like the Jarl he had been in the days when he served Ivar the Boneless before Ivar's son Hakon had betrayed him, and Ivar had cast Einar out of his service. He wiped the froth from his beard and looked across the table at Hundr. Einar's life had changed when they met, and now Hundr was Jarl and Einar was a ship's captain. Hundr was still young. He had not seen over twenty-six summers, but his missing eye and the scars on his face made

Hundr look older. He looked like what he was: a fearsome war Jarl and leader of five Viking warships. Einar gazed over at Hildr, and he reached below the table and squeezed her hand. She rewarded him with a smile.

She looks beautiful, he thought.

Her golden hair was brushed through with an ivory comb and piled atop her head in plaits. He wouldn't change his life, even though it hadn't gone as he had hoped it would. If he had never met Hundr, he would never have met Hildr or Finn, and they were his life.

"I'm bloody starving," grumbled Bush next to him. "I hope King Harald graces us with his presence before the meat goes cold."

"His men are all here, so he will arrive soon, I'm sure."

"Some of the King's men are all trussed up like women. They smell better than some whores I could name. It's no way for a man to live." Bush looked down at the table at Harald's courtiers in their fine tunics. Harald had also brought warriors, who sat in mail and leather like Hundr's men.

"Maybe you have your eye on one or two of them, with their soft hair and clean skin?" quipped Einar, and Bush laughed raucously, choking on his ale. "So, what do you make of this Rollo we have taken on as a shipmate?" asked

Einar. The tall, young warrior sat on the bench closest to the top table, where Einar sat with Hundr, Bush, Hildr, Finn, Rognvald and the other high-ranking men of Harald's retinue. An older man with an enormous belly held in by a thick belt sat at the far end of the table with a young, beautiful woman, and Einar assumed he was the Jarl of the fishing port.

"He fights well enough, I suppose," said Bush. "Dived into that freezing fjord after Hundr and Ragnhild. Hundr honours him, placing him in front of the men with Gorm and the other captains. He drinks now with a berserkers captain, Thorgrim, the son of Skapti far-sailor, and Kjartan Brandsson. All famous warriors and men to fear. He came to us chained and stinking of piss and shit. Now he wears a brynjar won at Vanylven. Maybe he's lucky?"

"Lucky, or as clever as a starving weasel."

"You don't like him then?"

Einar didn't have time to respond, for at the far side of the hall, two helmeted warriors dragged the wide doors open, and King Harald Fairhair strode inside. The warriors loyal to him stood from the benches and roared their approval, banging their fists on the table as he walked amongst them. He raised his hands, saluting their welcome, and spoke to men as he passed, leaning in to say a word in a man's ear or clapping another on the back.

"His men like him," shouted Bush above the din.

"He looks little more than a boy," Einar replied. The King was younger even than Hundr. His face was long and handsome, framed by a deep brown, neatly clipped beard. He was a short man, slight across the shoulders, but he had bright eyes and an open face. "He doesn't look like much of a fighter."

"Well, he has almost all of Norway under his rule. No man had ever been King of all Norway, so he must enjoy fighting, even for so small a man."

Which Einar supposed was true. King Harald approached the top table and paused, raising a hand to quiet the hall. Men sat, and the room went still.

"Thank you, Jarl Hrafn, for your hospitality. You are a fine host and a valued friend. Welcome, also, to new friends. To Jarl Hundr and his men, the heroes who put Vanylven to the sword when many said it could not be taken. Rognvald has told me of your bravery, and you have my thanks," said the King. He spoke well and confidently, his voice carrying across the room as clear as a Christian church bell. "I hear Jarl Rurik gave you his famed sword, Fenristooth. You may keep the blade as a token of my appreciation." The warriors banged on their tables again to support the decision.

"Generous of him, to give away that which he doesn't possess," whispered Bush.

"He's showing us who is the King here and who is the lowly sea Jarl," said Einar.

"I want you and your men to feel welcome in my kingdom and at our table. Many say you are the man who fought and bested Ivar the Boneless, the Champion of the North. I hear you also killed Eystein Longaxe and have killed lords in Frankia and the Saxon lands, a famous warrior indeed. Before we eat, I want to show you all something which has recently come into my possession." The King signalled to the side of the hall, and a boy ran over to him carrying a sword in a green scabbard. Its hilt shone with jewels and ivory. The King drew the blade and held it aloft. "Behold, the sword of Ynglings, my ancestors." All eyes in the room gazed upon the shining blade, and Harald turned slowly so that each man could witness its magnificence. "This is a sword of kings, first wielded by Fjolnir, son of Frey himself. The dwarves forged this blade for the Yngling Kings, and it is said that whoever wields it will be King of all Norway," he shouted these last words, and the hall erupted into raucous cheers. "Now, let's see how long Kjotve and his band of bastards can defy my rightful rule!" he bellowed, and his men continued their roars of support. "Come, let's eat and drink."

"A king with a magic sword," chuckled Bush through a mouthful of roast lamb. "Smells like silver to me," he grinned.

"Let's hope he fills our purses with silver and not our bellies with iron," said Einar. He took a bite of soft, white fish and watched Rollo. The warrior stared hungrily at Harald, ambition and envy dripping from him like the poison from the fangs of Jörmungandr, the world serpent.

SEVEN

"King Harald would like to talk to you privately after the feast," said Rognvald. His youthful face, free of the marks and scars of battle, glowed red on the cheeks.

"It would honour me to meet him," replied Hundr. The King's man smiled broadly, nodding at Hundr's response. The clamour and sweat of warriors and Harald's retinue, combined with the mammoth fire at the hall's centre, made for a close and hot room. Hundr felt a trickle of sweat roll down his face, across his dead eye. It snaked along his beard and down below his brynjar to tickle his chest. His face felt flushed, and he took a drink of ale. The brynjar was heavy, crafted from hundreds of metal rings forged together by a skilled smith. It was cumbersome to wear at a feast, but it was a symbol, as much as a piece of armour that would protect his body from a sword blow or spear thrust. Only a lord, or a successful warrior of reputation, could afford the armour or possess the fighting skill to stop another man from taking it from him. It spoke of wealth and that its wearer was a man of war. "You do not wear your mail for the feast?" he asked Rognvald.

"Not tonight; the King is here with his lords and advisors. With such men, one's cloth is as important as one's mail and weapons when in the company of warriors," Rognvald said, smiling again.

"You need to impress these men?"

"They are the Lords and Jarls of Norway, powerful men who lend their ships and warriors to Harald's cause. They are also as clever as rats and as cunning as foxes."

"The King must trust you to send you with his ships to carry out his work," said Hundr. Rognvald had led Harald's ships and warriors in the attack on Vanylven, and though both he and Harald were young men, that fact told Hundr that Rognvald was the right man to talk to if he wanted to learn more about the conquering King.

Rognvald's eyes searched Hundr's face as he chewed on a mouthful of fish. He took a bite of bread and washed it down with a drink of ale.

"We were boys together," he said, beckoning

to a slave girl for more ale for the table. "We are cousins. I helped make him King. When his father, Halfdan the Black, died, we fought alongside each other to ensure his succession."

"Was it contested?"

"Yes, Halfdan was a great warrior, and during his life, he doubled the size of his kingdom and made many enemies across Vingulmark and Hedmark. As a result, there was a lot of fighting, and many men died." Rognvald flashed a mirthless smile at Hundr. "Harald vowed not to cut his hair until he is King of all Norway, surpassing even his father's achievements. That is why he wears his hair so long."

"Forgive me for saying it, but you and Harald do not look like men of war, yet you have fought many battles?"

"Should a warrior look like you and Einar, scarred and huge? We have fought in many battles together, and Harald has the blessing of the gods. Holy men have prophesied it and seen it in their sacrifices, and we have luck on our side. I can fight with fury when I have to."
"I do not doubt it. So, you are a Jarl, then?"

"My father is a cousin of Halfdan the black and is Jarl in Vestfold. Harald honours me, and I will now be Jarl in Vanylven, even though my father still lives. Enough about me. Tell me, are the tales of your deeds true?"

"What tales?"

"Come now, Hundr, you are the famous man with the dog's name, killer of Ivar the Boneless and Eystein Longaxe. Champion of the North, some men say."

"I killed Ivar and Eystein. That much is true. I also killed Ivar's son on a blood-soaked jetty in Northumbria. It was fortunate we met you when we did," said Hundr, and he leant sideways to allow a servant to fill his cup with ale.

"Why was it fortunate?"

"We were sailing to meet King Harald, having heard of his war in the south."

"You want to fight for him, make yourselves rich?" Rognvald grinned again and wagged a finger at Hundr.

"We are Vikings," said Hundr with a shrug.

"Just so," nodded Rognvald, and he laughed. "What happened to your eye? If you don't mind the question."

"Ivar's son, Hakon, cut it out with a fiery red blade."

"So, you killed him?"

"I killed him. For that and other reasons." Hundr took a drink, and his left hand fell to the grip of his sword. He flexed his hands around the warm leather grip of Fenristooth, the sword Jarl

Rurik had handed him before Rognvald ordered his slaughter. "Does Harald have many loyal Jarls in the south? I hear Ketil Flatnose is his man." Hundr took a bite of fresh bread from a loaf woven in an intricate pattern. He watched closely for Rognvald's response to the mention of Ketil's name, hoping for a sign of Ketil's standing with the King.

"You fought like demons at Vanylven. I did not think to swim to the rope and cut it. I thought their archers would shoot us in the water if we tried such a thing. Maybe we would have never climbed their fjord wall if you had not made that swim." Rognvald plucked another chunk of steaming meat from his plate and took a bite of it from his small eating knife. "Ketil is a powerful man. His islands are the gateway to the Saxon lands and Ireland. He is not sworn to King Harald, but he does not fight against him, either. You know Ketil?"

"We have not met," said Hundr.

When everyone had eaten enough of Jarl Hrafn's food and drank enough of his ale, slaves came to clear the tables, and people moved about the hall freely, gathering in pockets to talk and continue to drink into the night. Men became raucous, shouting and boasting filled the hall, and Hundr found Einar standing with Bush and Hildr close to the door.

"I am sweating like a fat Christ priest in here," grumbled Bush, running a hand beneath his leather helmet liner.

"I will speak with King Harald this evening," said Hundr, mopping sweat from his own brow.

"I saw you talking to his pet, Rognvald," muttered Einar. "What news?"

"Ketil Flatnose is not sworn to Harald, so maybe he will not be offended when I tell him of the raid."

"You plan on telling him?" asked Hildr.

"I do. Better he hears it from me than from someone else weeks from now. Besides, I think we should stay and fight for Harald for a while. Fill the men's purses with silver."

"What do you make of Rognvald?" asked Einar.

"He and Harald are both young; they're cousins and friends. Harald is the son of Halfdan the Black and will be the King of Norway. Rognvald is his right-hand man, and they fought their way across Norway, subjugating powerful Jarls, men with reputation."

"So, they must both be savage and clever," said Einar. "I once met Halfdan the Black when I sailed for Ivar. Halfdan was a fearsome man, a conqueror in his own right."

"Just as Rollo told it, there is only one powerful Jarl left. Kjotve the Rich, and he has gathered other lesser Jarls and warriors to his banner to oppose Harald," Hundr explained.

"So, there will be a fight?" said Bush.

"There will, and that means plunder."

"And silver," chortled Bush, grinning his gap-toothed smile. "Maybe I could be Bush the Rich when we kill this Kjotve."

Hundr laughed.

"So, we will fight for Harald."

"But we won't swear to him," affirmed Einar. "We made that oath to ourselves in Northumbria. We will never swear to another Lord again. So, once this Kjotve is in the ground, we move on. And I'm still not happy about Rollo—he seems to know a lot for a man we found emptying Ketil's shit pail."

"He is more than he seems," agreed Hundr. "And we will move on after Harald defeats Kjotve. Maybe we will go east, back to my homelands."

"Maybe we could find some land with all the silver we plan to make," said Einar. "I am tired of foisting ourselves on unwitting Jarls for the winter and freezing my balls off. We should have a home, a base to spend each winter."

"If we have a home, our enemies can find us," said Hundr.

"Our enemies are dead." Einar smiled with a shrug, and they laughed together.

Hundr thought there was some sense in what Einar proposed. His old friend looked tired, and Einar had spoken before of his dream of having land of his own, to settle down by the fire with Hildr. It was a fine ambition and certainly one to be considered. Hundr's thoughts had only ever been of reputation, of making his name as a warrior and man to be feared. That had been his dream since he was a boy, roaming the streets of Novgorod as the bastard son of its Prince.

The life of a sea Jarl could not continue forever. He would either grow old, still sailing the Whale Road looking for battle, or he would find land and become a landed Jarl. Such was life, and he knew he owed it to his men to give them some sort of safety for their families. The warriors of his crews were sworn to Hundr, but more than half of those men would return to their families each winter, sailing to the lands of the Danes, Svears, or to Norway. Then they would return, at an agreed meeting point in Spring, ready for the next campaigning season. They owed Hundr their oaths and blades—in return, his duty was to reward them with rings and silver for their service. Such was the nature of the Lord and Warrior relationship. But to have land of his own would mean his men could bring their families together in a place of safety.

Hundr watched Einar and Hildr talking together, close to one another, touching a hand or dipping closer to speak into one another's ear.

Maybe it is time for me to find a woman, for a family.

The evening drew on, and men fell asleep on benches or stumbled to their ships or quarters, their bellies full and faces red from ale. One of the King's men summoned Hundr, and he followed the man along a dark, torch-lit corridor at the rear of the hall. It led to a chamber door, where the man knocked once. A voice responded, and Hundr pushed the door open to enter a wide room. At its centre was an enormous bed scattered with furs, and a warm fire glowed on its far side.

"Jarl Hundr, welcome," said the King, beaming. He strode to Hundr, and they clasped forearms. Harald had removed his brynjar and now wore a simple green tunic and trews. He was smaller than Hundr, of average height and build. He beckoned for Hundr to join him in two chairs positioned in front of the fire. As he followed the King, Hundr saw his famed long hair stretching down his back in a long plait, woven with silver wire so that his fair hair shone like water under a summer sun.

"Thank you, King Harald, for making my men and I so welcome."

"This is Jarl Hrafn's home and hospitality. But he is my man now, and you are most welcome. Rognvald tells me you fought like bears at Vanylven, that he might not have taken the place but for your heroics."

"He overplays it, King Harald. I could not have cut the rope if his men hadn't kept most of the archers on the walls busy."

"It is good to meet a warrior of such a famous reputation. The killer of Ivar the Boneless, no less. Was he as great a fighter as they say?"

"He was indeed very quick and very brave."

Halvdan smiled at that and clapped his hand on his knee. He reached forward to a small table between their chairs and took a sip of water from a horn cup.

"So, what can I do for you, Jarl Hundr?"

"I was on my way to see you, King Harald, when I came across Rognvald. There is something I must tell you before we speak openly and as friends."

Harald's eyes glinted, and he stroked his beard. He leant forward and reached to the side of his chair. He found his sword, the Yngling blade he had shown to his men in the hall, and rested it in front of him. The blade was naked and shone blue in the firelight, clouds and whorls visible in the metal, and its pommel glinting with precious stones.

"There is always something," said Harald. He placed the sword, tip-down, against the hard-packed earth floor and spun its hilt, so the weapon twirled in his hand. He raised his eyebrows and waited for Hundr to speak.

"It is not something I must ask of you, King Harald. But something I must confess." Hundr waited for Harald to speak, but the young king remained silent, staring deep into Hundr's eye. Hundr shuffled to change his seating position. "On my journey north, I raided the Orkney Islands and attacked the stronghold of Ketil Flatnose. I took his treasure but did not hurt his women or children."

A smile flickered at the corners of Harald's mouth.

"So, you attacked a man known to be loyal to my cause. And you come to me now to make sure you have not made of me an enemy? What if Ketil and I are like brothers, and your raid angers me? Would you attack me now? Could you kill me, Jarl Hundr?"

"I come to you to offer to fight for you. I will not swear an oath to you, but I will lend my blades to your cause and help make you King of all Norway. I wanted to tell you of my raid on Ketil's lands before you hear it from another."

"I am not angered. Ketil is not my oath man,

but nor is he, my enemy. We are Vikings, and such is our way of life. A man must protect that which is his from those who would take it from him. This is the way of the gods. If he knows you fight for me, Ketil will come looking for justice. He will want your head, and he is a dangerous man to have as an enemy."

"As are you, King Harald. Which is why I wanted to tell you in person."

Harald smiled and leant forward.

"I will need good men and famous warriors to finish this war with Kjotve. Therefore, I welcome you and your men and will reward you when we win. Ketil would not bring his ships to fight for me, but he would not oppose me, either. So, I would like you to do something for me. You say that you will not swear an oath, but ahead of Ketil coming to me, I must be sure of your loyalty before I accept you into my service."

Hundr mentally braced himself. *Here it comes, the price to pay not to have a king as an enemy.*

"Jarl Hrafn, whose hospitality we have enjoyed, is not a man I can trust. I hear he has sworn an oath to Kjotve in secret, and I do not want to march my army south and leave a potential enemy at my back."

Hundr scratched at his beard, and his dead eye pulsed in its empty socket.

"So, what would you have me do, King Harald?"

"Hrafn must die. Tonight. I will march tomorrow and leave one of my own men as Jarl in his place."

"It will be done," said Hundr. A knife in the dark was not the way of a drengr, but Hundr had killed many men, and so what was one more life amongst those others? "If we help make you King of all Norway, a suitable reward would be some land in your kingdom to rule as my own. Just like Rognvald will be Jarl in Vanylven, you will make a new Jarl in this place once Hrafn is gone."

"I have the sword of the Ynglings, the blade of my ancestors, which once belonged to Frey himself. The man who holds this sword will be the King of all of Norway. If the sword does not make it so, how can you, Jarl Hundr?"

"I have no deep magic but my sword and warriors."

"I jest, forgive me. Yes, if you help make me King of all Norway, I will grant you land of your own. I took this sword from a great barrow in the north. A ship sank below the earth in the time of my grandfather's grandfather. I went down there, amongst the decay, in the realm of Hel and her wraiths and pulled this blade from the bones and worm-eaten flesh. And I will be King. So, kill Hrafn for me, prove your loyalty, and you will help make me King of all Norway, and I will make you a landed Jarl in return."

The King called for his man, and Hundr left him in his bedchamber. He heard Harald give the Yngling sword to his man and order him to clean that and his mail to be ready to march the next day. The walls of the dark corridor felt close and cold as Hundr marched away from Harald. He must kill a man to earn the trust of a king.

That is not the way of the drengr.

His hand fell to the hilt of his sword, its grip comforting. Hundr had learned from great men such as Haesten, Ivar, and Bjorn Ironside that a leader must use all the tools available to him to accomplish his goals. Just as a King uses his Jarls, or a shipmaster uses his crew, Hundr must use his men to do what must be done. The leather grip was warm beneath his hand, and he rubbed his thumb across the ivory face etched into its pommel. The face was snarling and cruel, its mouth thin and hard. It was the face of a ruler carved into the bone ivory of a mighty sword. To lead meant to make hard decisions, and Hundr had to kill a Jarl in his bed.

EIGHT

"You want me to kill who?" said Rollo, rubbing the sleep from his eyes. He leant against the Windspear's mast, and his voice sounded loud, almost booming, in the chill quiet of the night. Clouds shrouded the moon, rendering the port town covered in total darkness, save where remnants of torches glowed in their iron holders along the quayside.

"King Harald wants Jarl Hrafn gone tonight. That is the price for our raid on Ketil and the price of your freedom," whispered Hundr. He looked across the dock to make sure no one overheard him. In the darkness, even a whisper felt like it could carry across the town like the flight of an owl.

"I am already free. Let the tyrant do his own dirty work. Do you have anything to drink?" Rollo clacked his dry tongue against the roof of his mouth and rubbed at his temples. His eyes searched the deck as though expecting to find a cup of cool, fresh water to drink.

"Tyrant? Listen," Hundr spoke louder, and he grabbed Rollo's arm. "I freed you from Ketil's chains, and this is what I ask of you in return. Take a blade and send Hrafn to the next life."

Rollo eyed him warily, looked down to where Hundr gripped his arm, and then smiled as he became fully awake.

"I can kill the Jarl for you, my lord. In return for the favour you did for me on Orkney. Can I take men with me in case there is a problem?"

"Take ten men with you, but stay hidden if you can."

"Killing Jarl Hrafn will not anger King Harald?"

"He will not be angry. Enough questions. Repay my generosity in freeing you and do as I ask," Hundr snapped.

"So, Harald sends another Jarl to the afterlife. Very well, my lord," said Rollo, holding Hundr's gaze for a moment before stalking away into the darkness.

Hundr thumbed the hilt of his sword as he watched Rollo disappear into the night. The cruel ivory face grinned beneath the callouses of his hand. He was alone with the soft crash of the sea on the Windspear's hull and the creaking of her timbers as she rocked on the gentle tide. He looked up at the dark silver sky, devoid of stars under the dense blanket of shadowed clouds. Killing the Jarl in the night wasn't right, and his guts broiled at the knowing of it. Hundr had made bad choices before, usually when he tried to do what seemed to be the right thing or when he followed his heart. Those choices had resulted in the death of his friends, like Sten Sleggya and Kolo, butchered in the streets of Dublin because Hundr wanted to fight for an Irish Queen. Killing Jarl Hrafn with a knife in the dark was not the way of the drengr. A warrior should challenge the Jarl in broad daylight and fight him in the Holmgang square. He looked down at Fenristooth, the ivory there glowing and grinning at him.

After the horror of Dublin, he had promised himself that he would think more like a ruthless leader and less like a boy pursuing a childish dream of honour and the warriors' code. All the great leaders he had met in his life—Ivar, Bjorn, Haesten, and Sigurd Snake Eye—had been cold and ruthless. They were men who did what must be done, no matter how hard or brutal it was. This was such a thing, Hundr told himself. One old Jarl must die so that Harald could bring his army south, knowing no enemy lurked at his back. When the army marched and Harald's fleet sailed, that would mean Hundr and his men also sailed towards battle, glory, and riches. Harald has promised land, and all Hundr had to do was fight to make Harald the King of all Norway and kill one old Jarl.

I should have done it myself, not sent Rollo to do my dirty work. Hundr listened to the lapping of the waves. He went to his sleeping quarters below the steerboard and lay down alone. Sleep was slow to enfold him in its embrace. He lay looking into the bleak, dark sky. Nótt, the night goddess, was up there riding her dark horse Hrímfaxi across the sky, and he thought of the gods and how they must judge the lives of men as he slipped into a fitful sleep, filled with thoughts of pale-faced ghouls with their throats cut in the darkness.

"Wake up, lord, wake up," said Bush, rocking Hundr's shoulder. Hundr opened his eye and rubbed the sleep from it, his head thick with the ale from Harald's feast.

"Is it morning?" he asked.

Bush shook his head. He took his leather helmet liner off and wrung it in his hands.

"No, it's still night. There is a problem, lord."

Hundr sat up from his bed beneath the steerboard platform and stood. The sky was still dark, and he could not have slept for long.

"What is it?"

"Listen," said Bush, pointing a shaking finger towards the town. Hund looked to where the buildings rose in shadow up the mountainside, and he could hear screaming. A pain-wracked screaming, like the sound of the underworld, the sound of murder and death. Torches sprang up across the settlement like fireflies as people woke to the terrible wailing and blood-curdling cries of terror.

What have I done? Hundr ran across the Windspear's deck to better understand what unfolded in the town. He had a hollow feeling in his chest, and although he couldn't see or know what had happened, he knew he had unleashed Rollo and ten of his warriors on the Jarl and the people of his household. *I should have killed the Jarl myself.*

"Lord, look," said Bush. Hundr peered across the port, where a dozen warriors came from the darkness. They held torches before them, and their calls of triumph and laughter lifted above even the cries of pain from the town beyond. "Oh shit. We might need to set sail, and quickly," Bush grumbled, and he looked expectantly at Hundr, waiting for an order, but Hundr just stared. He saw Rollo marching, his face and mail sheened in dark blood. Black Gorm strode beside him, and his berserkers trailed them, whooping for joy and brandishing their weapons. As the group turned a corner, Hundr saw they pulled along three women, rope around their necks and their hands tied.

"What in Odin's name have you done?" came a shout, Einar's voice peeling out from the deck of the Seaworm. Hundr saw him race down the gangplank of that ship, followed by Ragnhild and Hildr.

"Come on," Hundr said, and he sprinted from the Windspear, Bush trailing behind him. As they ran, a familiar rage-filled voice boomed over the cacophony of chaos.

"I don't answer to you," growled Gorm.

From ten paces away, Hundr saw the berserker captain reach out and shove Einar backwards. Einar rolled with the blow and returned to punch Gorm in the face. Hundr quickened his pace, but not before Gorm lunged at Einar with his axe, and Einar swayed away from the swing and kicked Gorm between the legs, dropping him to the timber jetty. Einar whipped a knife from his belt and held it to Gorm's throat.

"Easy, everyone. Stay calm," shouted Hundr as he leapt in front of Einar to get between him and Gorm's baying berserkers.

"We are dead men; these animals have broken the King's peace," said Ragnhild, her one eye blazing, and her left arm bound at the shoulder.

"Do you want to make the square?" growled Einar, glaring down at Gorm, who knelt with Einar's knife at his throat. The berserker captain was shaking with fury.

"I'll fight you anytime, greybeard. I'll kill you and take your ugly old whore to my bed," Gorm spat, and he grinned at Hildr.

"We'll make the square in the morning then, you and I," snarled Einar, and he flicked his knife across Gorm's face, slashing his cheek open in a line of dark blood. "That will remind you not to disrespect Hildr or me."

Gorm roared and lurched towards Einar, but Rollo held him back.

"Einar Rosti, the Brawler." Rollo grinned, his face half-lit by the flaming torch he held.

"Everyone move back," shouted Hundr, and pushed the berserkers away. Gorm shook free of Rollo's grip and stumbled after them, cursing them and holding his bloody face. Hundr turned to Einar. "You can fight him tomorrow if King Harald doesn't kill us first," he said.

"What have you done?" Ragnhild seethed at Rollo.

"Followed orders." He shrugged. "I went with Gorm and his men and killed Jarl Hrafn."

"You did what?" said Einar, looking from Rollo to Hundr.

"I killed Hrafn. Like Jarl Hundr asked me to, the King ordered it."

Hundr felt their eyes on him, judging him.

"Of all the men in my crews, did you have to take Black Gorm and his men with you?" he said.

"You told me to take ten men, so I took Gorm and his lot."

"What else did you do?" asked Hundr. His dead eye throbbed, and he kneaded it with his knuckles.

"We killed Hrafn's men, and it got nasty up there."

"Nasty how?"

"There were women there. A few of them died. It got messy." Rollo flashed a wolfish smile, a strange look of triumph playing at the corners of his mouth.

"You sent him to kill Jarl Hrafn, whose town we stand in and whose hospitality we have just enjoyed?" asked Einar, his broad flat face incredulous.

"Harald wanted it done. This was the price to show our loyalty and the price of the land and riches we seek," said Hundr.

"This is not drengskapr, axes in the darkness. This is Loki's work," hissed Ragnhild. She winced and raised her hand to support her injured shoulder.

"Jarl Hundr sent me, and I did what was asked. Jarl Hrafn is dead, his wife is dead, and his children are dead. I did not ask for this. This is the work of King Harald. This is how he becomes King of all Norway. He kills and takes men's land and will keep doing so until someone stops him. Maybe, now that Hrafn is dead, somebody will take notice. What if this sparks the flame that can grow into the fire of resistance?" said Rollo. His jaw was set firm, and his easy manner evaporated and turned into frowning anger. He loomed over them, the torchlight flickering across his face, his eyes dark and glaring.

"What is this talk of Harald and rebels, Rollo? You killed children?" asked Hundr. "Let those women go, now!" he bellowed at Gorm's men. They bunched in front of the captives, three women in ragged shirts, whimpering and broken. Hundr strode over to them. "Let them go," he said slowly and deliberately.

"Piss off; this is our prize," growled a berserker, standing out beyond Gorm and the others. He held his long axe, and even in the darkness, Hundr could see blood and chunks of flesh clinging to its curved blade. "Always, you stop us. We never get to take any women or slaves. I say you are no Viking. These are the old ways...the ways of the warrior and we..."

Hundr ripped Fenristooth from its scabbard at his waist and, in one fluid motion, slashed the bright blade across the berserker's throat, mid-sentence. The man fell to his knees, and his axe thudded as he dropped it. He clutched at his cut throat, blood welling and pouring down his bare chest. Then, Hundr looked at the remaining berserkers, stared each man in the eye, plunged his sword into the dying man's stomach, and ripped him open, the coils of his guts slopping onto the jetty.

"Anyone else got anything to say?" he snarled and pointed the blade at each man, including Rollo. "Let the women go, now. Everyone back to your ships. I will settle this in the morning." The berserker lay dead on the jetty, and he had died badly. The wounds were terrible to behold—gaping at neck and gut—but Hundr had to make an example of the man. To be a leader of fighters and killers, he had to be the worst and the best of them.

The rope tying the three women fell to the ground, and they sprang away, running for their lives back into the town beyond. Rollo put an arm around Black Gorm, who nursed his slashed face, and led them back to their ship. Gorm paused and turned to face Hundr.

"This is no way to treat warriors who follow orders. We are Vikings," he snarled.

Hundr let them go and slid his sword back into its fleece-lined scabbard.

"Is this what we are now?" said Ragnhild as he passed.

"It was a thing that had to be done. The King wanted it; it is the price for us joining his army. The price of our wealth." Hundr looked at Einar. "The King promises us land of our own if we help him win his crown. So, old friend, this is the price of your dream."

"Don't put this on my conscience," Einar muttered.

Hundr held his gaze for a heartbeat and then returned to bed. He lay there, looking at the night again. Eventually, he fell into a deep sleep, his mind wondering how King Harald would react to the slaughter. Much to his frustration, Hundr couldn't read the man. He could just as easily fly into a wrathful rage at the murderous turn his order had taken or be happy that his will was brutally carried out.

The following morning, Hundr woke below a clear sky, the light blue of springtime bluebells. Wisps of cloud floated along on a gentle, cool breeze. He went to the water barrel next to the mast and dipped his head in it, the refreshing water waking him fully and washing away the troubles of the night before. He brushed his wet hair away from his face and ran his fingers through his beard to comb the knots out. Hundr turned and was about to look for some food when he noticed his crew gathered at the prow. They spoke in hushed voices and went quiet when he approached. Hundr looked across the water and saw one of his ships was missing. The Sea-Stallion, a ship he had won fighting in Frankia alongside Haesten. Black Gorm and his berserkers crewed the Sea-Stallion. A cry rang out, followed by shouting, and Hundr dashed to port to see men aboard the Seaworm were running ashore, frantic and alarmed.

"What is it?" Hundr called to them, a sick feeling in his stomach.

"Finn is gone, taken in the night. They have stolen the boy and his priest," shouted a warrior. Then Hundr heard the wails of Hildr from the Seaworm deck, and he knew something terrible had happened.

"Gorm and his bastards have stolen the bloody Sea-Stallion," stormed Bush, marching across the deck, axe in hand. "They've taken young Finn and stolen your ship. We should have killed those Norse bastards in Ireland when we had the chance."

He is right; that was another grave decision. Hundr thought of the boy, son of Ivar the Boneless, huddled and afraid, a prisoner amongst wicked men, killers after all.

"Gorm and his men have broken their oath and stolen Finn Ivarsson," said Hundr, and he looked at Bush's lined face, his friend furious, looking to strike with his axe but with no one on whom to vent his anger. "Einar and Hildr will be beside themselves. What of Rollo?"

"Gone too, and some of Ivar's men, men who have sailed with us for years."

"I swear it now, an Odin oath that I will get that boy back. Rollo and Gorm will suffer for what they have done."

Bush did not have time to respond because King Harald marched from the town, flanked by a long hundred of his warriors. The King of War had come, wrathful and seeking Hundr and his men.

NINE

King Harald paced the hall, striding back and forth before a roaring fire. He walked with his hands clasped behind his back, his face drawn and concentrated. Muscles worked beneath his beard where he ground his teeth, his head occasionally nodding as though he was engaged in a debate with himself. Harald had said nothing since Hundr, Einar, Ragnhild, Hildr, and Bush had come before him. Rognvald had marched them in, and the young warrior sat at a bench, calmly watching his King pace back and forth.

Hundr observed Harald. There was a controlled malevolence on his face, his features set and grim, but his obvious anger was contained and managed. Harald had not spoken to Hundr as he and his men led them from the Windspear and Seaworm to what had been Jarl

Hrafn's hall. Einar was wide-eyed, chewing on his beard. Hundr could feel his rage pulsing like a ship in a storm, thrumming like the beat of the sea on a ship's hull. Finn was gone, and Hundr knew Einar would kill the men responsible. Einar loved the boy like a son and would not rest until Finn was safe.

A door at the rear of the hall creaked open, and four men shuffled through the space, carrying a bed between them. A groaning man lay upon it, and as they brought him closer, Hundr could see that the man clutched at a terrible wound in his guts. They had dressed the injury in cloth, but a wide, dark, blood stain seeped through it. His face was pale and sheeted in sweat, and his head bobbed frantically as he fought back the urge to cry out in pain.

"This is Arne," said Harald, making eye contact for the first time with Hundr. The King held his gaze and then flicked his stare to Einar. "Arne is the son of my mother's uncle. We are kin." Harald took a step towards Arne as his men lay the bed upon the floor rushes, and he bent to hold the wounded man's hand. "They wounded Arne as he defended my property from thieves and brigands. What do you know about this?"

Hundr opened his mouth to speak, but the King held up a finger and closed his eyes as though battling himself to be calm.

"I warn you. This is your one chance, to be honest with me. Tell me the truth, and some of you might yet live," said Harald.

"I will speak the truth, King Harald," Hundr replied earnestly. He swallowed hard, realising that the King was serious. Hundr had assumed that the carnage wrought by Rollo in his killing of Jarl Hrafn had enraged him, but clearly, there was something else at play here, some other unfortunate event which Hundr could not see. He did not yet know if the King was a gentle or brutal man—if he was prone to violence and killing or not. Hundr still knew very little about the King, but any man who, at so young an age, was on the verge of subjugating a Norway filled with Viking warlords, was not a man to be taken lightly. "Last night, some of my men broke their oaths to me. They have taken a boy, who is like a son to us, and stolen one of my ships, sneaking away in the night like nithings."

The King dropped Arne's hand and raced across the room, stopping at a handsbreadth in front of Hundr's face. His eyes were wide and wild, and his chin jutting.

"I don't give a whore's turd what your men took from you. They took my sword, the Yngling sword. A sword forged for the gods themselves, wielded by my ancestors, and its wielder will be the King of all Norway. I took it from the earth, risking curses and fetches, and now your shit-stinking men have stolen it." Harald was shaking, spittle flying from his mouth and his face as red as a summer apple.

"These men betrayed me also, King..."

"How do I know they do not wait for you out at sea? How do I know you are not Kjotve's man? It is not beyond that coward to send men to steal the Yngling sword, to make himself king." Harald shouted, interrupting Hundr again.

"You have my word. I had no part in this. I did as you asked. The Jarl is dead. I woke this morning to find my men gone, the boy and my ship taken. I am as angered as you are." Hundr met the King's stare with his one eye. Harald looked at each corner of Hundr's face as though he searched for the truth in his scarred features.

Before Hundr could say any more, Einar spoke up.

"The boy they took is the son of Ivar the Boneless and heir to the throne of Dublin. They mean to ransom him to his uncle, Halvdan Ragnarsson, who is now King in Dublin and would surely kill the lad. I am Einar Rosti, and I love that boy like a son. You have my word that I will wreak my vengeance upon these men, and I will retrieve the boy and the sword. This I swear," said Einar. His voice was low and sure.

Harald turned his attention to Einar, having to look up to meet that wind-burned, brutal, flat face. He nodded, seeming to find some level of trust in Einar's seething hate, which hung from him like Odin on the great tree Yggdrasil.

"Bring in the Sami," said the King, turning to Rognvald.

"Bavlos," Rognvald shouted, not stirring himself from his seat. A small man shambled into the room. He wore a thick blue coat and a hat of fur upon his head. His boots turned up at the toe, and his face was broad with dark skin, thin lips, and strange blue eyes which sat close together on his face. The short man came to stand next to the King and bowed his head.

"Find the truth of their words," hissed Harald.

Bavlos closed his strange eyes and nodded. He whispered to himself and walked in a slow circle around Hundr and Einar. Hundr shifted his weight from foot to foot, suddenly feeling hot beneath his brynjar. The Sami man fished his hand into his coat and pulled out a fearsome-looking animal claw and a handful of yellowed bones. He chanted to himself under his breath, and Einar glanced at Hundr, the corners of his mouth turned down in displeasure. Bavlos raised his hands to Einar, caressing them from Einar's forehead to his chest. He then wafted his hands towards him as though he tried to breathe in Einar's very essence. For a horrifying moment, Hundr thought Einar would headbutt the little man, but Einar just shook his head and glared at Harald. Bavlos repeated the same procedure over Hundr's face, let out a howl, and cast his bones onto the ground. He dropped to all fours and picked at the bones with his bear claw.

"Well?" said Harald, hands on his hips.

"They speak truth," muttered Bavlos in a heavily accented mumble, and he cackled, showing a mouth of pure white teeth. "There is a rage in these men and strength."

Hundr let out a breath he had not realised he was holding in and wondered what would have been his fate if the strange little man had said he was lying.

"So, you are wronged, as am I. The Yngling sword is missing, and your little prince is taken," said Harald.

"I will retrieve both. I will return your sword of kings to you. These were my men, and it is my responsibility to restore what was taken. These men will die, and you will be King of all Norway," vowed Hundr.

"I'll go with them," announced Rognvald, rising slowly to his feet and smiling at Hundr. "Let them take one ship, half of their men and half of mine. We will return the sword with the heads of its thieves."

Hundr frowned at that. He did not want a half

crew of men he didn't know aboard his ship. He felt it was his mess and wanted to clean it up himself.

"Very well. Take your fastest ship and your fiercest warriors," nodded Harald, pointing at Hundr. "Return the Yngling sword. Your other men and ships stay with me. If you fail, they will suffer for the insult against me by men under your command."

"We sail today," replied Hundr.

The morning was still young as men hustled around the Seaworm, making her ready for sea. The sky was a patchwork of dark clouds, pitted here and there with bright white shadows where the sun fought to break through. Hundr looked out to sea. The Whale Road looked calm. Shafts of light punched through the cloud to shine on the rolling waves as though the gods themselves were trying to pierce through the cloud cover.

"The Windspear is faster," tutted Ragnhild. She sat on a rowing bench, checking the feathers on her quiver full of arrows.

"On the Whale Road maybe," said Bush. "Her keel is longer, but the old Seaworm will attract less attention and is easier to row if we need to move faster around the coast or up a river. Thor only knows where Black Gorm and Rollo have gone." He shook his head and looked at Einar.

"I should have gutted Gorm last night, the

treacherous bastard," Einar spat. He slammed his fist into the Seaworm's mast and kicked at a coil of seal hide rope. "I knew Rollo was wrong. He had a look about him, sly and smiling all the time like a bloody fool."

"They have either gone south with Finn to sell him to Halvdan or east to this Jarl Kjotve with the Yngling sword," said Hundr.

"Gorm will have gone back to Dublin; it is a familiar ground for him. Like a rat returning to a midden heap," Bush uttered.

"Rollo leads them. Gorm wouldn't have had the idea, or the balls, to take that sword from Harald. That's Rollo's work. He goes to Kjotve," said Hundr.

"You have the right of it," nodded Einar. "Black Gorm is a lot of things, but he is not a man to run away from a fight. He and I were to fight today."

"Rollo must have talked Gorm around, dazzled him with promises of riches and reputation. Who else went with them?" asked Hundr.

"All of Eystein's berserkers," said Ragnhild. "And half a crew of Ivar's lot. Kjartan Oyvindsson was the captain of that ship. That's the one they took."

"Gorm and his men only swore to us last year when we defeated their Jarl. They were fiercely loyal to Eystein Longaxe. We should have killed them that day. But Kjartan and his men have fought for us for years, bled with us, sailed the Whale Road with us. So why would they take Finn?"

"They are oath breakers, all. Odin sees their deeds, and he will watch as we grind their bones into dust," said Hundr.

"Who will lead our men whilst we go after Rollo and Gorm?" asked Ragnhild. She looked pale, and the bandages were thick around her shoulder where Hildr had dug the arrowhead out of her flesh. Her mail had stopped the iron head from killing her, but it was still a painful wound.

"Don't look at me. I'm coming with you. I want them dead just as much as you do," said Bush as all eyes turned to him.

"Asbjorn will be in charge. Harald will march his army south, and Asbjorn will bring our three remaining ships with the king's fleet around the coast. They will be safe as long as Asbjorn stays calm and keeps to himself," said Hundr.

The others nodded at that. Asbjorn, too, had to come to Hundr's service following the defeat of Ivar the Boneless. He had sworn an oath to become Hundr's man following his Lord Ivar's death, and he had been loyal ever since. He was an experienced seaman, and had forgotten more than most men knew about sailing, and was already the captain of Hundr's ship, the Fjord-

Bear.

"Thank Odin, they are here at last," said Einar, and he pointed to the dock, where Rognvald came marching from the main street backed by ten warriors.

Hundr saw the shambling figure of Bavlos trotting along beside Rognvald, and the men behind them all carried shields bearing Harald's wolf sigil.

"He's got that little Sami he-witch with him. That can't be good. Women and holy men do not bring good luck at sea," grumbled Bush. "No offence, of course," he remembered to add, looking at Ragnhild and Hildr.

"Who or what is a Sami?" asked Hildr.

"A Finn, from the far north. They live in tents and roam the inhospitable land where the snow never stops and night can last for days. Powerful people of magic and spells, not to be messed with," said Bush.

"I don't give a shit whom he brings as long as he hurries up. We need to go after Rollo and Gorm," growled Einar.

"We will, old friend. We will hunt them without rest until we get the boy back," agreed Hundr.

TEN

The Windspear sped south, her sail full of Njorth's twin gifts of a favourable wind and a calm sea. Hundr had asked Einar to stand at the steerboard and take charge of the Seaworms tiller. His old friend was eating himself up with rage and ravenous hunger for revenge and giving him the focus of steering the long, sleek warship at least distracted from the pain of Finn's loss. The ship's timbers creaked, her rigging groaned, and the Seaworm dived into the white-tipped waves, chasing Black Gorm the berserker, and Rollo the betrayer, as the men now called him.

Hundr stood in at the mast alongside Rognvald and Ragnhild. He wore a bear fur cloak huddled around his shoulders, which had cost him three of Ketil Flatnose's arm rings. Bush had teased him about the trade, insisting the Hundr had let the merchant take his breeks down, but

Hundr was glad of the thing now that they were on the Whale Road once more.

"It is deep magic," muttered Ragnhild, clutching at the Odin spear amulet she wore around her neck. The trio watched the Sami at work in the shadow of the Seaworm's prow. He had made a small cairn of strange, coloured stones and pebbles, some the deep black of the dwarf kingdoms below the earth, some translucent and ethereal, and others the pure white of a spring cloud. Bavlos had adorned his cairn with animal claws, feathers, and small skulls and sat there rocking back and forth, chanting to his dark gods.

"Lucky for you, his gods say we are going the right way," said Rognvald.

Hundr looked at him sideways and then saw Ragnhild roll her eyes at Harald's man. *Lucky for you, I don't throw you and your arrogant bastard crew overboard.*

"Who does he pray to? This is not Odin, Thor, Njorth or Frey's work," asked Ragnhild, craning her neck to see what the Sami worked at.

"His gods are old gods," said Rognvald. "Gods of the earth, wind and sky. His gods are bears, wolves, birds and fish."

"How can a man who worships fish help us with what we must do?" Ragnhild pressed.

Rognvald smiled.

"He can see things. His gods whisper to him from beyond Midgard. And he has other uses. All the men I have brought to clean up your mess are useful."

"We need no help," snapped Hundr, bridling at Rognvald's words.

"Nevertheless, we will retrieve the sword before Kjotve the Rich can use its power to further his cause."

"So, who are these glorious warriors you have brought aboard the Seaworm?"

"Harald's own hearth troop, the best warriors from throughout his kingdom, brought together and sworn to protect and serve him even it means their own death. Leif Lokisword is a victor of a dozen Holmgangs and has the fastest blade in the north," Rognvald pointed to a tall, slim man with short-cropped blonde hair and a long thin face. "There is Afkar Magnusson, Unarr the bowman, and Valbrandr Kjartansson. All great warriors and men of reputation."

Harald's men looked formidable, Hundr had to admit. Valbrandr had the largest head, neck and shoulders Hundr had ever seen. His skull seemed twice the size of a normal man, and although he was not as tall as Hundr or Einar, he was twice as wide. His face was brutal, with a jutting forehead and flat, black eyes like a beast from the depths of the earth.

"I have never heard of them. The fastest blade in the north is a mighty claim," scoffed Ragnhild dismissively. "They, and you, Rognvald, were not with the great army when we invaded Northumbria and put King Aelle to the sword. I did not hear tell of your warriors in Frankia when we fought alongside Jarl Haesten and Bjorn Ironside when we battled and killed the Frankish Duke Robert the Strong. Vikings take to the Whale Road, and we bring our blades and courage to foreign shores to honour Odin and make for ourselves a place in Valhalla."

"That all sounds very exciting. I know you and your crews are famous warriors and veterans of countless campaigns. The deeds of the Man with the Dog's Name and how he killed Ivar the Boneless are told at firesides even in the cold north of Norway. But we have been fighting our own war. Harald and I have only seen twenty-two summers, and since Harald's Father, Halfdan the Black, died, we have seen nothing but war. So, we might not have travelled to distant shores and battled famous heroes, but I would wager that we have fought as many battles as you, and Harald has never lost. We need to get that sword back. The Yngling blade is the key to Harald becoming the first King of all Norway. My men and I will make sure that's done."

Hundr watched Rognvald's men. They worked

alongside the Seaworm crew, stowing the barrels of fish and ale securely in the bilge and responding without grumbles whenever Bush barked an order.

"Why so much war?" he asked. "When the old king died, was Harald not the heir?"

"He was the heir, but Harald was young when his father died, having only seen seventeen summers. Halfdan had increased the breadth of his Kingdom throughout his life. War had brought new lands to Rogaland and the Vestfold. So, when Halfdan died, those subjugated Jarls and Lords rose up, thinking Harald was but a pup and wanting to shake off the king's rule. Many of those men were kings themselves in all but name before Halfdan subjugated them, prideful and with powerful swords at their backs. The succession was a dark time, betrayals by those we thought were friends and loyalty from those we suspected to be enemies."

"How is it you came to be Harald's man?"

"We are cousins. We were raised together. They fostered Harald with my father when he was a boy, and we grew and learned to fight as brothers. But, as I said, when King Halfdan died, it was a dark time of betrayals and knives in the dark. Harald needed men he could trust, and I brought my blade and pledged it to his."

"And now you are a Jarl in your own right,

even though your father still lives?"

"Just so," nodded Rognvald.

"Tell us more about this sword. Is it truly the Yngling blade once wielded by Frey himself?" asked Ragnhild, and she touched the spear amulet at her chest.

"It is the sword of the Ynglings. I was there when Harald took it from a draugr beneath the earth. You are devoted to the gods?"

"I am, or was, a Valkyrie warrior priestess of Upsala. I am sworn to the service of Odin Allfather."

"I have heard of such things, a force of warrior priestesses who fight to honour the gods and reap souls for Odin's hall. I never thought those tales were true. How is it you came to be a priestess of Odin, and why do you now sail with these men?"

"It's a long tale," she said, sniffing and shifting her brynjar at the neck. "My father sent me to Upsala as a girl. I was his third daughter, and with two sons and two dowries already to be paid, he thought it best to pledge my life to the gods. I was raised to spear and axe, bow and horse, and fought wherever the High Priest of Upsala sent me. He tasked us to sail with the sons of Ragnar in the war of vengeance against the Saxon Kingdoms. Alas, during that fight, most of my sisters were killed in battle." She paused and looked wistfully out to sea as though the faces of her lost Valkyries were out there, peering at her across the waves. "During an ambush, I ended up with Hundr and Einar, and the rest is our saga. Now, only Hildr and I remain of our force who took to the Whale Road with Ivar the Boneless and Sigurd Snake Eye."

"Will you go back to your order at Upsala?" asked Rognvald, and Ragnhild looked at him. She held his eye and then looked at Hundr. For a moment, Hundr thought he saw moisture there, welling at the corner of her eye, but she turned away and walked towards the prow, leaving the question unanswered.

"She still holds an oath to Odin," said Hundr, feeling as though he must explain Ragnhild's abruptness. "Ragnhild will return to Upsala one day. Her loss does not end with the death of her sisters of the blade. Her lover died on the walls of Dublin last year. That death cut her as deep as a blow from a mighty war axe. She will not speak of it and holds it within her like a caged beast. Ragnhild fights like a demon, as you saw for yourself at Vanylven."

"She does, and she has not uttered a word of complaint about the arrow wound in her shoulder. Your crew are a strange lot, not least you. Surely you have a name other than a simple dog's name? Your accent is strange, from the east, I believe?"

"I had another name, once," said Hundr. For a moment, the sounds of the sea and the shouts of his crew paled as he remembered the boy he was when he was Velmud and roamed the corridors of Novgorod. He did not remember his childhood with fondness. As the bastard son of Novgorod's prince, the only thing of value his father had provided was his weapons' training. In those years, Hundr was Velmud, the bastard, and he had trained with sword, shield and spear from the time he could hold a blade steady. Besides that, his father shunned him as he whelped on a Norse concubine. "I was born in the east but left when I could to make my reputation. Einar Rosti became my Jarl when he allowed me to board this very ship as a bail boy. In those days, this was his ship, the Seaworm in which we now sail. The Norns spin our fates where they lie at the foot of mighty Yggdrasil, and they weft our lives in twists and turns."

"Just so," nodded Rognvald, and he smiled. "Just as when Harald took the Yngling sword from the earth, digging deep into a barrow to take it from the wights and the draugr below, wrenching it from their boney fingers to bring it forth and make himself King. Bavlos led him to it, his gods showing Harald the way to the tomb of the old kings."

"We will get the sword back. Does Harald not trust me to do it alone?" asked Hundr, and he carefully observed Rognvald for his reaction. Hundr had left most of his warriors with the King, and he was not sure what the King would do to those men if he did not retrieve his godly sword.

"No, he does not," said Rognvald, and he laughed to himself. "Harald is no fool. What could a man with your reputation do with such a blade, and how can a man know how he will react when he holds a sword forged for the gods, a blade which can make a man a king?"

Hundr smiled and looked around as shouts erupted across the deck. Towards the prow, Valbrandr had one of Hundr's crew gripped around the throat, and men erupted around the pair, shouting and pushing. Rognvald dashed to the scene and prised Valbrandr's thick fingers from around the crewman's neck. Hundr let the men sort the scuffle out themselves and moved towards the steerboard end of the ship. He picked his way amongst the barrels of dried fish and other supplies stacked in the ship's bilge. Two of his crewmen dashed past him with snarling faces towards the scuffle.

"Get back here," growled Einar at the men. "Do you want the bloody ship to capsize? Get back to work." The men grumbled but returned to their tasks, repairing frayed ropes or manning the ever-necessary, and much hated, bailing of the bilge. "Trouble between the men will spill over if we don't stop it quickly," Einar said, watching as Rognvald ordered Valbrandr and his men to back off.

"They look like dangerous men," Hundr remarked, stepping onto the platform to stand with Einar. The wind was stronger there, and he enjoyed the coolness on his face and hair. The chill drew water from his dead eye, and he cuffed it clear. "Though I dare say we are no soft-bellied traders ourselves."

"There are killers on both sides. It is always this way when crews mix. We should take away everyone's weapons and put them in a barrel. If someone draws a blade now, we will wade in blood."

"I'll talk to Rognvald and make sure that's done," agreed Hundr. Einar glanced at the coastline, craggy and faint in the distance as the ship raced along, its sail billowing and Hundr's one eye sigil snapped taut on the cloth. Hundr saw the worry etched on his friend's face and struggled to find words to ease his pain. "They won't hurt the boy. Finn is too valuable."

"He is just a boy, who happens to be the heir to the Kingdom of Dublin," said Einar, turning to Hundr. "We must stop them from taking Finn to his uncle."

Finn's uncle had already tried to kill the boy once. Hundr was as sure as Einar that if Rollo and

Gorm delivered Finn to him, Halvdan, King of Dublin, would finish the job and remove the true heir forever.

"They can only be half a day ahead of us," said Hundr. "They will have taken the sword to Kjotve first in search of that reward. An ambitious Jarl would pay a fortune for such a thing. So we will catch them there."

"Is that you talking, or that bear-worshipping Sami?"

"If I was Gorm, I would go to Kjotve first. There will be a bigger reward there. Then head south to Halvdan."

"They took Finn and broke their oaths. You should have killed Gorm when you killed his master outside Dublin."

"When I killed Eystein, Gorm and his men swore oaths to me, and we needed men. They are oath breakers, and we will kill them for what they have done."

"Killing Jarl Hrafn was not drengskapr. Warriors do not knife in the dark. You know we fight with blades in hand and let our enemies see our faces before we die."

"I know it, and if I could go back, I would do it differently." Hundr thumbed at the ivory hilt of his sword. The cruel face was rough under his touch.

"You would challenge the Jarl to fight?"

"No. Instead of sending Rollo to do it, I would have killed him myself."

"The gods do not reward such acts with luck. That is why young Finn and the sword were taken; the gods now punish both you and Harald."

"We have struck at night before, old friend. We raid, and we kill. When we killed Ketil Flatnose's warriors by surprise, we honoured Odin, and we were drengrs, but with Jarl Hrafn, it was a knife in the back and beneath drengskapr, not the warrior way. Nevertheless, we will retrieve the boy and the sword, and Black Gorm and Rollo will die."

"What of Harald?"

"We stay with him, make him King of all Norway and get rich. We deserve a good season of fighting and reward. That prospect binds these men to me, Einar, you know that. Harald will reward us with land, and our hulls will be heavy with silver."

"And they will make us sails of gold," jeered Einar, shaking his head. "When something sounds too good to be true, it's usually because it's a pile of horseshit. What if Harald does not become King? What if he doesn't honour his word? Do you really believe the sword is magic?"

"It doesn't matter what I think. A sword is a sword. It's the hand holding it that counts. What matters is what the other Jarls of Norway think. If they believe the sword makes Harald king, then so be it. As to Harald's word, I believe him. If he wanted to kill us or send us away, he would have done it already. He has an army of over one thousand warriors. I think he craves men he can trust and warriors who can win battles."

"He craves the throne and to be King of all Norway."

"And we will help him."

"You like that sword," said Einar, looking down to where Hundr fingered at the hilt.

"It's a fine blade," agreed Hundr, taking his hand away from Fenristooth and folding his arms. The hilt helped him think. It felt old and comforting. The cool, smooth ivory beneath his hand spoke to him of hard decisions, ancient war leaders, and the burden of leadership. Make a wrong decision, and his men would die. Hundr knew this all too well, and it weighed heavily on him. He had made the wrong decision before, taking his men to fight in Ireland. He would not take such decisions lightly again.

"As fine as your old swords?"

"Different," said Hundr. He had once wielded two swords, magnificent weapons taken in victory from Ivar the Boneless and his son, but he had lost them in the welter of death on Dublin's walls. "Hildr misses Finn?"

"She does. She blames herself for not protecting him. Finn slept under an awning on this very ship, and neither she nor I heard them take him. She will not talk. She is consumed with rage."

"Sail!" came a shout from the prow.

Hundr leant to peer around the sail. A karve warship, shorter and wider in the belly than a drakkar ship like the Seaworm, raced towards them from the coast.

"It's one of Kjotve's ships," yelled Rognvald from the prow.

"How can he tell?" asked Einar, shielding his eyes from the sun and staring at the ship.

"There's a sigil on the sail. I think it's a raven or an eagle," said Hundr.

"Let's see what kind of man this Jarl Kjotve is, then."

ELEVEN

Einar pulled back on the tiller to bring the ship about and ordered the crew to bring down her sail. They lowered her yard, hauling on both sides of her sheet so the heavy, sodden cloth did not flap loose. The crew rolled up the huge, heavy, woollen sailcloth, using the hemp ribbons sewn into its lines to tie it off as it came down. Bush barked and shouted at the men as they strained on the lines and busied at the spar, though Einar knew they didn't need the orders. The men of the Seaworm knew their business. Bush shouted again, and men followed his order, piling into the ship's port side as she banked, ducking under her halyard and brace ropes as they went. The deck was a mass of hemp, and seal hide ropes, each one serving its purpose to keep the ship sailing smoothly. Einar saw the small karve ship draw close, her own crew lowering their sail and sprouting oars from her sides. As the ships drew near, they would do so under the power of their oars to bring the vessels slowly together so they could talk across the waves.

Rognvald and his men huddled at the prow and left the Seaworm crew to their work. They eyed the approaching karve carefully across the swell—weapons kept low but ready in case the ship came with threat.

"Get us close," said Hundr as he helped Thorgrim and Kjartan take the oars from their resting callipers. They put only four oars out on each side of the ship, just enough to manoeuvre her and keep her steady.

"Close enough to touch?" asked Einar, and Hundr turned and flashed a grin at him. Einar knew that smile. He had seen it often in the last few years. He took a hand off the tiller and ensured his axe was loose in its loop at his belt. Hundr was a thoughtful man, and Einar respected his deep thinking, but the smile was wicked, and experience told Einar to be ready for trouble. Einar watched Hundr move across the deck, bracing himself with a hand on the sheet and shroud ropes and leaning to keep his balance as the weight of the men huddled together on the port side so that their weight would help the ship swing towards Kjotve's vessel. Hundr went to Bush, Hildr, and then Ragnhild to whisper in their ears. He also stopped to clap some of the crew on the back and talked to men busy at the ropes, Torsten, Trygve, and Kare—men Einar knew to be handy in a fight.

The karve drew close, and Einar could see men in the prow waving towards the Seaworm. He raised a hand in greeting. Both ships slowed as they came within an oars' length of one another. Einar saw bearded faces peering over the side at him, and he smiled at them.

"I am Birger Snorrisson. These are the lands of King Kjotve of Agder. State your name and your business," shouted a man in a blue cloak which flapped in the wind. He stood on the central platform around the ship's mast and cupped his hand to his mouth to shout across the gap between ships.

"I am Jarl Hundr, here to join my men to King Kjotve's in the fight against King Harald."

"You mean Harald the Tyrant?" shouted the man. "Where are you from?"

"From Ireland, we heard King Kjotve fights against Harald, and we come to join the fight," Hundr replied.

"Follow me into the fjord there…" the man pointed back towards the shore, "…and I will show you where you can moor your ship."

"Will there be a fight between Kjotve and Harald?"

"There will be a fight if you don't come about and follow me," shouted the man.

Hundr laughed at that, and Einar rested his hand on his axe.

"You should show more respect to a Jarl," said Hundr.

"You could be one of Harald's spies, and how do I know you are a Jarl? Just follow me and do as I say," the man insisted, and a line of his warriors appeared before him, making a small shield wall across the karve.

"Have you ever fought at sea before?" shouted Hundr.

The captain of the karve scratched his beard, looked down at his warriors, and then back to Hundr.

"No, just follow us in, and there won't be any trouble," he said. His tone had changed, and he spoke as though weary of the conversation, but his abrupt manner had slipped away.

"Good," smiled Hundr. "Now!" he shouted, and he pointed at Ragnhild.

Whilst Einar was staring at the disrespectful audacity of the karve's captain, Ragnhild, Bush, Hildr, Torsten, Trygve, and Kare had all gathered just below him, and each had a boot on the raised platform of the steerboard. Then, at Hundr's order, Ragnhild let out her Valkyrie war cry and launched herself over the gap, followed quickly by the others. Einar cursed as Hildr made the jump, and he held his breath as her arms flapped in the air before she landed to roll on the karve's deck, coming up with her axe in one hand and a short seax in the other. He cursed again to himself and leapt from the steerboard and down onto the deck. Einar heard the roar of the Seaworm men around him, supporting the attack, and the yelps of the karve's crew as their ship pitched in the water, overloaded at one end with the weight of the attackers' bodies, as Hundr knew she would be. Einar glanced across his shoulder and saw the line of warriors before the captain stumble and fall as their ship rolled, and Hundr leapt across the gap between the ships.

"You there, close your teeth and help," Einar snarled at a man watching him, open-mouthed and taken aback by the surprise attack. Einar was bent over, trying to lift the anchor stone from its place at the mast. It was too heavy for one man, and the staring warrior sprang forwards to help him. It was Valbrandr Kjartansson. "Throw it onto the other ship. You there, clear the way," he said to another of Rognvald's men as he strained with the rock, which was as wide around as a man's torso. Einar clenched his teeth and took small, stumbling steps across the ship with the weight in his hands. Valbrandr did the same; his face was red and strained. Finally, they reached the sheer strake and launched the rock over the gap, and Einar struggled to catch his breath as he heard it thud on the karve's deck. "Haul her close," he ordered, and the surrounding men grabbed the rope attached to the anchor stone and pulled, drawing the ships together.

The deck of the karve was a welter of blades, shields, shouting and confusion. Men sprawled on the deck, trying to recover from the sudden pitch in the water. They had tangled each other with spear shafts and shields and struggled to rise as Ragnhild, and the others tore into them with axe and knife. Einar searched for Hildr, and he watched her stab her seax into the face of an enemy before kicking another kneeling man in the groin. He hated it when she fought. She was his great love, and he could not contemplate life without her. But she was also a ferocious Valkyrie warrior, and battle was in her blood.

The ships banged together, and Einar heard the karve's oar blades crunching beneath the Seaworms hull. He drew his axe, put his boot on the sheer strake, and launched himself over the side. Einar landed in a crouch and came up snarling. A growling enemy reared up before him. The man dropped his spear, which was trapped in the legs of the man next to him. Einar was about to swing his axe at the enemy when a body thundered into his back, driving him forward and into the growling man. Einar pushed himself upwards, blood rushing in his ears, to see Valbrandr crack his axe across the skull of an axeman and kneel to stab a knife into the throat of the enemy with the spear beneath him.

Valbrandr let go of his knife and reached his hand out to Einar.

"I did not mean to crowd your kill," he said, and they pulled each other to their feet. Valbrandr ducked to avoid a spear thrust at his face, and Einar lunged forward and chopped his axe into the spearman's shoulder, dragging the blade towards him and spraying blood bright on the karve's deck. Einar felt the ship rock beneath him, reeling to port as its weight shifted under the attack from the Seaworm side. He bent his legs at the knees, an instinctive reaction from years of life on the Whale Road, and an enemy skittered towards him, falling and with his eyes wide in terror. The enemy flailed his arms, and Einar let the man fall onto his seax blade and then ripped it across his guts, feeling the gush of fiery blood across his hand. He swayed aside from another adversary who came hurtling across the deck, so off-balance he was almost running. Einar took a half step backwards, and the man went past him in a blur of white teeth and stinking leather. Einar reverse cut his axe to crack the blade on the back of the man's head, feeling his skull break under the blow.

Einar took a breath. He saw Hildr and Ragnhild moving down the keel, striking and lunging with skill and ferocity. Ragnhild's bandaged shoulder had not slowed her down, and men backed away from her viciousness. He saw Hundr exchanging blows with the karve's captain and then noticed three men coming to do what they should have done all along. They came towards him with shields raised. They would try to push Einar and Valbrandr back and overboard. If they had started the fight like that and made their shield wall tight to the port side, there would have been no fight, for they would have barged the Seaworm crew into Njorth's kingdom, and they would be food for crabs. Those three shield men came on, slow and deliberate, careful of their footing on the treacherous, blood-slicked deck. Einar braced himself with his axe and seax, ready to strike. His chest heaved with the exertion, and he felt the joy of it, the elation of battle. It took him away from his worry over Finn's safety, and the escape from that fear was welcome.

Einar let out his war cry, giving himself over to the battle fury, just as he had in his youth when he had earned his epithet, The Brawler. He charged them and slammed his shoulder into the central shield, its metal boss jarring and numbing his shoulder. Einar bent and chopped his axe into the boot of the leftmost axeman, seeing the warrior's toes bound away in a spurt of blood and mangled flesh as they sprang from the severed boot to roll onto the deck. That shieldman howled in pain, and his shield dropped, allowing Einar to rise from his crouch and slam his seax under the man's chin and into the soft flesh of his neck. Einar rose with the blow, and the power of it lifted the shieldman from the deck as Einar roared into his face. The seax blade passed into the man's skull, and its point pushed through the tissue of his face at the eye, leaving it a bloody mess of torn flesh and eye jelly. Valbrandr cannoned into the two remaining spearmen, snarling and spitting, using his immense strength to bully them backwards and then striking at them with his axe. Einar and Valbrandr fought them, shoulder to shoulder, hacking into the enemy crew until there was space around them, and their enemies lay dead or wounded at their feet.

"Stop!" bellowed Hundr, and Einar looked up to see he had the karve's captain kneeling before him on the mast platform with his sword at the man's throat. The fighting on the deck ceased. The only sound remaining was the groaning and whimpering of injured warriors. "Throw them all overboard, all except this one," said Hundr.

The captain closed his eyes and sobbed silent tears as the Seaworm crew, and Rognvald's men threw the dead and dying into the cold sea.

"Take anything of value—weapons, armour, coins," Einar ordered. Hildr ran to him and threw her arms around him.

"I like you, Seaworm men," grinned Valbrandr as he examined a short knife taken from a wounded man, its hilt carved into the shape of a boar. Hildr cleared her throat. "And women," Valbrandr added, with a polite nod to Hildr.

"I wasn't expecting to fight today," said Rognvald. He approached Einar, and his axe blade was red with enemy blood.

"No, but Hundr is a cunning dog. And now we have one of Kjotve's ships and some of his shields and armour." Einar smiled, and he pointed to where Rognvald's men and the Seaworm crew toppled the corpses of the karve crew overboard. "And we have a loud-mouthed bastard of a karve captain to tell us all about this Kjotve and what we are about to sail into. You never said he was a king?"

"He is no king, but he calls himself so to rally Harald's enemies to his banner."

"How many men can Kjotve the Rich call to arms?"

"Close to a thousand, he is, as his name suggests, wealthy and therefore attracts many crews to his cause for pay."

"Men like us," said Einar.

"Just so." Rognvald smiled. "But let's see what this captain can tell us."

Hundr had sheathed his sword, and the captain now stood leaning against his mast. Blood from his leaking nose was smeared across his face, and one eye swelled to closing. He watched, pale-faced, as the dead amongst his crew were stripped of anything of value and heaved overboard while the living lined up in the prow to be searched, heads hanging in shameful defeat.

"Let them live," the captain said, looking at Hundr's blood-spattered face.

"What is your name?" asked Hundr. He tore away the captain's cape with a vicious tug that almost drove the man to his knees. Then, Hundr used it to wipe the blood from his face and arms.

"Herjolf Herjolfsson, Jarl Hundr," the man mumbled.

"So, now you show me the respect you should have shown earlier," said Hundr. "Many of your men have died because of your disrespect."

"Will he let the survivors go?" asked Valbrandr, leaning close to whisper in Einar's ear.

"Yes," said Einar, after a moment's consideration. "Usually, at the end of such a fight, he will ask the survivors to swear to his service. They can then crew the captured ship, and we will mix in some of our own men to give her a full crew."

"Do such men not hold a grudge for their fallen friends?" Valbrandr questioned.

"Yes, they do," said Einar, and he scratched at his beard. Einar had never felt that Black Gorm and his berserkers had forgotten the defeat of their Lord, Eystein Longaxe. They had been like a rotten apple in the barrel, and an undertone of resentment had festered there to spill over into their recent oath-breaking. Ivar's men had been sullen at first, but they had been with Hundr's crews now for years, and it surprised Einar that some had broken their oaths and joined Rollo and Gorm.

"Where is Kjotve's stronghold? Tell us of it. How many men does he have?" Hundr asked Herjolf.

"Kjotve is my Jarl," Herjolf murmured, shaking his head with his eyes tightly closed.

"If you tell me what I want to know, I will spare the lives of your men," said Hundr. "There has been enough blood today. You caused this fight, disrespecting me in front of my men. I cannot ignore such an insult amongst warriors. Now, the strength of my sword forces you to kneel to me. You have a chance here to save the lives of your warriors; let them go home to their wives and children."

"I cannot," whispered Herjolf.

"Kill them all," ordered Hundr, and he wiped a hand across his tired face and brought it to rest on the hilt of his sword.

The order took Einar aback. It was ruthless and cruel. But it was precisely what everyone around Hundr had told him he should have done with the prisoners after their last battle. Had he done so, Finn would be safe, and Harald would not be missing his Yngling sword. There was a hesitation amongst the men, so surprised were they at the order.

"Forgive me, Odin," muttered Afkar Magnusson, one of Rognvald's men. He was a grizzled warrior with a bald head save for a trim of grey hair around his ears, which he gathered at the nape of his neck into a plait. Afkar slid a short knife from his belt and stalked over to the prisoner closest to him. The man shrieked and shook his head as he realised Afkar's intention. He went to raise his hands, but Afkar feinted and slid his knife into the panicked man's ribs. The man cried out, a high-pitched, frightened sound, as Afkar pitched him over the side to die ignominiously in the deep. Denied a warrior's death and denied an eternity in Valhalla. Once Afkar had started the work, the Seaworm crew joined in, and the enemy crew were swiftly cut down and thrown overboard. It was grim work, dark work, and there was no drengskapr in it. But Hundr had done the ruthless thing that must be done. He had made the hard decision, and men had died.

The captain knelt, hunched over, his body shuddering as he sobbed at the death of his men.

"Now you have caused the death of all your crew, and their blood is on your hands. Will you tell me what I want to know?" asked Hundr. The captain shook his head.

"I can make him talk," Einar spoke up. He felt men's eyes on him, as well as Hildr's, but he just looked at Hundr and nodded.

"He seems stubborn. You might have to whittle him down to the bone," said Valbrandr.

"I learned from the Boneless," Einar retorted. "He was not known for his gentle ways. He was good at making men talk." Einar remembered those days well. They were good years. He had been proud to be Ivar's man, and as they had sailed for Northumbria with the Great Army, Ivar had promised Einar land and that he would become a landed Jarl, not just the leader of men at sea. Land meant genuine power and wealth, rents and income, and property to pass down to an heir. Owning land was the dream of men of the Whale Road who sailed and fought for wealth. Some were landed already and hungered for more, but many others were ambitious wolves. Second sons, or sons of poor warriors who longed for land of their own. It was the sign of success, a man who could use the strength of his arm to win for himself a piece of land to rule as his own. Yet that dream had withered and died, trampled under the boots of the heirs of Ragnar Lothbrok.

"Did you see him cut the blood eagle?" asked Valbrandr, eyes wide with amazement.

"Once," Einar replied. Which was true, but he had not been there when Ivar carved his famous torture into the back of King Aelle of Northumbria. Einar had been sweating, bleeding, and close to death in a Saxon hovel. He strode to where the captain knelt, and Hundr left him to it, ordering the men to make the Seaworm and the captured karve ready to sail. Einar knelt and looked the captain in the eye. Tears stained his cheeks, and his face was a mask of pain.

"Tell us of Kjotve's stronghold, how to enter his fjord, and how many men he has."

The man shuddered and shook his head again. Einar placed a hand on his shoulder.

"If you don't tell me, I will cut out your eyes and cut off your nose. I will cut off your fingers and toes, and I will remove your manhood and use fire to seal the wounds so that you will live. Then, we will leave you ashore where you will need to be cared for like a child, a disgraced monster for the rest of your life, with the prospect of eternity as a nithing to haunt your dreams."

The captain shook his head and rocked back and forth on his knees. Einar tightened his grip on the seax and set his jaw. He had given the captain the opportunity to speak without enduring more pain, and the fool had refused. More than that, his arrogance had flared Hundr to violent anger, and the man deserved what was about to happen to him. Einar grabbed a fistful of the captain's hair and yanked his head forwards. He whipped his seax across the man's head, slicing off his right ear and tossing the ragged, bloody sliver of flesh into his lap. Herjolf screamed and clutched his hand to his injury; blood pumped around his fist in gushes.

"Tell me what I want to know. Tell me!" Einar bellowed, his anger becoming a furnace. This stubborn fool was keeping Einar from Finn, and the longer the boy was gone, the less likely it became that Einar could rescue him. If Rollo and Gorm delivered Finn to Halvdan Ragnarsson, the King of Dublin would kill the lad without hesitation or pity. Einar swung his seax up, so it sliced into the lobe of Herjolf's left ear, and he held it there, thick crimson oozing down the blade. Herjolf froze, his shaking eyes locked on Einar's. "Tell me, and this will be over quickly."

"King Kjotve had a thousand men to bring to battle," Herjolf stammered, thick snot clogging his nose and throat between sobs of pain. "His fjord is around that headland. The place is called Agder." He pointed to a hazy jut of land to the southeast. "Its bay is filled with ships, and Agder is full of those who would oppose King Harald and his bloodthirsty warmongering."

"Have you seen a ship arrive this last day? Men carrying a fabled sword and a young boy?"

Herjolf said nothing, and Einar thought he would faint, so he sliced his left ear deeper.

"I don't know, I don't know, please…" begged Herjolf.

"He knows no more," said Einar. Hundr nodded, and Einar pulled his seax away from Herjolf's ear. He dragged the captain to his feet by his leather breastplate and stared hard into his face. So much unnecessary blood spilt over one man's arrogant pride. Einar dragged him, flailing, to the bow and threw him over the side like an unwanted catch. Herjolf splashed into the grey waters to sink below to his doom.

"So, Kjotve has an army," said Hundr.

"Seems like it. But he can't keep such a force together for long. They need food and ale. A thousand men produce a lot of shit and piss. If they don't move, disease will kill more of them than Harald's blades."

"With so many men packed into Agder, we can't sail in and get Finn and the sword by force," said Hundr, looking across the waters towards the distant headland. "A few of us will go in quietly, steal the sword, and find the boy."

"I don't see any other way," agreed Einar. "We should go now, without delay."

"Bush," called Hundr, and he came across the deck of the small karve, stepping around blood splashes and fallen weapons. "Einar and I will go into Agder today. We go in quiet to find out the lay of the place. You will stay here with this ship and six men."

"But lord… I can help you…" Bush protested.

"We will miss your quick mind and your axe," said Hundr, putting a hand on Bush's shoulder. "But we have lost a ship to Gorm's treachery, and we can add this karve to our fleet. Keep it here on this stretch of coast, away from Kjotve's patrols, and she will be yours to captain."

"Mine?" gasped Bush, his eyes bright and flicking from Hundr to Einar.

"Yours. Keep her safe, though. We will meet you here when we have the boy and the sword."

TWELVE

The fjord at Agder wound around sheer mountainsides, where peaks rose from the flat, glassy water half-submerged, as though its bottom would stretch below Midgard and into the realm of the dwarves. The mountains were silvery grey in the afternoon sun, which was bright under a pale blue sky. Tufts of brown and green foliage spotted the harsh rock faces, and ahead of the lower peaks, Hundr could see farmland and pastures stretching beyond sight into the valleys afar. The sheer number of ships crammed into the fjord took Hundr's breath away. It was like a floating forest of masts and gently bobbing timber. Small faerings, four-oar rowboats, flitted between the huddled warships, trying to bring order to the chaos. Captains roared at one another as hulls clashed, and precious drakkars and karves tried to pole themselves off one another and avoid damage to their hull or keel.

"I have never seen so many ships in one place," Einar remarked.

"Harald should attack them now, from the sea," said Hundr. He pulled on his oar, keeping time with Valbrandr as they rowed their own small two-oar faering across the packed bay. The captured karve had towed the faering behind it, and Einar had hitched it to the Seaworm's stern before departing. Hundr had Hildr row the Seaworm as close to the fjord as they dared before he clambered into the faering with Einar, Rognvald, Valbrandr, and Ragnhild. Hildr then brought the Seaworm about and heaved seawards with orders to return at nightfall.

"If he knew that so many of his enemies gathered in one place, Harald would attack," said Rognvald. Harald's man craned his neck, searching each ship for a sigil or sign of whom they belonged to. Hundr saw ravens, bears, elks and axes painted on banners hung from mast posts, dangling limply in the light breeze.

"Harald has a lot of enemies," noted Hundr.

"To be the first King of all Norway is difficult. If it were easy, everybody would try it," said Rognvald, and he flashed Hundr his customary grin. "We have been at war for many years and made many enemies. Kjotve is rallying them all to him now for one last push against Harald."

"Men will flock to a man named Kjotve the Rich." Einar shrugged.

"Just so," replied Rognvald. "Kjotve isn't just rich, however. He is as cunning as a starving weasel. He would use these men to defeat Harald and then name himself King of all Norway. Which is why we must not allow him to have the Yngling sword."

Hundr leaned into his oar strokes, feeling the pull of the water across his back. They made for a gap between two beautifully sleek drakkars, one with a red hue from its hull timbers and the other with a golden wind vane atop its mast. It was a magnificent thing of runes and beasts shaped in a quarter circle.

"Fine ships," muttered Valbrandr as they rowed beneath the hulls, and bearded faces stared at them from aboard.

"What are you doing out here?" a voice cut through the sound of oars splashing and the gentle waters of the fjord lapping against the high hulls. Hundr looked over his shoulder and saw a red-faced man in a fine grey tunic kneeling in a faering. He was balding and pointing at Hundr, a paunch poking at his fine garments. "Whose men are you?"

"My name is Ragnar Ruriksson," lied Hundr, thinking of the first name which came to him.

"Our Jarl is Svart the Tall," shouted Rognvald.

"I saw his banner yonder, a prancing elk," he whispered.

"Svart and his men are inside the fortress for the Thing this afternoon," the man said, and he wagged a thick finger at Rognvald. "You should not be out here. Men are nervous about their ships and of men who would board them and steal their belongings."

"We are not thieves. We simply go to join our Lord ashore," said Rognvald, and he smiled at the man, holding his arms wide.

"We should row over to the stubby bastard and throw him overboard," whispered Einar, and Valbrandr laughed.

"Those two mutton heads behind him would drown quick enough," replied Valbrandr. Two men in mail rowed the grey-robed man's faering, which was not a good idea so deep in the fjord. Hundr and his men had left their mail brynjars aboard the Seaworm and came to Agder wearing only their tunics and hooded cloaks.

"Off with you then, head for shore," barked the man, and he grunted at his guards to row him in another direction.

Hundr and Valbrandr pulled again, and their faering lurched forward towards the port. As they neared the town, Hundr could smell fish and roasting meat, and the sounds of men shouting and talking came together into a continuous rumble of noise floating onto the still waters. The ships became tighter, and it was no simple thing to navigate their way through the hulls, which in some places were touch-tight.

"No sign of the Sea-Stallion," said Einar.

"The ship Rollo the Betrayer and Black Gorm, the berserker, stole from me," Hundr explained for Rognvald's benefit.

"They will be here somewhere in this midden heap. Rarely have so many turds gathered in one place before," said Rognvald. "They will have to sell the Yngling sword to Kjotve; otherwise, why steal it?"

It took an age for them to find a place to dock the faering, but eventually, they found a small opening on the far western end of the port, at a rotten, half-broken jetty where other such small vessels bobbed on the light tide, secured by ropes to timber posts. They came ashore and wandered along the bustling quayside, where merchants made the most of the throng of visiting warriors and sold fish, meat, and ale to the hungry horde. Ragnhild paid a piece of hack silver for a skin of ale and cuts of roasted pork, which the group ate hungrily as they weaved between the different crews.

Hundr saw men with shining mail, elaborately plaited beards with silver and gold rings, men with heads shaved apart from long knots of hair on one side hanging over their ears. Warriors strutted, eyeing each other carefully, keeping to their crews but marking each passer-by, judging his reputation and fighting prowess against his own based on the quality of his weapons, his bearing, and his cloth.

"This is a piss measuring contest and no mistake," said Ragnhild, taking a swig from her ale skin. She winced and rolled her injured shoulder and passed the ale to Hundr.

"A man could easily find trouble here if he wanted," agreed Einar. The words had only escaped his lips when a burly, red-haired man thundered a shoulder into Valbrandr, knocking him sideways.

"Watch where you're going, pup," barked the warrior, snarling at Valbrandr. He was a tall man, but nowhere near as broad or stocky as Rognvald's man.

"What did you say?" said Valbrandr, his voice low and measured. He righted himself, and Hundr saw the surprise on Red Beard's face when he noticed the abnormal size of Valbrandr's head and shoulders.

"I said watch where you are going," Red Beard blustered, and he crossed his arms in front of his chest in defiance. Men moved aside to create a space between the warriors, and Hundr sighed.

"We need to stay hidden and quiet. We don't

need trouble," Hundr said in a hushed voice, leaning close to Rognvald.

He nodded and placed a hand on Valbrandr's shoulder.

"Leave it, there will be a time to fight these men, but this is not it."

"Listen to your master and run along," jeered Red Beard, smiling at his victory as one of his shipmates clapped him on the shoulder.

Valbrandr turned away, and Hundr could feel the violence dripping from him like poison from a serpent's fangs. The quayside fell away into two streets of low houses, dark and topped with grey thatch. They stood at a crossroads between where the quay spread east around the fjord and further on beyond the two rows of houses. Ahead of that, a muddy street cut straight through two vast fields of bright green grass, dotted here and there with sheep munching on the cud. Then, a circular fortress rose from the sweeping valley, as wide as three drakkars with stout wooden walls as high as three men.

"Kjotve has built himself a castle," muttered Rognvald.

"And we must get in there if we want to find the sword," said Hundr.

"And Finn," added Einar, frowning.

"And Finn," Hundr agreed. He had not warmed

to the boy in the same way Einar had. Hildr and Einar had taken Finn under their wing and cared for him as though he were their son. Einar had no children, unlike most of the men in Hundr's crews who had wives and children in homes across the north. Einar had never settled, and Hundr knew Einar doted on the boy. Even so, Hundr found it uncomfortable to be in Finn's company. The lad was pleasant enough and mostly kept to himself, but Hundr had killed his father. That was no simple thing to bear, and Hundr knew that as Finn became older and grew into his strength, that knowledge would eat at him like cattle rot. Hundr would do all he could to get Finn back from Rollo and Gorm because he loved Einar like a brother, but he must get the sword for Harald first and foremost. That was the reason he risked his neck entering Agder and the reason he had killed those men in the sea off Agder's coast—to get the Yngling sword, make Harald King, and make his crews rich.

"He's not finished it," said Valbrandr, wiping the pork grease from his hands into his beard. "Look, they are still building the wall."

Sure enough, on the western side, there was a gap in the wall where men worked with axe and chisel to raise the sharpened timbers and complete the circular defences.

"We need to get a better look at the place," Hundr said. "If Rollo and Gorm have already given the sword to Kjotve, then we cannot take it by force. Instead, we'll need to steal it back."

"I am no sneak thief," growled Ragnhild, fixing Hundr with her one eye.

"And the gods know that. But we can't fight our way in. There are too many men," he said. "So, we steal the sword and the boy and then fight with honour alongside Harald in the war to come. There will be time for battle and glory, Ragnhild, but this is a time for cunning."

She snorted at that, but Hundr knew it was the only way. He was about to lead them towards the fortress when Einar nudged him with his elbow.

"Thor's balls, I don't believe it," Einar said, and he jutted his jaw towards the quayside. A column of warriors marched down a jetty, armed with spears and shields. Men moved out of their way as the column made a beeline for the fortress entrance. Hundr's breath caught in his chest as he saw the sigil on their shields. Each man's shield was painted bright white, and around each shield, two crossed axes were daubed across the linden wood.

"Ketil Flatnose," muttered Ragnhild. "Just when I thought things couldn't get any worse."

Hundr watched them march in perfect order, and the warriors came within ten paces of where Hundr stood. Ketil's crews had been away when Hundr raided his Orkney Island stronghold, so there would be no men amongst them who recognised Hundr's scarred, one-eyed face. But he still pulled his hood up to shadow his features, just in case. The column marched past, boots stomping in the mud, and Hundr saw a flash of gold amongst them, like a ray of sun bursting through a dark cloud. A woman with hair the colour of summer wheat strode in the centre of the warriors, her head held high and shoulders square. She turned to him as though she felt his gaze upon her, and for a gut-wrenching moment, Hundr thought she recognised him. Their eyes met, but she turned away before a heartbeat had passed. It was Sigrid Ketilsdottir, and she was as beautiful as ever.

"What in Frigg's name is she doing here?" said Ragnhild.

"Who was it?" asked Afka.

"The daughter of Ketil Flatnose, come to meet with Kjotve the Rich. No doubt to swell his ranks with Ketil's warriors," Rognvald deduced, and he frowned at Hundr.

"If Ketil has allied with Kjotve, that is not my doing," said Hundr. "He cannot yet know that I sailed to lend my ships to Harald's cause. Whatever reason Sigrid is here, it is not because of me."

Rognvald chewed on that. If Ketil Flatnose's daughter was in Agder, it could only signify one thing: a marriage. And that meant that Ketil was joining his forces to Kjotve's banner in the fight against Harald. It also meant that Ketil had planned to do that anyway, despite Hundr's raid. He would marry his daughter to Kjotve or one of his sons and forge an alliance. Looking at the massed warships in Agder's fjord and the warriors thronging the quayside, it seemed like a good gamble. Hundr had not seen King Harald's army, as he had not called his banners to marshal his forces at the time of their meeting. No doubt Harald could muster a sizeable force. And he had won glorious victories already, but Kjotve was assembling a mighty army of his own. Also, he would not have the Yngling sword, and if it held the power Harald believed it did, or the people of Norway believed it did, then perhaps Kjotve the Rich would become King of all Norway rather than Harald Fairhair.

As Hundr thought over that clash between the two great men, a horn sounded three long, low blasts from the walls of Agder's fortress. The warriors around the quayside and in front of the walls made their way either through the open gate of the fortress or around its sides. The sound of so many men talking rumbled around the fjord-like distant thunder.

"The Thing," said Rognvald. "We should hear what Kjotve has to say to his men."

"What if some of Ketil's men remember us? We

do not exactly blend in with the crews," uttered Ragnhild, pointing at her missing eye and nodding in Hundr's direction. They shared that Odin wound and its distinctive marking would make Hundr and Ragnhild easy to recognise. Ragnhild believed hers was Odin-sent in honour of her service to him. The All-Father sacrificed his eye in return for a drink from Mimir's well, whose water granted him wisdom. All Hundr had got from his dead eye was pain, and to remind him of that fact, the hollow socket pulsed, and Hundr rubbed at the aching scar tissue stretched across the bone and empty hole.

"We will avoid Ketil's men," said Hundr. "Keep your hood up. We will go and see what to make of this Kjotve. If he has the sword, he will probably parade it at the Thing. It is, after all, the gathering of all his lords and men to hear pronouncements and law-giving. If I had a magic, king-making sword of the gods, I would show it there."

"You put little stock in the Yngling sword?" chuckled Valbrandr. His laugh was like a wheeze which shook his shoulders.

"A sword is a sword. It's the hand that wields it, which kills," said Hundr. They followed the crowd around the western side of Agder's fortress, Hundr and Ragnhild walked with their hoods pulled up, and as they funnelled into the narrow space between Agder's high wall, and a steeply rising hill of dark rock, they fell into the crowd of warriors like so many fish in a shoal. There were big men and short men, warriors with elaborate beards and moustaches, and men of the Eastern Vikings of Hundr's homeland with shaved heads and topknots. There were warriors with baggy bright yellow and blue trews and brynjars dotted amongst the sweat-stinking leather armour most men wore.

Hundr glanced at the wall, which was still under construction. It was a window into how Kjotve's men constructed the circular fortress. It had a ditch dug around the perimeter and an entrance placed north, south, east and west. Beyond where that ditch rose on the side closest to the walls, rocks filled another deep ravine. The stout timbers soared from the deep bed of rocks, and each one sharpened into a point. On the town side of the walls, the ditch inclined on a grass-covered slope onto a fighting platform built so that two men could walk shoulder to shoulder.

"They know their business." Einar nodded as they marched past piles of logs and walked over a carpet of golden, curved wood shavings. The air was thick with the smell of freshly cut wood.

"When you are rich, you can hire the best men for such tasks: Danes and Saxons," said Rognvald.

"Saxons?" Ragnhild scoffed. "They fight like

children. Who would hire a Saxon to build a fortress?"

"Has not King Alfred built forts across his lands to keep our people out?" said Valbrandr.

Before Ragnhild could answer, three further horn blasts rang out, and silence spread across the crowd. They came to the southern side of the fortress, and Agder's valley stretched to where a set of hills punched out of the ground, covered in bright yellow flowers and marble-white rock. A short man in a red tunic and green cape stood atop the highest hill. He was rotund, and Hundr squinted his eye to see better, but was sure he wore a silver band around his forehead. Next to that finely dressed man were lords of war in mail, carrying fine swords, their arms thick with warrior rings.

"Thor's balls, look at the big bastard," said Einar. Hundr looked along the line of Lords, and there, towering above the other men by a full head, was Rollo the Betrayer.

"He has come a long way since we found him chained to Ketil's shit pail," sneered Ragnhild.

"He is the man who stole your precious sword," said Hundr.

"Just so," replied Rognvald. "And now Kjotve has it."

"And we have to get it back," grumbled Einar.

THIRTEEN

Kjotve strode forward on the hill and raised his hands to hush the crowds. Warriors were as thick in the valley as flies on shit, and Hundr wondered how Kjotve would keep so many men fed and watered. Such a crowd would eat Agder hungry in a matter of days. Kjotve was a small man in his fine clothes, not wearing a brynjar or carrying any weapons, and as he spoke, his voice belied his size and rolled across the crowd, as clear and resonant as a war horn.

"Lords and warriors, we gather here as loyal Northmen. We come together to throw back the greedy warmonger, Harald Fairhair." The valley erupted in raucous cheers, and Kjotve raised his hands to quieten them again. "The men gathered here are all that stands between Harald and his bloodthirsty ambition. He would sow the land with the blood of our people and bend us all to his will. We will not bend. We are warriors and freemen, Vikings, and we will crush Harald and dung the fields with the corpses of his warriors. Our kingdoms and jarldoms stretch back across the centuries. These lands are sacred; our forefathers are hewed up beneath the very earth we walk upon. Ancient kings and warriors, their draugrs now shaking at the prospect of Harald the Defiler disturbing their eternal slumber to steal their treasures." Kjotve reached behind him, and a warrior handed him a sword. Kjotve took the blade and held it out in front of him. "This sword is the key to our victory over the tyrant, this weapon which he dared to take from beneath the earth, defying the hard-earned sleep of an ancient draugr." The crowd was silent, and as Kjotve paused, the sound of gulls echoed from the coast beyond the town. They looked at Kjotve and the sword with open mouths and keen eyes, and when Kjotve held it aloft, there was a collective gasp as the blade caught the sun, gleaming blue and silver. "This is the Yngling blade, forged by dwarves beneath the mountains in deep history, wielded by Frey himself. Harald went beneath the ground, into the howe of King Fjolnir to take this sword from his dead hands, in violation of the laws of gods and men. This Yngling sword is said to make the man who wields it King of all Norway. The gods curse Harald, for now, I wield the Yngling blade, and with it, we will crush Harald, and I will unite the North against all tyrants!" Kjotve was shouting, and the warriors before him roared their approval, raising their fists and pumping them skywards.

"Rollo, the Betrayer stole the sword, is what he means. And Kjotve would destroy Harald and become a tyrant in his place," said Einar, leaning to speak into Hundr's ear above the tumult. Hundr saw Rollo grinning and applauding in the line of men who stood with Kjotve on the hill. The important men, the men who would become wealthy and powerful, should Kjotve be victorious.

Kjotve sheathed the sword and handed it back to his warriors. He raised his hands again to ask for calm from the throng. The hush descended once more.

"We rely not only on the gods and their sword to assure our victory. Every day, skilled warriors bring their reputations and their blades to our cause to fight for freedom. On this day, it is with pride and honour that I can announce a marriage between my son and a maiden of great lineage. Many of you know Thorir, famed for his berserkergang and deeds of bravery,"

"Thorir Haklag," said Valbrandr. Which meant hare-lipped. The men sniggered at the name.

Thorir strode forward to stand with his father. He wore the furs of a berserker and looked every inch the warrior, his arms thick with rings and his shoulders broad, in complete contrast to the slight figure of Kjotve, who looked more like a merchant than a warrior king.

"This very week, Thorir will be wed to Sigrid, daughter of the famed Jarl and warrior Ketil of Orkney. I welcome Sigrid Ketilsdottir to my family, and Jarl Ketil does us great honour by bringing his ships and his warriors to our cause. Death to Harald!" Kjotve bellowed those last words, and the warriors below the hill took up the chant, repeating it over and over, roaring in unison, shaking the very ground beneath Hundr's feet. Hundr remembered Sigrid from the moment they had spoken in her father's hall. She was a proud, beautiful, confident woman, and Hundr felt a pang of envy in his gut. He did not know Thorir, nor did he know Sigrid beyond their brief exchange of words as he raided her famous father's stronghold.

Hundr had not been close to a woman since the days in his past when he had loved and been betrayed by an Irish Queen. That love had burned him, scorched his soul, and left him cold and alone. But Sigrid might be a woman a man could live with that he could love, respect, and build a life with. For a normal man, perhaps, the son of a Jarl or nobleman. But not for a sea Jarl like Hundr. In the long nights at sea, sleepless and staring up at the stars, Hundr had reconciled himself to his fate. He was a warrior, a leader of men destined for a life alone and living by the blade, fighting for his place in Valhalla.

Hundr saw a movement in the corner of his eye. He turned to see a tall, thin man dodge behind a group of warriors. He didn't catch the man's face, but he had that feeling, that tingle at the back of the neck, a warning that someone was watching or that danger was near. Hundr stepped backwards and caught sight of a long, lantern-jawed face with close-cropped chestnut hair.

"What is it?" asked Einar, leaning back to see what had caught Hundr's attention.

"It's Mundi Fourfingers," said Hundr, moving off to follow the man.

"Of Ivar's old crew?"

"Yes. I'm going after him. I'll meet you at the quayside."

Hundr didn't wait for Einar to respond. He followed Mundi as he weaved between the crowd, heading towards Agder. Mundi stopped to look over his shoulder, and his face reddened when he saw Hundr behind him. Mundi ran, and Hundr set off after him. He shouldered his way through the crowd, and men grumbled and shouted curses after him. But Hundr had to catch Mundi and punish him for breaking his oath. He was one of the men who had sworn to Hundr years earlier after the defeat of Ivar the Boneless and had broken his oath and sailed away on a stolen ship with Rollo and Black Gorm.

Ahead, Hundr saw Mundi disappear around the corner of the fortress, heading towards the section of wall still under construction. Hundr followed him and burst through the press of men. There was a blur of movement from Hundr's blind side, which threw him off-balance, and he fell into the trampled grass. The surprise knocked the wind out of him, and he rose to a crouch, gasping for air. Hundr looked to see another of Ivar's old crewmen lunging at him with a short, wicked knife, so Hundr threw himself backwards and rose again in a half-crouch. He went for his sword but remembered he had left it aboard the Seaworm. He reached behind his back and whipped his seax from its leather scabbard hanging from the rear of his belt. The warrior came on, and men around shouted and pointed at the scuffle. Hundr launched himself forward at his attacker when the man was in mid-thrust with his knife hand. Hundr got inside that blow, headbutted the man full in the nose, and stabbed him with four quick, shallow blows to his guts with the seax. The man gasped and sagged to his knees, and Hundr left him bleeding to follow Mundi.

The men behind Hundr were in an uproar, but Hundr ignored them, turning to continue the chase. He stumbled, collided with a warrior, fell to one knee, and got up again, cursing. Hundr broke into a run, searching for Mundi as he raced around Agder's walls. It didn't take long before he saw Mundi bolting into the piles of trimmed timber, waiting to be placed into the fortress walls. Hundr skipped between the stacks of tall stakes and off-cuts and saw Mundi leap up and climb onto the half-constructed wall, clambering over the inner timber construction and up onto the bare planking where the fighting platform would be. Hundr ran and leapt onto the wall, grasping the roughly hewn wood with both hands to hoist himself up. He cursed as slivers of splinters stabbed into his palm, and he hauled himself up onto the planking. He ducked just in time as a log tossed across the gap by Mundi sailed over his head, but he could not move fast enough to avoid a second, which slammed into the side of his skull. Hundr fell to his knees, clinging to the planking.

"You broke your oath, Mundi. I curse you as a nithing," he called.

"You are too soft, Dog's Name. A real Jarl wouldn't allow beaten men to live. You dragged us to Ireland chasing a whore Queen. A pox on you and your oath," Mundi snarled, and he dropped from the planking and went inside the fortress.

Hundr leapt after him and yelped as his shin

thumped into a sawhorse. Mundi was running again, and Hundr sped after him, fisting a carpenter in the chest to move him out of the way. Hundr chased him down a mud-slicked street and into a long building, its door wide open. Hundr ducked inside, pausing as his eye adjusted to the gloom. A pot crashed into the wall over Hundr's shoulder, and he ducked before Mundi launched any more missiles. Hundr's vision became accustomed to the darkness just in time to see Mundi disappear through a door at the rear of the room, which stank of damp animals. Hundr went to follow him, but three goats came bleating from the doorway, and he saw Mundi leave the adjacent room through an open shutter on his right. Hundr leapt through the open window, landing in a roll and rising in a crouch. He sucked air into his gasping lungs and launched his seax at the fleeing oath-breaker. The weapon flew and clattered into Mundi's back. He fell with a yelp, rolling in the mud and struggling to feel for the wound on his back. Hundr strode over to his former man and knelt to pick up the seax.

"There is no wound. It's not a throwing axe," Hundr said. The hilt of the thing had hit Mundi between the shoulder blades, but the worst he would feel of it would be a welt of a bruise. "This is a wound." Hundr dropped to his knees and let his bodyweight drive the seax into Mundi's thigh. He screamed, and the people in the muddy laneway scattered from the violence. Hundr punched Mundi twice in the face, more from anger at the chase than to torture the man. "Rollo gave Kjotve King Harald's sword. Where does he keep it?"

"Stick the sword up your arse," Mundi hissed, his mouth clogged with blood. He was about to spit a mouthful of it into Hundr's face before Hundr wrapped his hands around Mundi's throat.

"Where is it?" Mundi shook and jerked in his grip, but Hundr squeezed tighter.

"In his hall, he hung it in his bedroom, so his maids say, anyways," croaked Mundi.

"Where is the boy?"

Mundi's eyes went wide, and his tongue protruded from his mouth. His hands tore at Hundr's arms, and a four-fingered hand grabbed his wrist.

"Where is Finn Ivarsson?" Hundr let his throat go, and Mundi gasped and coughed for air.

"He's gone. Black Gorm took the little bastard."

"Gorm has sailed away in the Sea-Stallion?"

"Piss off, dog," said Mundi, scrambling away. Hundr grabbed the hilt of his seax, which was still stuck in Mundi's leg, and ripped it free. Mundi howled like a kicked dog.

"Where has he gone? Tell me, and I will give you your life."

"See, you are weak. Bloody easterner. You are no…"

He didn't have time to finish. Hundr leapt upon him and cut his throat before he could get his words out.

Not that weak.

Hundr sat back against the building to catch his breath. Gorm was gone with Finn, and Kjotve had the Yngling sword in his bedchamber. Just when he thought he was close to finding the boy and the sword, they were further away than ever.

FOURTEEN

Einar knelt on the cold stone. The bones in his knees ached from the chill, and he shifted so that his weight was on one knee only, bringing the other up and leaning his arms against it. Darkness had fallen upon Agder, and Einar looked down over the fortress and its bay. It was a clear, still night, and the sea's glassy surface reflected the stars where the fleet of warships bobbed gently on a light swell. He could hear the creaking of timbers and the occasional shouts of a warrior up late, drinking ale and wandering the quayside.

"Kjotve keeps the sword in his bedchamber," said Hundr. "It is in a building adjoining his feasting hall. His warriors guard it, and we will need to get in and out without raising the alarm if we want to live."

"If they see or hear us, we won't get out

of here alive," agreed Rognvald, scratching his thin beard thoughtfully. "We would need to fight our way out of his chambers, through the stronghold, hope they don't bar the gate, and then battle our way across the quays, into our faering, and row amongst the ships which will no doubt do their utmost to sink us or skewer us with spears and arrows as we pass."

"So, best to get the sword without waking Kjotve or his men then," said Valbrandr with a wry grin.

Einar shook his head and wiped a hand across his eyes and beard. "Gorm has already left with Finn. Every moment we waste here brings the lad closer to his doom."

"We will go for Finn, Einar. I give you my word," Hundr promised. "But we are here now, and we must get the sword. We gave our word as drengrs to King Harald."

Einar closed his eyes and thought of Finn, small and gentle. Raised in the halls of Dublin as a lordling, soft and kind. Nightmares had plagued Einar's sleep—dreams of Finn huddled crying on a storm-swept deck, hungry and treated cruelly by Gorm and his vicious berserkers. Finn had Father Darragh for company if the priest still lived, but he was alone in a cruel world, and every minute Einar delayed at Agder brought Finn closer to those who wanted to kill him.

Einar understood it made little sense to leave Agder now when the sword was so close, but once they had secured the Yngling blade, and if they survived the near-impossible task of breaking into Kjotve's bedchamber, then he would go for Finn. And Black Gorm would die.

"Seems like certain death, to get in and out without being seen. We can't fight our way out, and none of us here is known for being so fleet of foot that we could sneak into a man's bedchamber. We can walk into the fortress. It's not guarded nor barred nor even finished," Einar said. "So, getting to his rooms won't be difficult. But getting into his bedchamber will be, especially without being seen."

"Kjotve's rooms can be entered either from the front door, which will be guarded, or through the hall," said Hundr. "I looked over the buildings after I chased Mundi into the fortress. Seems to me there are two ways we can do this. One is we get onto the roof, cut away the thatch and drop into his chamber. The other is to go in through the hall, which is unguarded."

"It's unguarded because his younger hearth warriors who don't have a home of their own, and the people of his household will sleep in there, just as in any hall," said Ragnhild. "We would be walking through a long room of people sleeping, and if one wakes, then we are done for."

"Just so." Rognvald nodded. "There might be another way, though. Yet it would mean more risk to us and placing our lives in the hands of Loki chaos: we burn the place, and in the pandemonium of the burning hall, we go in for the sword." Rognvald stared into the fortress with a gleam in his eye and a smile playing at the corners of his mouth. It was a clever but dangerous plan. They would create a storm within the fortress and burn Kjotve's hall, and in the maelstrom of that burning, there would be an opportunity for them to brave the flames and go in for the sword.

"Whatever way we do it, it will be a risk," said Einar. "If we go in through the thatch or the hall, and they catch us, we are all dead. With the fire, they will not be looking for an attacker, nor will the warriors be searching for us. Fires start all the time, a candle toppled from a table, a torch blown over by the wind. If we don't kill anyone or need to fight, then we might get in and out without being noticed."

It seemed like a good plan. Einar was not a man averse to risk. He had fought in more Holmgangs than he could remember, and one does not earn a name like The Brawler by being timid. But he had to live. He had to get out of Agder alive to be able to rescue Finn. If Einar died, Finn would die at the hands of his uncle. Without Einar, there would be no one to go after the boy. Hundr would honour his word and hunt down Gorm, but Einar was under no illusion that Hundr's promise was primarily to aid Harald. Einar doubted that Hundr would take up Finn's pursuit if Einar himself died. Of course, he knew that when Hundr looked at Finn, he saw the boy's mother and father, and that attachment brought only painful memories of dead friends and lost love.

"Fire it is then," said Hundr, and he and Rognvald decided between them how they would steal a god's sword from under the nose of the King of Agder and escape his army of warriors.

Later that same night, Einar huddled with his back against a low stone wall. He looked up at the clear, bright night and wondered at the stars as they shone above him. Einar waited for the signal, for the flaming arrows which would soar across the night sky and set Kjotve's hall aflame. He looked at the eagle constellation of Veðrfölnir and wondered at the bird perched atop the great tree of Yggdrasil. On such a clear night, men believed the stars contained messages, signs that holy men could only interpret. Einar hoped the eagle held a message of hope for young Finn and a message of luck for the feat of daring he must accomplish that evening to retrieve the Yngling sword. Twinkling beyond the majestic eagle was the collection of stars which formed the shape of Nithad, the evil king who wielded a mighty sword forged by Völund. Nithad had imprisoned Völund and forced him to craft that blade and other such treasures, but Völund had captured the wicked king's children and made drinking cups of their skulls and jewels from their eyes, and Völund then escaped on wings crafted in the heat of his forge. There was some god-magic in that message. *A cruel king and a magic sword,* Einar thought.

Before he could dwell any longer on the stars and their hidden messages, a bowshot hissed across the sky above him. It seemed to pause there, hanging beneath the jewelled sky, but then fell along its arc to plunge silently into the dark thatch of Kjotve's hall.

Another arrow flew and landed with a crunch in the thatch of the outbuilding behind the great hall, which contained Kjotve's living quarters and bedchambers. Ragnhild was fulfilling her part of the plan, and as the warriors of Agder slept, the Valkyrie archer fired another four shots into the night sky. Einar watched the silhouetted thatch, waiting to see if the flaming arrows would take effect and catch alight. He held his breath, for this was a dangerous part of Hundr and Rognvald's scheme. They had sent Ragnhild to Agder's walls to shoot her fire arrows out of sight of Kjotve's warriors who guarded his door facing west. Without the fire, they could not get the sword. Rognvald had shown himself to be both cunning and clever in his plan. There was evidently a reason Harald and Rognvald had been so successful in their war to rule Norway— they could not have done that without having deep cunning between them.

Einar held his breath, waiting for the roar of alarm to go up from the guards, but they were silent and had not seen the arrows. He breathed out slowly and rolled his shoulders. It would soon be time for Einar to play his part in the plan. For what seemed like an age, nothing happened. The arrows had landed in the thatch as planned, and there had been no rain that day, so the roofing would be dry. But there was no flame. He waited, wondering if the cursed building would ever catch fire, or if he would need to climb in through the roof after all, but then he saw a glow atop Kjotve's hall. It started small, a faint orange hue above the shadows, but then the sea breeze wafted it, and the embers grew. Soon the glow turned into flame—Einar could hear its crackle—and then another fire sprang up on the outbuilding. He clenched his teeth. It was almost time.

Singing broke out across the courtyard in front of Kjotve's outbuilding, and two men emerged from a laneway, arms draped around each other, belting out a rowing shanty. They both held pots of ale and swayed as they stumbled across the moonlit pathway. Einar saw the two guards stiffen and their spears straighten as the inebriated men crossed in front of them.

"Fire, look, there!" called one of the drunkards, pointing up at Kjotve's hall. It was Hundr; his arm draped around Valbrandr's enormous shoulders. The guards spun, leaping backwards as they saw the fire spreading its venom across the roof, casting a flickering light on their startled faces. The guards looked at each other and then back to Hundr and Valbrandr, hesitant about what to do.

"Sound the alarm! We need water; someone forgot to put a torch out," shouted Valbrandr, and the guards dropped their spears.

"Fire, fire, we need water," yelled one guard, and the other ran for the doors to Kjotve's rooms to get his Lord out of danger. Dry thatch would burn fast and fierce, and that was the plan. Once it caught fire, it would collapse into the building itself and burn alive anybody unfortunate enough to be inside, which was not a death worthy of Valhalla. Einar waited as men emerged from buildings, knuckling the sleep from their eyes and springing into action, searching for vessels to carry water. Finally, Einar launched himself to his feet and sprinted across the lane from where he had crouched. He ran towards Kjotve's hall and cursed himself for a fool, for he was about to charge into a burning building and risk his life, his place in Valhalla, and his chance to rescue Finn Ivarsson.

Einar did not break stride and crashed his shoulder into the timber shutters of the outbuilding's window. He burst through it with a grunt and collapsed onto the hard-packed earth floor. Einar rose to his feet, and already the place was thick with smoke. His eyes itched with the sting of it, and his throat scratched from the filthy air. He tried to see through the smoke, and a man hurtled past him towards the window. Einar couldn't make out his face. He walked down a narrow corridor, tracing the lines of the walls with his hands and coughing as the smoke caught in his chest. His hand found a door, and he pushed it open. A man jumped to his feet, springing from his bed.

"Fire, get out of the building, quickly," Einar said, and he left the man, continuing down the hall. His eyes streamed with water, and he could feel heat above him, and the sound of the fire roared, filling his ears with its rushing growl. He found another door, but it was locked.

"King Kjotve, Lord King," a man shouted somewhere, lost in the smoke-filled building.

Einar jumped as a section of the roof collapsed on his right. Flaming, searing hot thatch fell to the floor, and Einar put his arm up to shield his face from the fierce heat. He stepped back and crashed his boot into the door, smashing it open. A small man and a plump woman were inside, both with looks of panic on their faces, covering each other with cloaks.

"Lord King, the building is on fire. We must go," said Einar, recognising Kjotve. He dropped his hand to the axe at his belt. The war would be over if he could just kill the bastard in his bedchamber. He drew his axe and took a half pace forward.

"Are we under attack?" gasped Kjotve, pulling his wife close to him.

"No, Lord King. It's just a fire—a torch or candle in the thatch," he said. He released his axe. Killing Kjotve now would rouse the fortress to arms, and Einar knew he would never get out of the place alive, and Finn would be lost to his bloodthirsty uncle. He saw Kjotve glance at the wall of his bedchamber. Einar couldn't see in the smoke, but he knew from the look on Kjotve's face that was where the Yngling sword rested. Another crash of flaming thatch thundered into the hall outside the bedchamber. "We must go now, Lord King." Einar ran to Kjotve and ushered him from the room.

"The sword," gasped the King of Agder, looking back over his shoulder.

"Save your wife. I will go back for the sword," said Einar. He pushed Kjotve down the hall,

all three of them coughing and struggling to breathe in the cloying smoke, which was now as thick and heavy as a dragon's breath. "Get him out," Einar commanded, thrusting Kjotve into the arms of a warrior who appeared before them. Kjotve's wife yelped as they had to jump over the flaming thatch that had fallen in from above. Einar turned around and made his way back to the bedchamber. His heart raced, but he felt tired. The smoke was too thick, and he wanted to sit down for a rest, just to catch his breath. But he knew that if he did that, he would never get up again. So, he growled and forced himself back into Kjotve's room. He ran in and surged for the rear wall, grasping for the Yngling sword, but his hand fell upon the cold iron of a warrior's brynjar mail coat. The man turned to him, holding the sword in two hands, his face blackened with soot.

"I have it, come on," shouted the warrior above the roar of the fire. Einar nodded, but he headbutted the man in the nose and ripped the sword from his grasp. The warrior had thought Einar, a friend, another of Kjotve's men, had come to rescue the sword of kings, but Einar was not his friend; he was his doom. He crashed his knee into the man's head and kicked him brutally to the ground. Einar spun on his heel and raced from the doorway, leaving the enemy warrior to die in the horrors of the fire. Einar came into the hallway, but more thatch had fallen in, and the whole corridor was ablaze, the heat searing and oppressive. He stuffed the scabbard into his belt and ran the opposite way down the corridor towards the hall. That too would be on fire, but he had no choice, and he began to believe he would die in the flames.

Einar bellowed his war cry as he pounded down the hallway. He crashed through a heavy door and stumbled into the cavernous hall itself. Einar gasped because the inside of Kjotve's hall was a vision of hel itself. The roof had collapsed in large sections, and the hall's interior was a horror of screaming people pinned under roof beams, roaring fire, and bodies running here and there, trying desperately to help their burning friends and loved ones. Einar thanked the gods, however, because the collapsed roof allowed most of the smoke to billow out into the night sky, the glorious stars now cloaked in a grey, swirling cloud. A figure loomed above Einar, enormous and terrible in the dancing firelight.

"Leave the sword, bastard," the monstrous figure growled, and as the firelight flickered across its face, Einar recognised Rollo The Betrayer.

FIFTEEN

Einar whipped his axe free from its belt loop, and at the same time, he punched Rollo in the throat. Then, as the big man staggered, Einar brought his axe down hard, intending to crush the Betrayer's skull. Rollo, however, was as fast as he was big, and he caught Einar's wrist and drove his arm back. Next, Einar thrust his knee into Rollo's chest, causing him to stagger backwards, releasing Einar's arm. Rollo reeled away but came around with a knife in his hand. He grinned and knelt to pick up a flaming timber, waving it before him like a sword.

"So, you are Harald's war dogs now?" Rollo shouted above the din of the burning hall. "You fight for a tyrant, an evil man. What does that say about your honour?"

"What do you know of honour, of drengskapr, Rollo the Betrayer?" sneered Einar, and he lunged at Rollo with his axe. Rollo parried the blow with his timber, and sparks from its flaming end flew into Einar's face and beard. He crashed into Rollo, the two men tumbling to the floor. They rolled together, intertwined and clawing at each other. Einar let go of his axe and caught a fistful of Rollo's hair just as Rollo punched him in the face. Einar slammed his head into the floor, but Rollo still had the flaming timber in his hand, and he twisted and thrust it towards Einar's face. Einar let go of Rollo's hair and caught the timber just as it singed his beard. The heat was unbearable, and Einar screamed because it felt as though the skin of his face was melting. Einar roared with pain as the timber burned his hand, where he gripped it to stop Rollo from beating him with it. The fire raged around the two warriors, and somewhere beyond Einar's vision, another part of the roof collapsed with an almighty crash. Blood pounded in Einar's ears, and for a terrible moment, he thought he would die in that place, killed by a betrayer and without a blade in his hand. Yet he pulled himself together, rolled Rollo's hips, and drove the timber away from his face. Einar came up on top of Rollo and twisted the wooden stave out of his hand. He elbowed Rollo in the nose and clamped his hands around Rollo's throat. Rollo was big and strong, but Einar had over thirty summers of rowing power locked up in his arms and shoulders, and his shovel-like hands were calloused and brutal. He squeezed, and Rollo's eyes bulged.

"Tell me where Gorm has taken the boy," Einar snarled.

"I didn't want to steal the lad away; that was Gorm…"

Einar headbutted Rollo before he could finish, and then butted him again.

"Where is he?" he bellowed, spittle flying from his ash-blackened mouth and into Rollo's beard.

"He's taken him to King Bjorn Ironside."

"You lie. Has he sailed to Dublin?"

"To Bjorn, he goes to Bjorn," Rollo spluttered through a choking gurgle. Flaming thatch floated down from the ruined roof and landed next to where the two men fought. Einar released Rollo and lunged to his feet. He stamped on Rollo's groin and raced towards a gap in the wall, which the collapsing roof had torn away.

"You fight for a usurper and a tyrant. We will free the people of Norway," Rollo shouted, but Einar didn't turn. Instead, he scrambled up the collapsed wall and leapt into the night air. Einar dropped through the glowing embers and drifting smoke to land in a crouch in the street. All around him, men ran and shouted in panic, trying to organise themselves to put out the roaring fire and save their freshly constructed fortress from Loki's fire hunger. Einar's hand pulsed from the pain, and he looked at it to see blisters already forming from the burn. He reached to his back and breathed a sigh of relief that the Yngling blade was still there, and without hesitation, he ran through the streets of Agder, pounding towards the quayside.

At last, Einar reached the docks. There, a pale red sunrise was begging to spill above the far horizon beyond the forest of masts and ships' prows. Behind him, Agder burned, and its people rushed to save their town. Einar reached to his back once more and clutched the sword of ancient kings. He bent over, hands on his knees, to catch his breath. His eyes stung still from the appalling smoke in Kjotve's chambers, and his burnt hand felt twice its normal size. He coughed and hawked up a gob of thick black phlegm. Einar shook his head to awake his senses because he had to find their faering and get out of Agder alive. Then, ahead of him, he heard the clash of arms, the ring of iron on iron. He peered through the gloom and saw Hundr furiously battling two spearmen who bullied him back with their shields. Einar, Hundr and the others had come ashore without their brynjars, and for a split second, Einar thought Hundr would die as he fell to one knee. But it was just a feint, and Hundr came up as an attacker lunged at him, cracking the man across the skull with his axe. Einar ran towards Hundr to help him deal with the second spearman, and as he drew close, he heard the man shouting, calling for aid in his fight. But the burning town and its chaos drowned out his voice.

"I have the sword," Einar called as he rushed to Hundr's aid, his axe drawn and ready to strike.

"Go to Valbrandr; he needs you more than I," said Hundr as he saw Einar approaching. It was only at that moment that Einar noticed a woman in a white nightdress behind Hundr. She was backed right onto the quayside, and the battling warriors had hidden her from view. It surprised Einar to see a woman standing there, watching the warriors fight, but she did not look afraid. On the contrary, she was stern and proud, clutching a small box to her chest. Einar looked along the quayside where Valbrandr was hard-pressed indeed. Three warriors hacked at him, and he looked to be injured, stumbling backwards and catching their attacks on his shield. Einar charged forward, his axe in one hand and his seax in the other. Valbrandr fell to one knee, and an enemy warrior pierced his shoulder with a spear thrust. Einar let out a war cry, and the spearman looked up in surprise to see Einar bearing down upon him. He tried to raise his spear to defend himself, but it was too late, and Einar buried his axe head in the man's face. It made a wet slapping sound as the blade chopped through the fat and gristle of his nose and cheek, and Einar left it there, allowing his momentum to carry him, thundering into the second attacker. That warrior fell to the cold stone of the quayside, and Einar stamped on his throat and slammed his seax into the choking man's chest. Blood oozed from the wound, and Einar ripped his short seax free to face the last attacker. The third warrior was about to strike his axe on Valbrandr's splintered shield, and he looked at Einar just as a white-feathered arrow plunged into his stomach, throwing him backwards.

"Let's get out of this place," Ragnhild shouted as she came running from the darkness, her bow in hand.

Einar bent to help Valbrandr to his feet, and the big man groaned from the pain of his wounds. The spear thrust to his shoulder had spread blood like a blooming flower across his tunic.

"Thank you, Einar Rosti. I owe you my life," he said through clenched teeth. "They saw us fighting their men in the streets and followed us here. More will come. We should go."

"Did you get it?" asked Ragnhild, clapping Einar on the shoulder as she drew close.

"Here is the cursed thing. Enough men have died for it today," said Einar, and he drew forth the scabbard, handing it to Ragnhild.

"There is Rognvald," Hundr called, pointing down into the shining blackness of the sea, the shadows from the burning town flickering on its surface. Then, sure enough, Einar heard oar splashes, and the faering came into view, rowed by Rognvald.

"Who is the woman?" asked Ragnhild.

"I am Sigrid Ketilsdottir," the woman retorted, raising her chin as she spoke.

"As in, the daughter of Ketil Flatnose?" said Ragnhild, looking at Hundr and throwing her arms up.

"She comes with us," Hundr announced, and he helped Sigrid down into the small boat. She stepped into it and kept her box close as she sat next to Rognvald. Einar tossed the Yngling sword to Rognvald, and the young warrior's face lit up as he turned the thing over in his hands. They clambered into the boat and pulled out into the shadowy dark spaces between the moored warships in Agder's bay. Einar looked back at the orange and red flames licking above the high walls of Kjotve's fortress. Men had died for that sword; the blade Harald had taken from a draugr who slept peacefully in his howe. He wondered if the thing was cursed, but they had done their job and would return the sword to King Harald, and Einar wanted that done quickly. Black Gorm was out there with Finn, and the longer Einar was delayed, the closer the boy came to his murderous uncle.

The next day, the Seaworm tacked northeast, following Norway's rugged coastline and heading back to King Harald to bring him the Yngling sword. There was a strong wind at their backs, and the drakkar sliced through the Whale Road, rising and falling on the soft swell. Einar drank from a tankard of ale and sat on a rowing bench with Bush. They watched as Ragnhild showed her skills as a healer. Valbrandr grunted as Ragnhild pulled the catgut thread through the flaps of his leg wound with a bone needle. She tutted and shook her head as he jerked, and a pulse of blood washed over his thigh.

"Keep still. You moan like a child," she tutted, and Valbrandr nodded, grimacing. She had already sewed up the wound in his shoulder, the cut looking like a ragged smile at the centre of raised purple and blue bruising.

"She's some healer," said Bush, raising his cup in salute at Ragnhild's work. "Reminds me of watching her sew you back together after your fight with Ivar. Now, that was a wound."

"Aye," agreed Einar softly, placing his hand on his stomach. "I should have died with Ivar's blade in my guts. Thank the gods that Ragnhild and Hildr saved me." He remembered the pain and suffering of that terrible wound, the fevered sweating and weakness, and bone-crunching pain as his body repaired itself.

"They sewed up your insides, as I remember it, and yes, you should have died," Bush gibed, and he cackled as Einar punched him on the shoulder.

"I should have died many times. I'm too old for this horseshit. Running into burning buildings to get magic swords!" He frowned, looking down at his bandaged hand. Hildr had gently rubbed a soothing salve into the burn and wrapped it with some clean cloth, but it still felt as hot as hel. His back ached, his knees throbbed, and he felt like he could sleep for a week.

"She's a fine-looking woman," said Bush, nodding his head to where Sigrid Ketilsdottir stood with one hand on the sheet rope, looking back towards where Agder's coast fell from view beyond the retreating headland. Her long golden hair whipped in the wind, and along with her nightdress, she wore spare leg wraps and a jerkin provided by Ragnhild and Hildr.

"She is," Einar agreed. "But what is she doing here with us? It wasn't long ago that we climbed her father's walls and plundered his hoard."

"I can hear you," Sigrid shouted above the din of the sea, crashing against the hull.

"Shit," mumbled Bush, and he sidled away

from Einar and went to where the men coiled seal hide rope at the prow.

"Why did you leave your husband?" Einar called to her. If she had heard his question, she might as well tell them what she was doing by running away with men whom her father surely hated.

"Leave her," chided Hildr, coming to sit next to him.

"I left Agder because I want to be mistress of my fate," Sigrid proclaimed. She let go of the rope and came towards Einar. She stumbled amidst the ship's rocking on the waves and almost crashed into Einar before Hildr caught her.

"You will find your sea legs soon, sit," said Hildr warmly, helping Sigrid sit beside her on the bench. "It is difficult for a woman to control her destiny. Ours is a world of men, as much as they are prideful fools." She smiled at Einar.

"You are a warrior?" asked Sigrid.

"I am. But I was raised to it at the temple of Odin at Upsala. Ragnhild and I are warrior priestesses of the Valkyrie order."

"I, too, can be a warrior. I can fight. My father had his men teach me. Even though they didn't like it."

"Becoming a Valkyrie was not my choice. My father left me at the temple when I was but a girl."

"Better to be a warrior than to be traded to a man like a cow at market," said Sigrid. "I would rather die than let that pig Thorir sweat and drool over me, stuff his child into me and close me away in a gloomy chamber, my only fate to die birthing his brat or die old and sad in the hall of a man I do not love."

"So that is why you run away?" asked Einar.

"I want to be free to choose my path. I can be a warrior, just like you. Why can't a woman have reputation? Like your scarred Jarl there, the man with the dog's name."

"Even if that path lies with the crews who stole from your father?" asked Hildr.

Sigrid frowned at that. She looked at her boots.

"He hates you. My father has sworn an oath of vengeance against Jarl Hundr and all of you. He says he will dance in your blood and decorate his hall with your bones." She looked at Hildr, her eyes wide and mouth quivering. "I saw a chance, and I took it. I saw Jarl Hundr in the street outside the burning hall and knew he was there to attack. It was the only chance to escape my life, to change my fate."

Hildr held her hand and smiled.

"I understand. I think the gods will smile upon your courage. Men use the strength of their arms and their weapon skill to forge their own path, so why shouldn't we?"

Einar rose to his feet and looked to the steerboard where the Sami shaman knelt over the Yngling sword, murmuring in a guttural voice and rocking back and forth. Hundr and Rognvald watched him, Hundr at the tiller and Rognvald intent on the strange little sorcerer. Einar went to join them.

"What does your seer say?" asked Einar, leaning back onto the sheer strake so the wind could blow through his hair.

"He says Harald will be King now that we have sword back," Rognvald answered with a smile. "How is your hand?"

Einar flexed his burned hand beneath its wrappings.

"I'll live. Seems to me that Kjotve has an army already gathered at Agder. He can't keep all those ships and warriors in place for long. The fight for Norway must come soon."

"Just so," said Rognvald. "Better to have the last of Harald's enemies together to be defeated in one final battle. Harald will be pleased and will bring his army south to make himself King of all Norway."

"Are they his enemies?" said Einar, and he watched as Bavlos shook and rattled a length of rope with bones and bits of iron tied to it.

"They are if they oppose him," Rognvald remarked, smiling at Einar.

"Seems to me that those men would live in peace if Harald hadn't made war upon them."

"Live in peace? Are we not Northmen? You are a drengr, Einar Rosti. Have you lived a life of peace? When you sailed with Ivar the Boneless, did you allow men to live in peace, or did you fight and kill to burnish your reputation bright and honour Odin and Thor?"

Einar thought that was fair, and he raised his hand to acknowledge the logic in what Rognvald had said.

"I just want to get the sword back to King Harald so that we can sail after Gorm and his men."

"You will not join the fight against Kjotve the Rich?" asked Rognvald, and he cocked his eyebrow at Hundr.

"We will find and kill Black Gorm and his oath breakers first," said Hundr.

"Harald has promised you land if you help him win the war," Rognvald reminded him.

"I know it, and we will fight alongside Harald. But first, we must kill Gorm and free the boy," affirmed Hundr, meeting Einar's gaze with his one eye.

"Who is this boy who is so important to you? He is not your son, Einar?"

"We are all a family, bonded by blood," said Hundr before Einar could answer. "Einar is my brother, as is Bush. Ragnhild and Hildr are my sisters, and Finn is part of that family. We have fought across the Whale Road and endured blades and torture. We have killed sons of Ragnar Lothbrok and Frankish Lords. I will not let young Finn suffer at the hands of Gorm and his savages. They are oath breakers, and I will kill them for that treachery."

Rognvald nodded at the power of Hundr's words.

"What about the woman, Ketil's daughter?"

"She came running to me whilst Kjotve's hall burned," shrugged Hundr. "Valbrandr and I were watching the buildings whilst Einar went in. We followed the plan, ready to strike and fight our way out if Kjotve's men realised they were under attack. Sigrid came from the flames, clutching her treasures to her chest. She asked me to take her with me, away from Thorir Haklag. She wants to make her own fate."

"Her father is powerful. Ketil Flatnose hates you already. Now that you have his daughter, he will do all he can to kill you," said Rognvald.

"I do not have her. She can leave whenever she wishes."

"He will not see it that way."

"He can see it whatever way he wants. I, too, fled my home, running from my people. I wanted to change my fate, to force the Norns to change the thread they wove for my life. Then I met Einar, and he took me in when I had nothing. Einar gave me a chance, and I will give Sigrid a chance."

"It helps that she is not difficult to look upon," Rognvald quipped, and he winked at Hundr.

Einar looked out at the white-tipped waves and wondered where Finn was at that moment. He desperately hoped the boy was not afraid or hurt. He gripped the mast rope until his knuckles turned white, and Einar promised himself that he would kill Gorm and his berserkers. He imagined Finn cold and huddled on their ship, and he knew they would not treat the boy softly. Einar would kill them and get Finn to safety, or he would die trying.

SIXTEEN

The Seaworm met King Harald's fleet off western Norway. They had unknowingly sailed past the King's fleet and his army, losing half a day before turning about to search again amongst the puzzle of islands, mountainous fjords, and inlets which made up the coast of Rogaland. Rognvald went straight to the King with the Yngling sword, informing him of Kjotve's army mustered at Agder. Hundr had let Rognvald go, putting him and his men ashore on a flat island covered in lush green foliage, perched in a fjord of water so clear it shone green under the sun. Ragnhild had warned Hundr to go to Harald himself with the sword and ensure the King recognised him for the glory of its rescue. However, Hundr preferred to find Asbjorn and his precious ships and ensure all was well.

"The ships are out in the fjord with Harald's

ships," she said. "We did what Harald asked, and he should reward us."

"We will be rewarded, and I will go to Harald. But first, I want to check on the ships. We have four left since Gorm stole the Sea-Stallion. They are our wealth and our lifeblood. Also, the men will be unsettled after Black Gorm's betrayal. I worry that others might get the same idea. The last thing we need is another ship disappearing in the night with a full crew."

"None of the others will leave. They have sworn oaths."

"So had Gorm and the dogs who ran with him; they still left at the first opportunity."

They rowed the Seaworm out into the wide fjord beyond the island and around the ships of Harald's fleet. Bush called a gentle pace, and the vessel moved slowly across the still water. Einar approached, with Hildr alongside. They picked their way between the rowing benches from the stern, and, as he came close, Hundr noticed that Einar's jaw was set firm, and his brows were knitted together.

"We should talk to Harald today," Einar said, ducking his head under the sheet rope and leaning on the furled yard.

"We will," said Hundr. "I know you want to be off searching for Finn as soon as we can."

"When I fought Rollo in Kjotve's hall, he said Gorm would take Finn to Bjorn Ironside. You know well that Bjorn is the King of the Svears now."

"I do. If we can catch Gorm whilst he is with Bjorn, then I will talk to Bjorn."

"Good. Hopefully, Bjorn remembers how you and he fought back-to-back in Frankia and killed Duke Robert the Strong together. We should head out today if we can."

"I need to talk to the men first, then Harald. Then we go."

"Do you think we can trust King Harald?" asked Hildr. She wrapped one arm around Einar's waist and shielded the sun from her blue eyes with her other hand.

"As much as any king," Hundr said. He did not trust anyone beyond his family of Einar, Ragnhild, Hildr and Bush, and he had learned that the hard way. "Why do you ask?"

"Something Rollo said to Einar at Agder," she replied, nudging Einar to speak.

Einar frowned at her. It was a look that said this was a conversation he had hoped would remain between him and Hildr.

"It's nothing really," Hildr shrugged. "He just said that Harald was a tyrant and usurper. Of course, we have heard that before about him. It got me thinking, that's all."

Hundr watched the Windspear come into view across the fjord. Asbjorn waved at him from the prow, and Hundr returned the salute.

"Thinking about what?"

"Well…are we on the right side of this thing?"

"When has that bothered you before? What is the right side of things? We are drengr, men of war. We fight, and we kill. If the right of things is fighting on the side of the weak or not fighting for a conqueror, that is not the life we have chosen or the life Odin would have us live in his honour. Were you ever on this right side of things with Ivar?"

"I never thought of it like that back then. But should we not consider now if we are fighting on the right side?"

"There is no right side. There is only the side that wins and the side that is vanquished." Hundr moved closer to Einar and rubbed his thumb across the carved ivory face on Fenristooth's hilt. "We fight for reputation and silver and to honour the gods. You know this; it has always been so. Odin does not care if one man wins a kingdom from another. He cares only that men fight bravely and die with honour so he can fill Valhalla with warriors to fight for him at the end of days when Ragnarök tears the world apart. Harald is a war-king. He is a conqueror. You ran into that burning building to get the Yngling sword because Harald promised to reward us for fighting for him. He will grant us land, what you have always wanted, Einar. That is why we fight. I don't care if Harald kills a Jarl or takes land from Rollo's people. Neither should you." He clapped Einar on the shoulder. "Don't get soft on me in your old age. Talk to him," he said, smiling at Hildr.

"I am not getting soft," Einar scowled, thrusting his hands into his belt and straightening his back. "Let's just talk to Harald and get after Gorm."

Hundr went aboard the Windspear, and Asbjorn met him with a skin of ale and a wooden plate filled with fish and fresh bread.

"Well met, lord," said Asbjorn, a wide smile splitting his handsome face. He was a man of average height and build but had a glossy black beard and long raven black hair, like an animal's pelt. He was well-liked amongst the crews for his calm manner, had a reputation for bravery, and was a front-line fighter.

"I see Harald is looking after us," smiled Hundr, drinking from the ale.

"He is. His men make sure that we are well provisioned."

"How are the men?"

Asbjorn chewed at his beard.

"They worry when you are away, lord. We sail up and down the coast, shadowing the march of Harald's army. But the march is slow, and it doesn't feel like we are going anywhere. The men want to fight. They are hungry for it."

"Have they spent Ketil's silver already?"

"No, lord. Well, some have..." Asbjorn said with a smile, and Hundr laughed at the thought of his men losing their wealth gambling and whoring in ports across Norway.

"We will fight soon. First, I must talk with King Harald; then, we will put to sea. Do I need to talk to the men, tell them of our plans?"

"That would help—having sight of you will give them hope we will soon be back to arms."

Hundr ordered his captains to row their ships away from Harald's fleet and towards a beach on the opposite side of the fjord from Harald's island camp. It was a small beach of shale and large boulders, surrounded on each side by sloping hills of wild grasses and briars, which rose into mountainous, stone-covered hills enveloping the fjord. Hundr clambered up one such hillside, the sun warmed the grass, and yellow and blue flowers dotted the field here and there. The smell of grass was light and refreshing after being at sea.

The wind blew the salt from his hair, and he watched as his men came ashore. He had two hundred men still under his command, Northmen, the hard men who took to the Whale Road in search of their fortunes. They were men who lived by axe and shield, entrusting their lives to the Norns and Njorth's fickle weather-fury, trying to earn a place in Valhalla or Thor's hall of heroes, Thruthvangar. Many wore brynjar mail coats, the sign of successful and wealthy warriors. They massed below and looked up at him from their scarred, weather-beaten faces, and he marvelled at so many having sworn to serve him, to be his men until they died, or he released them from their oaths. Hundr had come from nothing, and now, as he looked down upon his men, he felt like a leader for the first time, like a Jarl.

"Warriors, oath men..." he shouted, towering above them. He cleared his throat, hoping they could hear him. Hundr was not fond of making speeches to his men and only did it rarely. He felt himself sweating. Taking a deep breath, he raised his voice and continued. "We have sailed together across the great green. From Ireland to Norway, we bring our blades and shields. We fought hard in Ireland. Many of our oar mates died, good friends and hardy warriors gone to the afterlife. We left Dublin with our purses empty and in need of filling." He paused. A tide of indistinct murmuring rumbled across the beach, and he saw men shift their feet and shake their heads. "We showed our mettle by raiding Orkney, the island of the famed warrior Ketil Flatnose, and we took his silver." There were a few grunts of dissension amongst the throng at the mention of that, yet there were more nods than shaking heads. "Black Gorm and Rollo the Betrayer broke their oaths, and they stole the Sea-Stallion, along with King Harald's sword of kings, the Yngling blade of his ancestors. Today, I have returned that sword to Harald. Einar Rosti himself fought his way into a burning hall to retrieve it, adding more lustre to his already burnished reputation." The men thumped their chests and stamped their feet at the mention of Einar's name. "King Harald has the sword and will make himself King of all Norway. We will fight for Harald and lend our blades to his cause."

"What do we care if Harald Fairhair is King of the North?" called a voice.

Hundr couldn't place it but saw the men turn to it and nod to one another.

"You are right. It is nothing to us if Harald becomes the King of all Norway. But he will reward us if we fight for him."

"What if he loses? I hear Kjotve the Rich has twice the men that Harald does," came another voice.

"Harald has the sword of kings," said Hundr. He did not believe in the sword's magic, but he knew his men were a superstitious lot, and a blade of the gods would give them confidence. "When he is King, he will grant us land, a place of our own in Norway."

"What do we want with land?" called a different man.

"You can't hump land," came another, and there was a ripple of laughter.

"With land, we have a safe base each winter. I grow tired of spending long cold winters with Jarls and Lords who only feed us begrudgingly because we pay and because they fear us. Many of you have wives on distant shores. We can have our own land and winter together. Bring all of your families there; there will be farms and good land for all of us."

"If I wanted to be a farmer, I would have stayed with my father and mother in Jutland," said a man.

"I should have stayed in Jutland with your mother," replied a warrior, causing raucous laughter.

"Land gives us wealth," said Hundr. "It gives us security and a future. Each summer, we can sail the Whale Road for silver and blood. We will still honour Odin and bring our blades to foreign shores, but while we do it, our wives and families will be safe on land. We have won with our bravery and battle skill. Life is short and grim in this world. Let us master it whilst we still draw breath. Let us be warriors, but also landowners." He paused, but there was no comment from the men this time. He let his eye pass over them, his brave warriors, and they looked at him with hope. Hundr thought his ambition was now their ambition, a future for them and their families, and the promise of more adventures on the Whale Road. "So, now we find Black Gorm and punish him for his betrayal. We will kill Gorm and return to Harald. We will fight to become the richest Vikings in all of Midgard!"

The men roared their approval, and Hundr strode down the slope. The men greeted him warmly, clasping his hand and slapping him on the back. His heart leapt as he marched. He had the loyalty of his men; he was part of something and the leader.

Rain fell onto the still waters of the fjord, pitting its surface with myriad circles and filling the bay with a soft rustling sound. The afternoon had turned to early evening as the Seaworm had rowed across the still waters to bring Hundr and Einar to the island where King Harald had made his temporary headquarters. They stood beneath a clutch of tall spruce trees, and Hundr leant against a rough trunk, watching as Harald exchanged pleasantries with a group of finely garbed men.

"Easterners," said Einar, arms folded across his chest, glaring at the King.

"Rus," Hundr agreed, recognising the people of his homeland with their shaved heads and topknots ringed with silver. They wore bright tunics beneath fine mail, and Hundr's dead eye socket pulsed as he watched them.

"Your people?"

"You are my people now, Einar. But yes, I grew up amongst such men."

"When you were the son of a Prince?"

"Something like that," said Hundr, and he sighed. He rarely spoke of his childhood. Only once, during a desperate time in Northumbria, had he let slip that he was the son of a Prince of the Rus. However, he had failed to disclose that he was one of many bastard sons of the prince of a great Rus city. Seeing the Rus warriors with Harald brought back memories of those sad and agonising days.

"I wish they would stop wagging their cheese pipes so we can get on this," grumbled Einar.

"We will be away soon. We will take the Windspear, she is faster than the Sea-Stallion, and we will make up ground on them." Hundr could see the taut frustration on Einar's face. It was understandable—they had retrieved the

Yngling sword, and Hundr had promised Einar they would now be off in pursuit of Black Gorm the berserker and Finn Ivarsson. First, however, he must talk to Harald. There was praise to receive for recovering the blade, and they required permission for the journey they must make.

There was bowing and clasping of forearms between Harald, Rognvald and the Rus before the latter strode away towards the area where Harald's men had stretched sailcloth to make tents, and the smell of roasting meat and burning wood beckoned invitingly across the island. Rognvald leant into Harald and whispered in his ear, and the King turned to where Hundr and Einar waited. He smiled broadly and spread his arms wide.

"The great adventurers return," Harald bellowed. He waved them towards him and shouted for ale. He wore a brynjar which filled out his slight frame, and his famously long hair was braided at his back in intricate plaits with silver thread running through it. "Rognvald has told me everything, Einar. How is your hand?"

"I'll live," Einar said, holding up his bandaged hand.

"Rognvald also tells me Kjotve has assembled an army."

"Yes, King Harald," Hundr affirmed. "He has

many ships and many men. He has more ships than you, I think."

"This is good news. Finally, the turd comes out to fight. I never thought he had it in him. We can finish this in one battle, with one strike of the Yngling sword."

"So, you will fight, then?"

"Of course," said Harald, his bright eyes narrowing. "But we must be careful. Kjotve has many men, as you say. More than us, maybe. We must bring them to war, but war isn't only battles. It is food, sickness, water and ships. We must fight them at a place of our choosing and at a time of our choosing. Leading them to the right ground is as important as bravery in the shield wall, but more subtle."

"They were Rus?" said Hundr, nodding at the backs of the retreating men.

"They were. They share your accent. Aren't you a man of the East?"

"I am. What news have they of the river cities?" Hundr spoke of Kyiv and Novgorod, the mighty cities built along the trade routes between the West and East. All manner of goods came up the wide rivers which cut through the lands of the Rus and Khazars, silks and spices from the East, and furs and blades from the west. Such trade had made the Rus rich and powerful. It had been the place of Hundr's birth in what seemed like a different life when he bore a different name and longed for the sea.

"They say they come to assure me of peace between my kingdom and theirs and to keep the trade routes open. They bring gifts of silver coins bearing the strange marks of the mussel-folk, better silver than our coins and even better than those of Frankia and Wessex." Harald touched a finger to his nose and winked at Hundr. "But they really want to see what kind of man I am and how strong my army is. They will report back to their Prince. He will decide if I am a threat to his kingdom or not."

"Are you?"

"No," said Harald, and he laughed to himself. "Not yet anyway."

"Their Prince is still Rurik?"

"Yes, Rurik rules in Novgorod and all the Rus, or so his men say. What do you know of Prince Rurik?"

He is my father, even though he never treated me as such. "Just his reputation, nothing more."

"One of his sons is here, Yaroslav. The man with the fish scale armour and the long moustaches," said Harald, and he pointed at one of the Rus.

Hundr looked across the green, luscious grass of the island to where the Rus took plates of food from Harald's men. He had not recognised his half-brother at first, but looking at him there across the camp, snatched Hundr's breath away. Hundr clenched his hand around the hilt of his sword and tried his best to keep his face steady and free from emotion. He did not want Harald to see his reaction. The King had shown himself to be both clever and cunning, and it would not serve for him to suspect Hundr's past. Hundr was sweating and tore his eyes away from Yaroslav, forcing down the memories which threatened to flood his mind and cloud his thinking.

"You have the Yngling blade back, and the misdeeds of the oath breakers amongst my crew are now washed clean," said Hundr.

"The blade is returned, and Bavlos assures me that the ancient god magic is still within it. Its wielder will be King of all Norway."

"Good. We must leave today, Lord King. One of the oath breakers, Rollo, remains with Kjotve," said Hundr, careful not to address Harald's enemy as King. "But the other, Black Gorm, the berserker, has taken a boy under our protection. We must pursue Gorm and the remaining oath breakers. Gorm sails to King Bjorn Ironside in the land of the Svear. I fear that travelling to Upsala is no small journey."

"It is not. You must either sail around the southern tip of Gotland and through islands of treacherous marauders or travel overland. Either way, you would not get there and back in time to fight for me against Kjotve. However, Bjorn is not at Upsala."

"What do you mean, he is King of the Svear, and his fortress is at Upsala?"

"He is King, but I am reliably informed that Bjorn builds a new trading town at the mouth of the River of the Geats, on the west of Svealand. Lödöse is its name, or so I am told. Bjorn would have a trading town nestled between his kingdom and that of the west. He is a clever man. His travels west and south have taught him of the wealth there, so he now builds a town to develop trade nestled in between Denmark and Norway, easily accessible from Frankia and the lands of the Saxons. The Svear always looked to the east for trade and battle. Bjorn realised that the real wealth now lies in the west."

"Which is why Gorm seeks Bjorn." It all suddenly became clear. Hundr had wondered why Gorm would make the long journey around the hook of the lands of the Geats and then around the Svear islands, a journey plagued with danger. A man must sail through the lands of countless Jarls, each one warlike and hungry for plunder. The passage to Dublin would take a few days more, but the reward from Halvdan Ragnarsson would undoubtedly be many times that which Bjorn might pay for his nephew.

"Your oath breaker sees a chance to sell his stolen boy for some quick silver, and then he can be on his way, rich and free of your grasp. Interesting that the son of Ivar the Boneless sails with you, the man who killed his father. There are many sides to you, my one-eyed friend."

Einar shifted his feet and growled, and Hundr smiled at Harald. The King seemingly knew much more of Hundr's business, and no doubt that information had come from Rognvald. But, as the two men were both cunning and well informed, Einar's wariness grew. *A thing to mark for the future.*

Harald looked out at the ships on the fjord.

"Ketil Flatnose has brought his ships and warriors to Kjotve's banner?"

"He has. We saw his men at Agder."

"And his daughter is aboard your ship?"

"She is," said Hundr, and he glanced at Rognvald. Ragnhild had been right. He should have come ashore with Rognvald and presented Harald with the sword and news himself. Now, the King had been afforded time to hear all the details of Agder and Ketil, with time to think on the warp and weft of what all that meant for his war.

"Ketil will hate you even more now. I have met Ketil and thought he would fight for me. But he has chosen a different path. He is your enemy now. I hear she is beautiful?"

"She is easy to look upon, Lord King."

Harald sighed and looked up at the darkening sky.

"Go, chase your prey and save your boy. But I need you with me when I do battle with Kjotve. You are cunning, and you have battle luck. Such things are difficult to come by. You returned the sword, so there is nothing left between us, no oaths and nothing owed. But my offer stands. Help make me King of all Norway, and I will reward you with land. So, kill your berserker, but come back to me in time to do battle."

Hundr nodded.

"I will leave you two of my ships and warriors as a sign of my respect for you, Lord King, and to show my commitment to return and fight in your battle."

The King inclined his head and marched off to join his Rus guests at their meal.

"We might need those men," said Einar as they walked back to shore.

"We won't. Gorm only has one ship, and the Windspear will catch him. We'll take the Seaworm too, in case we get in trouble. We will hunt him, Einar, and I will kill him for breaking his oath. I promise we will get Finn back and return here to make Harald King of all Norway. We sail tonight on the tide."

SEVENTEEN

The Windspear crashed into the trough, and then her prow rose high, pitching to her stern before dipping again. Her crew laughed and roared at the thrilling and frightening strength of the rolling brown sea, vast and powerful beyond measure. The Windpsear tossed around on the surface like a twig bobbing along a babbling brook, and the younger men of the crew bailed her bilge with red-raw hands, just as Hundr had done years earlier when he had first joined the Seaworm crew.

The wind blew hard and fierce, and Bush sat on his arse in the sloshing water, hauling on a seal hide rope, bellowing orders which were snapped away between the roar of the wind and the mighty crash of the waves on the oak hull. The sail was full, and most of the crew huddled close to the steerboard to keep the ship's bow high. Einar fought with the steerboard, one moment leaning into its spar and then hauling it back, red-faced and teeth bared, fighting to keep her on course towards his prey.

Hundr tilted his head against the stinging rain as it whipped his face, and the air was thick with the creaking of ropes and the groaning of her hull timbers carved from sturdy oak. They raced south on the wind, around Norway's coastline and towards the lands of the Svear. A figure huddled in a fox fur cloak waddled along the deck, passing a hand from rope to rope and reeling from the roll of the ship. The hood fell back, and Hundr's stomach somersaulted as he saw Sigrid grimacing at the Whale Road's embrace. He cursed himself for a fool, feeling as nervous as a bold child at her approach. Then, just as she came within two paces of him, the ship pitched forwards violently. Sigrid let out a yelp as a surge of water splashed across the deck, spraying them both with ice-cold salt water. She fell forward, and Hundr caught her in his arms, then helped her to her feet to hold on to the mast.

"I am sorry. I do not mean to be a burden," she apologised, pulling the hood about her face. Her eyes were piercing blue, pale with pure black at their centre.

"You are no burden. Even old sea dogs like Einar and Bush could not walk the deck steadily in this storm," Hundr replied.

"Tell me how I can earn my place," she said, wiping a slender hand down her face to wash away the seawater. "The men contribute. They work the rigging and bail the bilge. They clean the timbers and furl the sail. How can I help?"

"You said before that you know weapons?"

"I do. My father's men taught me the bow and the spear," she said, lifting her chin.

"Do you know how to bind a wound or set a broken bone?"

"Yes, I have helped tend to my father's wounded warriors many times."

"Then that is how you will earn your keep. You should stay close to Ragnhild. She will keep you busy."

"I have tried. She is not an easy person to talk to."

"True," Hundr laughed. "Ragnhild is a famous warrior, and she can be as spiky as a hedgehog's arse, but she will come around, don't worry. I can talk to her for you?"

"No. If she is going to respect me, I must win her over myself."

"Well, the best way to do that is through action, not words," he said.

Sigrid thought about that, looking across the deck to where Ragnhild tied off a loose halyard rope.

"Do you regret your decision to leave Agder?" Hundr asked.

"No, I do not. I am not destined to be a peace cow or a vessel for a man's child." She pulled her cloak around her and stared hard into Hundr's one eye. "My father built a glorious name for himself. Why should I not do the same?"

"You will prove your mettle soon enough. Why did your father ally with Kjotve?"

"King Kjotve the Rich, you mean?"

Hundr smiled and shrugged his shoulders at that.

"Why not ally himself with Harald?"

"Harald is ruthless and greedy. He's already a king, yet he wants to make himself King of all Norway when there has never been one before. My father feared that if he fought for Harald and helped him win the throne, Harald would soon come for Orkney and take it for himself. Men die, and women and children suffer for Harald's ambition. I think my father had the right of it. Harald should be fought."

"Did Ketil come to that decision himself, or did Rollo pour it into his head?"

"Rollo came to speak for Kjotve, and my father made him a prisoner to punish his arrogance. But, yes, Rollo and my father often talked, late at night, by the roar of the fire."

"What was so wrong with Thorir Haklag that you would run away and join the men who stole your father's hoard? Ketil is furious, no doubt."

"Thorir is a famous warrior, building his own reputation as a berserker and brave fighter. But I do not love him; I barely know him. He is a brutal man, and a life lying underneath him, being his lady, is not the life for me. It is not the life I am meant for; I feel it. The gods have more planned for me."

She stared at the sea, her pale eyes quivering and her jaw set firm.

"I too ran away from my home, long ago, to make my path," Hundr said, surprising himself that he was so forthcoming. He rarely spoke of the days before he had joined Einar's crew. But he sensed something in Sigrid, a similarity. He knew how she felt and the courage it must have taken for her to run away.

"Where was your home?"

"East. An unhappy place. I think the gods reward us for bravery and daring. They bring us luck and strength if we defy the world and do them honour with our deeds. You have made enemies, I fear. It will shame Thorir that his wife-to-be left with a sea Jarl. Kjotve will be maddened that we shame his son, and it dishonours your father. His situation with

Kjotve will now be a difficult one."

"I know," Sigrid said, and suddenly her shoulders sagged, and she looked at the deck. She leant against the mast carved from a golden fir tree, and Hundr thought he saw a tear roll down her cheek. She cuffed at it and pushed loose strands of hair away from her face. The sea sprayed them again with its icy spit, and Sigrid looked at Hundr through hooded eyes. "I love my father, and I have dishonoured him. The gods laid an opportunity before me when I saw you that night, standing ready to fight. I know your reputation. Men tell tales of the Man with the Dog's Name and his crew of fighters. The man who killed Ivar the Boneless and Eystein Longaxe. Some say you are the champion of all the Northmen. I wanted that life, a life at sea and at war. I want to go to Valhalla when I die. Mine is not a life for weaving, smiling, and being humped by Thorir Haklag. Your face is cruel, but I think you have a good heart."

She said those last words and let her eyes wander across Hundr's scarred face, and he wanted to raise his hand to cover the ruin of his empty eye socket. It ached in the cold, and the salt water stung deep inside it. And then, they stood together in silence for some time, shivering in the wind's whip and the sea's spite.

They chased Black Gorm the berserker across a ferocious sea, speeding across the Whale

Road towards Bjorn Ironside, another son of Ragnar Lothbrok and the only one of those famous sons who wasn't an enemy of Hundr. Finally, the day turned to night, and the sea calmed. The crew threw the sail across the deck to make an awning and settled down to sleep between watches. Each man had a meal of fish, hard bread, and a cup of ale. Hundr slept beneath the steerboard, and as he drifted off amidst the sway of the boat, he thought of Sigrid and her golden hair, and of his old life, in the time before he was Hundr.

The boy was shivering, clothed in light trews and a jerkin which was too short in the arms and at the waist. They were child's clothes, summer clothes. Yet it was winter, and a thick white blanket of snow covered the city. His breath misted in the air before his face, and his ears hurt because they were so cold. Velmud huddled with the hunting dogs in a long kennel close to his father's stables. The dogs were warm at night and did not scorn his presence. It was morning, and the light shone through the cracks in the faded wooden planking that formed the kennels' walls. The dogs stirred from their slumber as Velmud awoke. His stomach growled, and his mouth was dry. There was a low trough of water which the dogs drank from, and Velmud crawled to it to take a drink. The surface of the trough was frozen in a sheet of ice, and Velmud leant over it to use his elbow to break through the frozen cap and get through to the water beneath, but he fell back, surprised at the face staring back at him.

Velmud thought of himself as a boy, a lad who still mourned each day and night for his dead mother. She had passed away in the summer of that year. Pain had eaten her up from the inside out, and she had died in her bed. The person he saw in the trough's fog-ice was a young man with a broad face framed by a wispy beard. He looked at himself again, a boy no longer. He had grown tall, that much he knew. Since his mother had died, no one had brought him winter clothes to keep him warm, and the only food he ate was what he could scrounge up for himself amongst the scraps of the palace kitchen and the food thrown out for the animals.

He smashed his elbow through the ice and plunged his head into the freezing water, its icy sting both refreshing and painful on his frozen ears and face. Velmud drank deep of the water and came up short of breath from the cold. He brushed his long hair back from his face and stroked the dogs who had kept him warm during the night and likely stopped him from freezing to death. Finally, Velmud left the kennel and made his way to the practice square. He had not attended his daily practice for weeks and knew his master would scold him. Velmud wrapped his arms around himself, shivering as he stalked through the city streets—the mud of its lanes and streets frozen solid and hard under his feet. Velmud did not have boots. Instead, he wore leather shoes, soft and worn from use. Summer shoes. His toes curled up at the ends as the shoes were too tight on the sides, and one had ripped open at the seam a week earlier.

Velmud arrived at the training square and paused, watching the weapons master at his practice. He moved through the movements of the sword, slowly and deliberately. His form was perfect, and he moved as gracefully as one of the court dancers. Velmud shuffled over to him, head bowed and wringing his hands. He knelt on the hard, cold floor.

"Ah, Velmud, you see fit to return to your training," said the master, stopping his movements and standing before Velmud with the tip of his sword resting on the ground. "Your father, the prince, has allowed you to practice with your noble brothers all these years, and this is how you repay him? By not turning up and skulking in the shadows?" He leant forward and wrinkled his nose. "By the gods, but you stink. I told you to find suitable clothes." The master's words trailed off as Velmud met his gaze. Anger turned to a nod of understanding and a shake of his head. "You are here now, so let's practice. The next time you fail to present yourself will be the last."

Velmud rose to his feet, and the master looked up at him and took a small step backwards. "Thank you, master. I will not be absent again," he promised.

"You are still growing. If we feed you properly, you will make a mighty man indeed," said the master, gripping Velmud's shoulder. Velmud looked down at him. The weapons master was greying, and his hair was thinning on top. He had to look up to meet Velmud's gaze. "Very well, sword first."

Velmud picked a practice blade from the master's table. It was a wooden sword filled with lead to give the weight of a proper weapon. The grip was smooth to the touch. He held it out before him and loosened his muscles. For longer than he could remember, Velmud had practised daily with sword, spear, axe, and shield. The feel of the weapon was familiar, and Velmud closed his eyes, controlling his hunger and focusing on the weapon, its balance and forms.

"Begin," barked the master. Velmud moved through the cuts, thrust, parry, lunge. He went through the guards, high and low, and brought himself into a controlled stance, panting and sweating. The master came for him, feinting high and striking low, but Velmud blocked the cut and came about and inside the master's guard to hold the wooden blade at his throat. "Good," said the master, and he rewarded Velmud with a rare smile.

"Try that on me, bastard," came a drawling voice across the square. Velmud turned to see his half-brothers watching him. The three young men were armed with their training weapons, and Velmud sighed, wishing they had learned by now not to challenge him. There were the pure blood sons of

the prince, where Velmud was his bastard to a slave woman. Bastard or not, he was their better when it came to fighting.

"If I win, I get your coat and your boots," said Velmud, pointing his sword at the elder of the three. He was the prince's heir, dark-haired and strutting with the confidence of wealth and royalty. The heir laughed, and his brothers laughed with him.

"Very well. You look like a beggar, and you need the clothes. When you lose, you will not return here again. We had thought you had left already, to take up your life as a nithing. Digging holes, tending to pigs, or carrying rocks. Or whatever other drudgery peasants and slaves do for work." He sneered, and his brothers laughed again. "Lose, and you will begone from this place. You will never amount to anything. You are a lowborn bastard and will always be nothing."

The boots were trimmed with fur, as was the thick coat, and Velmud beckoned his half-brother on. He screamed like a wolf and came at Velmud smiling and swinging his sword expertly, each lunge straight and perfect, each cut controlled and powerful. Velmud danced away from him with ease, enjoying the strain on his face as he tried desperately to strike a blow. His brother snarled and overreached with a lunge, but Velmud stepped in and headbutted him hard and square on the nose. His brother fell to his knees and dropped his practice sword, covering his ruined nose with his hands. The other two took *a step forward, but Velmud warned them back with an outstretched sword. He had always been better than them, always faster, stronger and more ruthless.*

"Coat and boots," Velmud hissed. His brother pulled them off, keeping one hand on his nose, which poured thick, dark blood across his mouth and splashed on the cold ground.

"Your name will never be known," spat his brother, his speech muffled by the cloying blood in his throat. "My name will be roared by armies and known across the world when I am the prince of this city. No one will know your name, you will never have a reputation, and you will live as a nithing, denied Valhalla. I am the son of a prince, and you are the son of a whore. You are nothing," he bellowed.

The other brothers ran to help him to his feet. Velmud dropped his practice sword. He pulled on the boots and coat and ran. As he dashed through the city, his brother's words rang around his head. He cannoned into people rising to their morning's work, traders and soldiers. They cursed him as he ran. Eventually, Velmud reached his hovel and scrambled at the frozen earth with his hands, his nails splitting on the hard soil. He wept, then sobbed. Tears flooded down his face, and snot dribbled into his wispy beard. Velmud found his small box of treasures—a brooch and some hack silver given to him by his mother and kept safe for such a moment. He stuffed the trinkets into his coat and set off running again. Velmud was determined to become something. He ran from the city gates, then along the wide riverbank and travelled for days, and weeks, ever northwards. He would forge a reputation; he would become someone. He would show his brothers what a warrior like him could achieve, and he would earn a place in Valhalla.

Hundr woke with a start, jerking up from his blanket. The memories of himself as Velmud were thick in his mind, and he shook them away with the sleep from his eyes.

"Svealand," came a shout from the prow, and that man blew a long low note on a horn to wake the crew. They had sighted the coast of the Svear. Soon, they would reach Lödöse and the kingdom of King Bjorn Ironside, son of Ragnar Lothbrok.

EIGHTEEN

Einar watched the low, brown coastline of western Sweden come into view from the horizon's haze. The ships had emerged from the previous day's storm unscathed other than some loose ropes and a lost oar. He steered the Windspear towards the estuary mouth of a river, visible from the sea as a gash carved into the landscape, but which Ragnhild and Hildr had assured him was the mouth of the River of the Geats and where they would find Bjorn's town of Lödöse.

"Let's hope Finn is here," said Hildr. She sat on the edge of the steerboard platform, working at new fletchings on some worn arrows in her leather quiver. She had already checked the spare strings of her recurved bow and wiped the stave clean to keep the corrosive seawater out of the wood and horn construct, which gave the weapon its immense power.

"If he is, we will get him to safety." Einar nodded. The sail snapped taut under a gust of wind, and Einar leant into the tiller as the ship lurched off course under the wind's power. The eye sigil on the lofty sail stood high and bright as they made course for the river ahead.

"Do you think Bjorn would ransom him?"

"He will pay Gorm for his nephew, I think. He is blood, the grandson of Ragnar Lothbrok. Bjorn would not leave his blood in the hands of a man like Black Gorm. But I do not know if he would keep him safe or return Finn to Halvdan. There was no love lost between Bjorn and Ivar. In the end, they almost came to blows in Frankia. You saw it as well as I."

"I did," she said, pulling a fletch tight with her teeth. "Bjorn and Hundr liked each other in Frankia. They fought back-to-back to kill Duke Robert the Strong. Gorm might not find Bjorn so welcoming when he learns how he came by his nephew."

"Maybe. I just wish we hadn't taken so long to get here. We spent too long chasing that bloody sword for Hundr's King." Einar had kept his frustration quiet, but it had eaten away at him like a dog gnawing on a bone. He could not sleep; his dreams were plagued by visions of Finn crying and afraid amongst Gorm and his savage crew.

"Hundr's King?"

"He's not my King. We swore an oath after Northumbria never to swear to another Lord again. You were there, you remember?"

"We haven't sworn to King Harald. Hundr is fighting for the King to get what we've always wanted; what you say you want. Land of our own."

"He fights for his own reputation," Einar tutted, yet he regretted the words the moment they escaped his lips. Hildr stopped her work and shot him an angry look. Einar stiffened. "We should have gone after Finn first, then gone after the sword. The boy could be dead. He has harmed no one in his life. I promised to take care of him."

"As did I, and we will." She stood and put her arms around him, nestling her head on his chest. He stroked her soft hair with a calloused hand.

"A ship approaches," came a call from the bow. Einar leant around the sheet rope and shielded his eyes from the sun to look towards the river mouth.

"It doesn't come from the river," he said.

"It must be one of Bjorn's ships patrolling the bay," Hildr reckoned.

"Lower the spar and furl the sail," Einar bellowed to the crew. "Ready the oars."

The crew busied themselves at the rigging and mast, and Einar turned to see Bush had ordered the Seaworm's crew to do the same. Their spar came down in jerking pulls, and Hundr's sigil of the eye collapsed under the weight of the heavy wool sail. The approaching ship bore no standard that Einar could see, and it glided towards them with efficient and well-timed oar strokes, the blades on each side of the hull rising and falling in unison, droplets of shining water dripping from the rising strokes. Hundr was in the bilge. He helped the men tie off the sail and then remove the wooden oar hole plugs along the hull, leaving them dangling on strings.

"Must be one of Bjorn's ships," Hundr called down, cupping his hand around his mouth to shout above the din of the men at work.

Einar nodded. The ship came closer but wasn't showing any signs of slowing down. Her hull became clearer as she drew close, and she was a sleek drakkar similar in size to the Seaworm but smaller than the Windspear. A silver wind vane was at her mast, and that fine piece of carved metal caused Einar to frown. It was familiar. The curve of its prow beast was something he recognised. He squinted and thought that the beast was a horse, arcing towards its own deck with snarling teeth and a flowing mane. Einar felt a hollow drop in the pit of his stomach. It was the Sea-Stallion. Before Einar could roar his warning, he saw Black Gorm lean over the prow. He was stripped to the waist, and Einar thought he saw blood on Gorm's face and chest— the sign of a berserker ready to fight in their wild, ferocious abandon, daubed with blood to spur them on to fight with daring and savagery. Gorm held onto the prow with one arm and lowered himself towards the glistening water. He stretched out his huge, long-handled war-axe and let the blade drag in the water, creating a ripple and then raising the fearsome blade above his head.

"It's Gorm! It's the Sea-Stallion," Einar bellowed, pointing. "Hold the oars, hold the oars!"

The Windspear's crew stared at him open-mouthed, and then, moving slower than time, they turned to look at the ship racing toward them. A dozen oars were already in their holes and prepared to pull, and Einar saw what Gorm intended. The berserkers heaved frantically, ready to ram the Windspear head-on.

"Get the oars in, now!" Hundr roared, scrambling across the deck. He leapt for the chests in the bilge, frantically searching for his mail and tossing weapons to the men.

"Bastard," hissed Hildr, and she wrapped a leg around her bow stave and bent it over her hip to nock a string to the horn hook at its tip. She tested its pull once and then drew an arrow from her quiver.

"The boy," Einar said, suddenly concerned that a stray arrow might kill Finn as readily as one of Gorm's axes.

Hildr nodded and loosed her shaft. It sang across the water, and for a moment, Einar thought it would take Gorm in the chest, but he swayed away, and it flew high over the approaching ship. Gorm laughed and brandished his axe. They were within four strokes now, and Einar let them give one more long pull, and then they swiftly yanked their oars in. Aboard the Sea-Stallion, in one swift and impressive manoeuvre, the two banks of oars slipped inside the ship like the legs of a mighty beetle curling in on itself.

"Get the bastard oars in, now!" Einar shouted, and the crew of the Windspear withdrew their oars, but it was too slow. "Brace yourself."

Hildr loosed another shaft, and a warrior yelped in pain from the Sea-Stallion. She lowered her bow and held onto the sheer strake.

The Sea-Stallion swerved at the last moment, and her hull smashed into the Windspear, raking along her side in a stomach-churning crunch of snapping and splintering timber. Men cried out as oars snapped back with immense force to stave in their ribs like the punch of a giant.

The Windspear canted in the water, and it threw Einar from his feet. For a horrifying moment, he thought she would completely roll over before she righted herself and threw men in the other direction like rags. In one fell swoop, the deck was a shouting, screaming chaos of flying ropes and painful disarray. Gorm's crew poured missiles onto the deck of the Windspear as they scraped along the length of her hull. Arrows and spears thudded home with bloody efficiency.

Kjartan Brandsson fell over the side with a spear sunk deep and bloody in his chest. Einar saw the savage delight on Black Gorm's face as he sailed past, and they locked eyes. The look of triumph turned the berserker's face into a picture of pure joy. Then, as the ships crossed and Einar surged to his feet, he glimpsed a boy hugging the Sea-Stallion's mast. It was Finn Ivarsson, and he was crying. The anguished look of fear on his boyish face forced the war rage to burst explosively from Einar, and it smothered him with anger. He could feel his chest roar before the noise of it left his mouth. He launched himself into a run, and in three strides, he leapt from the deck of the Windspear, surprising even himself with the foolishness as the wind whipped his hair before he landed crashing into the stern of the Sea-Stallion. A thud in his ribs stabbed at him, but he rose, snarling with his axe in one hand while he ripped his seax free with the other. Bearded faces stared at him in surprise, and he suddenly realised he was not wearing his mail and had leapt into a ship of enemy berserkers alone.

Einar stood to his full height, and from the corner of his eye, he saw Hildr staring at him open-mouthed as she and the Windspear sailed beyond the stern of the Sea-Stallion.

"Einar," a small voice cried out, and though he couldn't see him through the gathering line of Gorm's men, he knew it was Finn. Einar heard fear and hope in that voice wrapped up in a desperate scream. A berserker came at him; blood smeared on his scarred face. He had his long-handled war axe in both hands and stepped carefully over a rowing bench before ducking under the halyard. Einar looked beyond his attacker and saw that the Seaworm approached and was ten oar strokes away. The berserker emerged like a wolf from under the halyard. Einar laughed as he glanced at the deck to make sure of his footing. He laughed at the release of his horror at making the rash jump into an enemy ship, from the sheer suicide of facing thirty warriors alone, but also because the berserker was a fool. He came on with a long-handled axe with its enormous blade, the weapon all Gorm's men carried. It was the wrong weapon to wield on a drakkar warship—a vessel narrow across the deck and a criss-cross of rigging, spars and benches. Einar leapt forward and hooked the beard of his axe over the long axe haft. He laughed raucously at the surprise on the berserker's face while he slammed his seax into the side of his head. The broken-backed blade punched through the berserker's temple as though it was rotten wood, and when Einar yanked it free, a spurt of thick red blood flew into the air. Einar kicked the corpse back into the berserkers, crowding them even further so that they had the bleeding body of their crewmate to climb around, as well as the cluttered deck when they came to kill him.

"Kill that bastard," he heard a voice roar from the prow. It was Black Gorm, and his time would come. Two more came forward, and Einar threw his axe at the first man, a short hard throw to bury his axe head in the man's bare chest. The enemy looked down at the weapon protruding from his own body, choked on his own blood, and pitched forward. The second attacker's foot slipped on the glistening blood, which now pooled on the deck, and as he raised a hand to brace himself on the halyard rope, Einar stabbed him in the armpit and then in the neck in two quick blows.

"Odin!" Einar roared. "I am Einar Rosti. I send you warriors for your Einherjar. Bring me luck, bring me strength." He felt the Odin strength in his ageing arms and legs. Suddenly, Einar felt like a young man again, like he had been when he had served Ivar the Boneless as his enforcer. He was a fighter then, famous for Holmgang duelling and fighting when there was no need. But there was a need now. Finn needed him, and Einar howled at the sky like a wolf and brought death to Gorm's berserkers on the deck of the Sea-Stallion. Another snarling warrior came at him, thrusting his axe forward like a spear. Einar grabbed it behind its head and pulled it wide. He stepped in and stabbed his seax into the warrior's guts in four fast blows, ripping open his stomach to slop blue-pink coils onto the deck. The Seaworm came close. He could hear her men shouting, but Gorm's men had learned from the deaths of their shipmates and came at him now holding short knives, rage twisting their faces into masks of hate. They came in a line of three, spanning the deck, the shouts of their men behind them raucous and thumping in Einar's ears. The three approached him as one, stabbing and lunging with their bright blades. He batted one aside with his forearm, and its edge sliced into a line of fire there that made him cry out. Another blade cut across his chest before he could avoid it, and Einar slashed his seax across that man's face to send him reeling. The central warrior lunged, and Einar dodged backwards and struck with the speed of a serpent, thudding his blade into the warrior's hip. The man screamed and grabbed Einar's hair to pull him into a headbutt, and

Einar's vision went black. He fell to his knees, and the first warrior cut across his back with his knife.

Einar felt himself slipping into the dark and thought he must die there under the berserker attack. But then he remembered Finn, the boy who could have been his own son in a different life—the boy who needed him. The Odin rage pumped into his legs, and Einar drove himself upwards, his vision clearing and his seax coming up to cut into the soft flesh beneath his enemy's jaw. He felt another cut on his back and turned to grab that attacker by his beard, clutching a handful of greasy, matted hair in his calloused fist. He dragged the man across the deck in two long steps and threw him overboard. The berserker screamed as he hit the water because the Seaworm was upon him, and Einar turned away before her hull crushed the man's skull. Bush had brought the Seaworm about, and she was bearing down on the Sea-Stallion at an angle so that she would ram the ship, which was no longer under oars, as her crew abandoned their benches to face the wrath of Einar.

The men on the deck cleared, and within four heartbeats, Einar saw Black Gorm grinning at him. He had Finn Ivarsson clasped around the neck and a knife held at his little throat. Gorm opened his mouth to caw his triumph, but the words were snatched away as the Seaworm crashed into the hull of the Sea-Stallion, pitching the ship savagely so that it rolled like a pestle in a bowl. The berserker crew screamed and roared as the impact threw them across the deck, and they ran and slid under the force of it as the ship rolled. Most of them fell into the sea, splashing and thrashing for their lives in the icy salt water, but some, like Einar, had grasped ropes to steady themselves. Einar saw that Gorm had fallen as the ship rolled, and he lay sprawled in the bilge, trying to regain his feet. The men of the Seaworm leapt aboard the Sea-Stallion, and Einar saw Bush and Thorgrim getting amongst the fallen berserkers, hacking at them with their axes. Einar seized his moment. He sprang forward, kicked Gorm in the face to send him flailing, and jumped over him to where Finn was huddled, curled into a ball beneath the mast post. Einar put a bloody hand on the boy's head and stood between him and Black Gorm.

"So, we get to finish our quarrel, Einar Rosti," spat Gorm through bloody teeth as he scrambled to his knees and searched for his weapons in the deck's chaos. The ship still pitched back and forth on the water, and Gorm's knife and axe had slid away from him. "We agreed to fight, to make the square, warrior against wa...."

Einar tensed his shoulders and grabbed the back of Gorm's head with his left hand, and with his right, he stabbed his seax underhand into

Gorm's eye. It was a savage blow, filled with hate and the last of his Odin strength. Gorm wanted one last chance at Valhalla, to fight Einar in the Holmgang they had agreed to fight before he fled his oath on a stolen ship. But now he was dead, his muscled body twitching on the deck of that very drakkar. He had died without a blade, and Einar had denied Gorm the glory of Valhalla. He turned and knelt, wrapping his aching arms around Finn's tiny shoulders.

"It's alright now, boy," he said amongst the cries and shouts of Bush and his crew as they dispatched the last of Gorm's men. There could be no mercy for them, no second chance for oath breakers.

"You came for me," whimpered Finn, looking up at him with a tear-streaked face.

"I came for you. You are safe now, lad."

NINETEEN

"At least we have four ships again," said Ragnhild as they drew close to the Seaworm and Sea-Stallion. The men backed oars as they came alongside the Sea-Stallion, where the deck was a mess of splintered wood and tangled rigging. Hundr could smell the iron tang of blood and the shit stink of dead men who had voided their bowels before death.

"There he is," shouted Hundr, and he blew his cheeks out with relief to see that Einar was still alive. The old warrior stood leaning against the Sea-Stallion's mast with his arm around Finn Ivarsson's shoulders. "He looks pale...like he has seen Valhalla and comes back amongst us."

"He is very brave or very stupid. Jumping onto a ship full of berserkers like that," Ragnhild said, but she was smiling at Einar and would have appreciated the Odin bravery in him making the jump.

"Einar!" Hildr called, and she scrambled across the deck, clambering over the side and onto the Sea-Stallion. She ran to Einar, threw her arms around him, and then knelt to hug Finn. Though she hardly needed to kneel to get to him, Hundr noted, the boy had grown tall. He had tousled chestnut-coloured hair and hugged Hildr close to him as the ships were lashed together.

"Einar looks injured," said Ragnhild. "Where is that weasel of a priest who is always around the boy?" They both swept the deck with their eyes, but there was no sign of Father Darragh. Hundr did not care for the fate of the priest. The boy was safe, which made Einar and Hildr happy, and Hundr had fulfilled his commitments to his crewmates and family.

"We have Ivar's son back now. Let's see what the damage is, and then we can get back to Harald before the war is over," he said.

"It was strange that Gorm came from the south like he was returning from Bjorn rather than heading towards him."

"Looks like we will find out if he spoke to Bjorn or not," Hundr pointed to Lödöse's distant shore from where three ships approached. "Like as not, he never made it to Bjorn. We would not have known where his new trading town was if Harald had not told us. I doubt Bjorn would have let Black Gorm leave Lödöse with his nephew as a prisoner."

"You liked Bjorn. Maybe we should have come to him instead of King Harald for this year's fighting season."

"I did like Bjorn," Hundr admitted. "He was so different from his brothers Ivar and Sigurd. He was as great a fighter as them, a true Lothbrok, but he was also warm and loved by his men. We went to Harald because we knew there was a war in Norway. Where there is war, there is an opportunity for us. We were right to go to Harald. We can get that which we have never had, land and a home for ourselves. Bjorn is building, not fighting, and we are not builders."

Ragnhild smiled at that.

"My home is the Odin temple at Upsala, but you are right in what you say. The crews need a home, for their families, and a base for the winter months."

"You used to speak of returning to your order. Would the Valkyrie take you back after all this time?"

Ragnhild looked at him, and the corners of her mouth turned down as she shook her head softly.

"I do not think so. It has been eight years since most of the sisters died, and I left the High Priest's ranks to fight for you. I have broken my oath during that time. I am more Viking now than Valkyrie."

They both looked out at the light swell of the sea, and a moment of silence passed between them, the comfortable silence only possible between friends. Hundr thought of the friends they had lost in those eight years, especially Kolo, who had been Ragnhild's lover and with whom she had broken her oath of virginity.

"I do not think Odin will hold that oath against you," said Hundr. "You have sent many souls to Valhalla this last eight years. You honour the gods, Ragnhild."

She inclined her head but said nothing and continued staring at the sea's grey swell. The crew busied themselves securing ropes and removing the detritus of the fight from the deck of the Sea-Stallion.

"I told Sigrid that you would look out for her, teach her the ways of the sea," Hundr continued.

"I thought as much," Ragnhild said, tilting her head with a wry grin.

"What do you make of her?"

"She will do, I suppose. She knows weapons, though that is still to be put to the test. Sigrid wants to learn, but she is no Valkyrie. She is the daughter of a Jarl, raised soft."

"She wants to be free of her past. She wants to

carve out her own destiny."

"Just like you."

"I suppose so, yes. The Norns spin our fates, but we can alter what they weave for us. We can force those three hags beneath Yggdrasil to change the pattern of our lives."

"Unless what you see as the change in the weave was actually their plan for your destiny all along."

"You are wiser than you look," Hundr teased, and she punched him in the stomach. He laughed for a moment, enjoying the closeness with Ragnhild. They had shared many moments of danger together, and Hundr loved her like a sister. She was often hard and removed herself from idle conversation, but then Hundr knew he was like that himself. He thought about telling her how much he valued her skills as a fighter and her friendship, but Bush came hirpling up the deck, scratching at his beard and shaking his head.

"We lost four oars, which will need replacing. The hulls of all three ships are scratched, but the timbers are not cracked. We lost Kjartan, and only five men are injured," Bush said, removing his leather helmet lined to run his hand over his pure white scalp.

"Who is injured?" Hundr asked.

"Orm Ruriksson took an axe to his foot. Bloody thing is hanging off. Kare has a nasty gash on his arm. The others are not seriously injured. There are five prisoners."

"Kill them."

"We are light on crew members for the Sea-Stallion; we will need to take men from the Windspear and the Seaworm to man her for the journey back north. That means we will be short on all three ships," said Bush.

"Oathbreakers can't be allowed to live. They betrayed us, and we must show the men that when they swear to me as their Jarl, they are swearing to Odin to serve me until I release them from that oath. If the men don't think I take that oath seriously, it isn't worth anything."

"Very well," sighed Bush, shrugging his shoulders. "Who will do it then?"

Hundr paused and glanced at Ragnhild out of the corner of his eye. Usually, she would leap at the chance to sacrifice to the gods, sing her prayers to the heavens and send souls to honour Odin, Thor, Frey or Freya. But instead, she looked at her boots and kept silent.

"I will do it," Hundr said. "Their oath was to me, so I'll do them all."

Killing a man is no straightforward matter. Hundr did not pity the men he killed in battle.

They were warriors, and all men knew the risks when taking up arms. But to kill a man—to rip his life from the world of men outside of the clash of arms—was something different. Killing men stayed with him. Their faces haunted his dreams. Men slain outside combat were not men he would see again in Valhalla, to drink and feast with, and fight again together. These men, who must be executed for their betrayal, would not go to Valhalla. They were destined for the Skuld world to wander there as nithings for eternity.

"I, too, am an oath-breaker," whispered Ragnhild once Bush had stalked away, barking at a man for tying a loose knot. "I broke my oath to Odin, to my order."

"You are no oath-breaker, Ragnhild," said Hundr.

"I left my order in Northumbria, yet I swore to fight to the death when I took my vows as a girl."

"You came to get me out of Hakon's fortress, fought your way in, and sent many warriors to Valhalla. You saved my life, just as I had saved yours. Odin would surely see it that way. It was a fight of few against many, and you returned the blood debt owed to me."

"One does not simply put an oath aside."

"When we are done here and have won our reward from Harald, if you wish it, we will go to Upsala, and you can ask Odin yourself."

"I should go to Upsala," she agreed, looking at him. Her scarred face was washed free of anger and strength. She looked like an ageing woman, standing there on the deck before the power of the sea. Hundr saw Ragnhild as a warrior, pure and simple. But standing there, she appeared different as she contemplated her life. She had the soft lines of a woman's face; her hair showed grey at the temples, and, were it not for her battle scarring and one eye, she could have been someone's wife or mother. "I should make my peace with Odin."

Hundr held out his hand, and she clasped it in the warriors' grip.

"So be it," he said, and they exchanged a look of friendship, a lingering wordless meeting of their shared single eyes.

Hundr moved down the ship, picking his way around the men who knelt, washing the blood from the deck with bail buckets. He passed by Einar, who sat with his back against the mast. His face was as pale as a fetch, and he grimaced as Hildr washed and tended his wounds. Hundr nodded to Einar, and his old friend nodded back through clenched teeth. The boy, Finn Ivarsson, huddled with his arms around Einar's waist, and he looked at Hundr beneath the wings of his ruffled hair. Hundr tried to smile at him, but it was an awkward gesture. He still couldn't get past the fact that Finn was the son of his greatest enemy, and as the boy grew, Hundr feared he would want revenge for his slain father. He saw the five prisoners kneeling in the prow, their heads bowed and the berserker blood on their faces and chests dried and crusting into tiny flakes.

He could feel the eyes of the crew on him as he moved around benches and ducked under ropes. Grim faces peered at him from across the bows, where the men onboard the Windspear and Seaworm watched to see what he would do. Hundr glanced back across the bay, where the three ships drew closer. He could see the raven banner fluttering from their masts on large triangular standards. A black flag with a white raven flying in the wind, the sign of the sons of Ragnar Lothbrok.

"All you men have sworn to serve me. I am Jarl Hundr, your Lord. You pledge your lives to me as oath men, to fight and crew my ships until you die or until I release you from that oath." He ducked under the spar of the furled mast and came up, meeting Sigrid's blue eyes. Hundr lingered on her. She was a vision of golden-haired beauty amongst the acrid stink of sweat and leather, the ferrous redolence of blood, and his men's bearded, grim faces. He wrapped his right hand around the hilt of his sword, Fenristooth, the cruel ivory carved face warm and rough beneath his palm. Hundr sighed and looked upon the prisoners, the survivors of Black Gorm's crew of betrayers. He thought of the words Mundi had spat at him at Agder—that he was too weak and too forgiving.

"I took these men in when they were defeated outside Dublin city," he shouted so all the crews could hear. "I let them live after I had killed their Lord, Eystein of the Long Axe. They were broken men, then. I let them live because they swore to serve me. They have rewarded that forgiveness with betrayal. I am your Jarl, and my duty is to reward your oaths with silver, war, and reputation. That is why we sail the Whale Road. It is also my duty to uphold and honour our oaths sworn in front of the gods. Without oaths, there is nothing to separate us from beasts in the ditch. So, I condemn these traitors to the Skuld world, to wander there as wraiths for all time."

There was a murmur and a sucking in of breath across the crews, audible above the caw of the seagulls in the sky and the constant sigh of the sea. The berserkers snapped their heads to look at him. Some were twisted in anger, and others became panicked and drawn tight with terror. Hundr drew Fenristooth slowly, letting the hilt scrape against the wooden rim of its fleece-lined scabbard.

"Behold Odin, how we honour you by punishing oath breakers." He whipped the sword across the throat of a frightened man and then brought it back around to plunge it into the chest of a second. His heart raced, and his stomach felt sour as the men died without a blade in their hand, in dishonour. He rested his sword on the throat of the third and laid it open in a wash of blood. Hundr cut the throats of the final two men, and they flopped, thrashing to the deck, pumping their lifeblood onto the dark timbers. "Back to work," Hundr snapped at the open-mouthed, gawping crews. Hundr felt sick. He had to suck in long, slow breaths of sea air to calm himself. It had felt like murder, not like fighting. Such were the hardships of being a leader of men. This was the price, he knew, of his thirst for reputation and silver.

Leading so many hard men, warriors, and killers led Hundr to glory. It had brought him five ships and a small army of men to crew them. He had a reputation, and men knew his name wherever Vikings sailed. Some even said he was the champion of all Northmen. The price of all that was the burden of leadership and the necessity of cruelty. He had not realised that before. Hundr had thought that by forgiving his enemies, his men would think him just and fair, making them fight harder for him. But now he knew they wanted a hard leader, a man who brooked no dissent or betrayal. He had never thought himself such a man, but he supposed that was what he had become.

The three ships came close, and they removed the shields from their sheer strakes to show they came in peace. Hundr watched their oars rise and fall in time, and he wondered if he was any different now from Ivar the Boneless, Eystein, or any of the other men he had fought in his life. He had always considered them evil or as monsters that he should fight and destroy, like the hero in one of his mother's old stories. Maybe they were just men, leaders of Vikings. Hard men like him.

"Is that you, Man with the Dog's Name?" A booming voice called across the distance between the raven ships and his own, snapping Hundr from his thoughts. Hundr saw Bjorn at the prow of the largest ship, a thirty-oar drakkar. He was unmistakable, with his thick, bushy beard and enormous frame.

"It is I, Lord King," Hundr shouted back, raising an arm in salute.

"What are you doing fighting in my waters? Do you come here as a friend or foe?"

"As a friend, King Bjorn. We fought a crew of my own men, oath breakers. Black Gorm, the berserker, was the name of their leader."

"Never heard of him. Must have the reputation of a piece of goat shit," Bjorn shouted, and the men around Hundr sniggered. "I see you showed them the error of their ways." Bjorn pointed to the prow of the Sea-Stallion, where Bush and

Trygve threw the prisoner's bodies overboard.

"When their ship came towards us, I thought he came from your new town."

"No, he did not. I imagine he saw your horrible eye sigil and wanted to kill you for its ugliness. Your man did not set foot in Lödöse."

Hundr was relieved that Gorm had not found succour with Bjorn. If he had sold the boy to his uncle, or if Bjorn had taken Finn by force, it would have made the situation impossible.

"You have fared well, King Bjorn, since last I saw you."

"It did not sit well with me, how it ended in Frankia, with my brother," said Bjorn Ironside as his men brought his drakkar alongside the Sea-Stallion. Bjorn had grown wider around the midriff, but other than that, the last eight years had been kind to the son of Ragnar.

"You had no choice. You had to side with your brother. I was worried you might be my enemy, King Bjorn."

"Ha!" roared Bjorn. He laughed with his head thrown back, pulling the nearest of his crew close to him with one brawny arm, and he pointed across to the Sea-Stallion. "Do you see that scarred pup there? He looks like a piece of weasel shit, but that's the Man with the Dog's Name. Hundr. He and I fought together in

Frankia, alongside Jarl Haesten. He is the man who killed my brother, Ivar the Boneless. We make legends, Hundr, do we not?"

"You are now another son of Ragnar Lothbrok, who is a king. You must be drowning in silver, King Bjorn."

Bjorn laughed again and clapped the hapless man next to him on the back so hard he almost fell overboard.

"Will you stay and feast with me tonight in Lödöse? My new town is just there at the mouth of the river. It will soon rival Birka and Dublin for trade."

"I would love nothing more, but I cannot. I must return to King Harald to help him win a war."

"Harald Fairhair? You serve him?"

"No, Lord King. I do not serve him, but I have committed to help him win his war against Kjotve the Rich."

"Your Harald wants to be king of the world, I hear. He had better not turn his eye to my lands," said Bjorn wagging a thick finger at Hundr.

"No man would fight you willingly, Lord King."

"If you will not stay, how can I help you before you leave?" asked Bjorn, and Hundr smiled. He had feared Bjorn might be his enemy, but he was as warm and welcoming as ever. Hundr asked Bjorn for replacement oars and some food and ale for the journey north. He also promised to visit Bjorn again once the war with Kjotve was over—the war that would see Hundr become a landed Jarl if the fight had not already happened without him.

TWENTY

Bjorn Ironside was as famous for his generosity as he was for his ferocious skill in battle. Hundr drank fine honeyed ale from a cup carved of pale horn. It was thick and delicious, and he wiped the foam from his beard and smiled as he watched his men drink and eat their fill. Bjorn had furnished Hundr with oars to replace those damaged during the fight with Gorm, spare hemp ropes, and an extra woollen sail for the Sea-Stallion. The men had cheered Bjorn as his crew had loaded barrels of beer and steaming joints of pork and lamb aboard the Windspear.

Hundr had thanked Bjorn, and they'd made their friendship good. He looked forward to returning to visit Bjorn again, as he'd promised. It was a promise Hundr had been happy to make. He liked Bjorn, but he was a simple man to like.

He was brave and had earned a reputation as a fighter, yet he was also kind, full of laughter, and loved nothing more than drinking and wrestling with his men. It was a trait Hundr saw lacking in himself. Hundr knew himself to be cold and withdrawn. He had always been alone and did not find it easy being close to and amongst others.

A strong westerly wind blew, so Hundr had not waited off Lödöse to allow his men to enjoy Bjorn's ale and food. Instead, he had ordered the sails hoisted, and the three ships had begun their journey back towards Harald in Rogaland on Norway's west coast. That first day, sailing had been good, with a fair wind and calm sea, and the ships had glided across the Whale Road like ravens on the wing, crossing the Skagerrak in excellent time. Hundr had ordered the small fleet to anchor close to shore off the coast of what he thought was somewhere between Grimstad and Kjevik. The waters were choppy, and the night was clear, with a hint of red on the horizon. He'd broken open Bjorn's ale and food and let the men eat and drink their fill.

The crews sang and told tales of old battles and stories of the gods. Hundr did his best to follow Bjorn's example and move amongst them, sharing a drink with men he rarely spoke to, men like Sigvarth Trollhands, so named for his huge and strong hands, Amundr Ravnsson, and

Skapti the Geat. All good men and warriors of reputation. They laughed and drank, and Hundr fell asleep on the Windspear, under the sail awning spread across the deck. The Norns had brought him luck, and the wrongs of Gorm and Rollo's betrayal had been made right. *There would be one more hard fight,* he thought, and then Harald would be the King of all Norway. Then, Hundr and Einar would have what they had always wanted. Hundr closed his eye and hoped for dreams of what that place might be like, perhaps a fine harbour with good fishing and a long hall with a warm fire. He imagined flocks of sheep in the hills and men to till and farm the land who would pay him tithes. It was a dream worth fighting for, worth dying for.

The next morning was filled with headaches and groans. It was a chill morning, and a fog rested above the sea to the south. Droplets of its moisture made Hundr's hair and beard damp. He rose from the deep sleep that comes from having too much ale and searched the deck for the water barrel. He stepped around snoring bodies and found it behind the mast post. Hundr skimmed the floaters from the top with his hand and dunked his head into the cold, fresh water. It was icy, and as he rose, he gasped from its chill and wiped the water from his face. The three ships were moored and lashed together to allow the crew to move across the decks during the previous night's festivities, and Hundr saw movement on the deck of the Seaworm and the Sea-Stallion. He felt a clap on his shoulder and turned to see Bush grinning at him from under his stained helmet liner.

"Some amount of ale supped last night," he said, and he hawked up a gobbet of phlegm. Then, he let out a monstrous fart and splashed his own face from the water barrel. "Does the lads good, a good night's drinking."

"But not our heads," muttered Hundr, wincing as the words rattled around his skull. "Best get them up. The wind is not with us today, so we'll need the oars."

Bush looked up at the wind vane atop the Windspear's mast post, a curved piece of silver inlaid with a boar's head. It signalled a light wind blowing north, yet they must head west.

"Not a day to pull an oar," he grumbled and set about rousing the crew with shouts and more than a few friendly kicks in the arse.

Hundr saw Ragnhild and Sigrid leaning on the bows and looking out into the fog. They were talking together, out of his hearing, but he was glad to see them talking at least. Hundr stepped over Kare and Ingolfr, who had fallen asleep with their heads resting on each other and their horns of ale still beside them.

"Did you enjoy the ale?" he said, standing next

to Sigrid and smiling down at her. She glanced up at him, and he saw her gaze again, exploring his dead eye and scarred face. Hundr turned away, feeling his face flush. Bush had often told him to wear a patch and that his face put the men off their food, albeit only in jest. Hundr did not care; he felt the scarring added to his reputation and gave him authority beyond his years. But now that Sigrid's blue eyes found the empty socket and jagged line where Hakon Ivarsson had cut him with a red-hot knife, he suddenly felt his face reddening, and before he realised it, he had reached up to cover the hollow eye with his hand.

"It was delicious," Sigrid nodded. "But I think some of the crew might have enjoyed it a little too much." She smiled and looked back at the groaning men, rising gingerly under Bush's orders.

"Where's Einar?" asked Ragnhild, not taking her eyes off the rolls of fog.

"He slept under the steerboard with Hildr and the boy," Hundr answered. "I didn't get to talk to him last night." He had wanted to talk to Einar to ensure his wounds were cleaned and not too painful. But Einar had seemed at peace and happy to spend the evening with Finn and Hildr, so Hundr had left him alone. At the stern, he heard the cry of Orm Ruriksson, who had lost half his foot in the fight with Gorm. It was a terrible wound, and Hildr and Ragnhild had done their best to clean and bind it.

"That man will be lucky to survive. He had his wound in the bilge's filth when he fell. If it smells today, he's done for," said Ragnhild, and she touched her silver Odin spear amulet for luck. "What's that?" she pointed out towards the depths of the sea fog.

A shadow appeared there, the mist shifting around it like the fetch of a great giant of legend. Hundr leant forward to stare hard at the shape, but it disappeared into wet clouds. He could hear the grunts of his men and the creaks of his ship's timbers, but out there in the shrouded waters; he was sure he heard the shouts of a man, a coarse and muffled order barked by an unseen captain.

"Did you hear that?" he asked, whispering. Hundr held his breath, looking at Ragnhild and Sigrid for acknowledgement that they, too, had heard it.

"It's a ship," said Ragnhild. "It's more than one ship."

"Get the ships untied, make the oars ready," Hundr shouted, turning towards the deck.

"Thor save us," gasped Sigrid. "It's my father."

"Bush, Einar!" Hundr bellowed. "It's Ketil Flatnose and his fleet. Get the ships under oar now!" But he knew it was too late. His stomach turned over, and he gripped the sheer strake as five curved hulls slid from the mists, black sails flapping in the light wind but full enough to drive them forward and stretch the wool to show Ketil's sigil of two crossed axes.

"I'll take the Seaworm," Einar said, dashing across the deck and using his axe to hack at the ropes which tied Hundr's ships together.

"Bush, get to the Sea-Stallion. Get her moving; get the oars out. We move, or we die," stressed Hundr. Ketil Flatnose had hunted him, and the wily old sea-Jarl had taken his opportunity to fall on his prey like an eagle. Hundr was outnumbered and stuck like a pig in a pen. His ships were stationary, and even if they could get the oars into the water and the anchors up, Ketil was too close. Hundr looked at Ragnhild, and she had her eyes raised to the heavens, her lips moving silently in prayer to Odin.

"Ragnhild, take Sigrid and Hildr and start shooting at the bastards. Skapti, Sigvarth, make a shield wall on this side," Hundr ordered. The Windspear was side on to Ketil's fleet, and they would never be able to move in time to get away. Hundr doubted Ketil would ram them. He was a Viking, and he would love his ships as much as he loved his wife, and to ram them would sink the Windspear, but it would cost Ketil a vessel or two. The Windspear was a beautiful, long drakkar warship, larger than any of the ships Hundr saw approaching. Ketil would lick his lips at the prospect of taking her, of killing Hundr and raising his black sail on her mast.

Ragnhild, Sigrid, and Hildr were at the prow and had fired their arrows across the waters. One slammed into the hull of the leading ship, and another whistled over the enemy deck and out of sight. Sigvarth came next to Hundr and grinned up at him. He was a short man, but he was barrel-chested and a fierce fighter. An arrow thudded into the hull, only a handsbreadth from where Hundr stood, and he showed his teeth in a grimace.

"Get that shield wall here, now!" he roared. A warrior in the stern yelped, and Hundr saw him fall with an arrow in his chest. They were at sea, and so none of the men wore mail or breastplates, which meant they were susceptible to missile strikes. "Break out the chests, fetch my brynjar," he ordered. To fall into the sea wearing a coat of mail meant death. It would sink a man faster than a stone, but Hundr did not plan to fall into the sea, and nor did he want to die with an arrow in his chest.

Ketil's ships split. Two came for the Windspear, aiming right where Hundr stood behind Sigvarth's shield, one from each end veered away to come about the sides of Hundr's ships to attack them from the opposite side, and one other came for the lashed prows. Ketil was no fool. He knew his work, and he had come to kill. Hundr had raided his hall, stolen his silver, and taken his daughter away from her betrothal. He saw a baleful figure with a grey beard and shining helmet on the deck of the leading ship. The warrior wore mail and held a bright sword aloft. Hundr knew he was Ketil without ever having met the man. He was a great sea Lord, who had come for vengeance and blood.

"They are wearing mail," said Hundr to the rank of men who had made the shield wall across the Windspear's deck. "When they try to board, throw them into Njorth's embrace, let the bastards drown."

Ingolfr hefted a spear, took two quick steps and launched the weapon across the water. It sailed through the air in a bright arc, and Hundr thought it would take Ketil in the chest before an arm snapped out to catch it mid-flight. That warrior spun and launched the weapon back towards the Windspear, and it thudded into the trunk of the warrior next to Sigvarth, throwing him backwards and spraying blood on Hundr's face. He wiped the hot liquid from his cheek, heart racing from the shock of the strength of the spear throw. Hundr looked back at the black-sailed ship and took a step backwards. The thrower was Rollo the Betrayer, mailed and ready to fight alongside the man who had held him prisoner on Orkney before Hundr had freed him. *Another man I saved and should have let die.*

A young warrior scampered to Hundr with his eyes lowered, and he flinched as an arrow whipped past his head. He carried Hundr's mail and a shield. Hundr bent to pull his brynjar over his shoulders and took the shield from the warrior, clasping his hand around the wooden grip inside the bowl of its lime wood boards. The warrior grinned at him, a toothless, mirthless grin, and then died as the black feathers of an arrow shot from his throat in a wash of scarlet. Hundr roared his anger and turned to face Ketil and Rollo, ready to fight and die. Then without hesitation, he barged his way into the shield wall and overlapped his shield with Sigvarth's.

"Are you ready to fight?" he shouted to his men, and they responded with a clipped roar. "These men come for our blood and our lives, but we are not easy men to kill. We are the sea wolves of the one eye, and we will send these whoresons to the Skuld world." Hundr ripped his sword free of its scabbard and banged its steel on the iron boss of his shield. His warriors roared and bellowed their defiance, and the black ship swung her bows to face the Windspear, rocking her hull and making Hundr stumble backwards under the wave of her coming.

The whole shield wall line had tripped backwards as the Windspear canted before the force of Ketil's ship, and Flatnose's warriors leapt to board her. A man screamed as he misjudged the distance and fell into the gap between the ships, sinking to his death. A tall, thin man landed heavily on the deck in front of Hundr and came up brandishing a spear before his hook-nosed face. Hundr put his shoulder behind his shield and charged at him. He thrust the iron boss upwards to smash the hooked nose and drove the warrior over the bows and into the water to join his shipmate.

"Kill the bastards," Hundr shouted, and he stabbed the tip of his sword into the throat of a man who stumbled as he landed on the Windspear's deck. The deck surged beneath his feet, throwing Hundr sideways as the second of Ketil's ships came alongside the Windspear. His arm hit a rigging line, and Fenristooth dropped from his grip to clatter on the deck. Hundr knelt and scrambled for its hilt, but a warrior stamped on his forearm, and Hundr looked up to see a short, hafted axe coming for his head. He closed his eyes, but the blow did not come. He rolled away and saw Sigvarth hacking into his attacker with his seax, blood spattering his face and chest. Hundr snatched up Fenristooth and crashed into the chest of the nearest enemy.

The deck of the Windspear was chaos. The shield wall had failed to thrust Ketil's men back as the clash of ships on the water had thrown warriors around like a rabbit in a hunting dog's jaws.

"Bastard," a voice boomed, and an axe came

for him. Hundr parried it with his sword and pushed his attacker back with his foot. "You took my silver and stole my daughter. Die now, dog's name." The man was of a similar size as Hundr but with a silver beard and a shining helmet which ringed his eyes. He was broad across the shoulder, and his mail stretched across a heavy paunch. Behind the helmet, Hundr could see a nose like a turnip, spread across the old warrior's face, broken in some fight long ago. It was Ketil Flatnose, and he came at Hundr again, chopping down with his axe. Hundr swayed to one side to avoid the blow and made to sweep up his sword, but the blow became fouled in the fight's crush as a falling man trapped his blade. Hundr cursed and drew his seax from where it hung by two thongs from the rear of his belt. Ketil punched him in the face, and it was like a hammer blow. He dropped to one knee, his vision blurred, and a dull ringing thudded around his skull. The axe came again, and Hundr grabbed a thick, brawny wrist in his hand and elbowed Ketil in his belly. His men dragged the old warrior away before Hundr could kill him, and a gap opened on the deck as the Windspear crew withdrew, leaving bodies dead or writhing on the blood-slicked planking.

Hundr saw Rollo kill Kare with his axe and then push his way to the front of Ketil's warriors. He grinned and pointed his axe at Hundr.

"This is the fate of men who fight for tyrants and murderers. You will all die here today, and then we will kill Harald the Usurper," Rollo said, edging forward, his axe and mail thick with the blood of Hundr's crew.

"Murderers? Are you a child to talk this way whilst you kill my men?" Hundr snarled. "You are back where I found you, emptying Ketil's shit pail." He looked over his shoulder with his one eye. His men were crammed onto the Seaworm, and the Windspear was lost. The Sea-Stallion was also under heavy attack. Hundr saw Ragnhild, Hildr, and Sigrid leap onto the Seaworm to join the survivors of his men. His enemies had found him and taken him by surprise. Hundr was surrounded and outnumbered, and he braced himself for his journey to Valhalla.

TWENTY-ONE

Rollo edged forward with his axe held before him, his size dominating the Windspear's deck. Ketil's men were with him, armed with axes and spears and ready to kill. Hundr readied Fenristooth for the attack and was about to launch himself into those deadly blades and meet his fate when he heard Ragnhild's voice shouting behind him.

"We can get away, cut them loose, cut the Windspear loose," she was repeatedly shouting. Hundr could hear the thud of an axe on wood where she chopped through the ropes which had lashed the ships together during the previous night's festivities.

"Ragnhild," Hundr shouted, tightening his grip on the ivory hilt of his sword. "Cut a hole in the hull. Sink the Windspear. Sigvarth, I need three good men to die in the shield wall with me." Hundr flicked his sword out with all the speed his lifetime of training had gifted him, and the tip licked at Rollo's face like a dragon's tongue. It nicked his cheek, and the giant warrior lost his balance as he recoiled from the blow. An attacker lunged a spear at Hundr, but it was a nervous strike, and he batted it away easily. "Come and fight with Hundr, champion of all the Northmen. Make your reputation," he said, waving them on, battle-lust and warrior pride flowing through him.

Ketil's men huddled together on the ship's port side, snarling and poised for the attack. But ship fighting was a dangerous business. The deck was a treacherous mess of slick timbers, sloshing blood, myriad rigging ropes and benches. An attack can be just as easily foiled by a trip or slip as by an enemy blade.

"I found some warriors worthy of Valhalla, lord," piped Sigvarth, standing alongside Hundr with his shield. Two grim-faced warriors stood with him.

"We must hold them back whilst Ragnhild fouls the Windpsear. Will you stand with me?" said Hundr, and the three warriors responded with a clipped roar in unison. Hundr risked a glance behind, and Ragnhild, Hildr, and Sigrid were chopping frantically at the Windspear's hull, leaning over the side of the Seaworm to strike as close to the water as possible. Beyond them, Einar and Bush battled on the deck of the Sea-Stallion against Ketil's ships there. One of those ships had drifted away from the Stallion, and its men were shouting and roaring at one another in a maelstrom of flailing arms as they tried to get oars to bear to bring them back alongside Hundr's third ship. There was a chance to live, a chance to escape Ketil and Rollo's murderous trap, but it must be now, and it must be fast.

"Sigvarth, when I fall back, you must drive forward and hold them here. Can you do that?"

"I can hold them, lord," he said and flashed his teeth.

"Ragnhild, how much longer?"

"We are almost through," she called.

Hundr gripped his sword in two hands and darted towards the enemy, where Rollo had righted himself and rose to meet him with a blood-smeared cheek. Hundr cut and slashed at them, more to keep them back with his speed and skill than to kill them. All the time, he could hear the chop of axe blades on the hull, like a drum beating in his head, each blow bringing the beautiful Windspear closer to her doom. Hundr saw Ketil rise amongst his men, baleful and bellowing his anger as he shouldered through his warriors to come alongside Rollo.

"I want this man dead; I want to piss down

his dead throat and dance on his bones," Ketil shouted, and he came on, lunging at Hundr with his sword. Hundr parried it and then ducked under a sweep of Rollo's axe. He cut at Ketil's ankles, but the Jarl leapt over the blow, and Hundr shouldered into him, throwing him back amongst his men. Hundr thrust his sword at Rollo, and the blade scraped across the big man's mail rings without cutting through. A fist grabbed the neck of Hundr's own brynjar, trying to haul him towards Ketil's men. For a moment, Hundr felt the gorge of his throat rise in panic as another hand grabbed a fistful of his hair. He thought they would pull him into their midst, where their sharp blades would cut, stab and slash at him until he was dead. But he twisted away, sliced the blade of his sword hard on the first hand, and heard a scream as the warrior fell away clutching it, two fingers of which rolled on the deck beneath Hundr's boots.

Hundr rolled aside, ducking below a chopping swing of Rollo's axe. Then, bent over, he ran beyond the three shields of his waiting warriors.

"Hold them, Sigvarth," he panted, adrenaline coursing through his veins.

"We'll hold the bastards, lord." Sigvarth nodded, and with shields raised, the three men moved forward in unison, blocking the space on deck between the mast yard and the side.

"We are through!" Hundr heard Ragnhild shout and knew they had cut a hole in the Windspear, and that seawater would flood her bilge.

"Start shooting at the other ship. Tell Einar to break away. He must get under sail, now," Hundr called. He brought his sword down twice to cut the thick rope of the brace and halyard, sheathed Fenristooth and pushed on the yard timber itself. The long pole of fir began to move slowly, and Hundr cried out with the strain and shoved with his legs. It moved again, and he pushed harder and then laughed as, on the port side of the Windspear's deck, the turning spar crashed into Ketil's warriors, crowding them and forcing them to bunch against the side. Hundr stumbled as the long drakkar leaned in the water, and he felt cold seawater through his boots as water flooded the deck from Ragnhild's hole. The yard came back as Ketil's men pushed it away from them, but in the lean of the Windspear, it became tangled in the rigging of Ketil's own ship. Suddenly where Ketil had been so sure he was about to kill his enemy, now all was confusion and uncertainty. Hundr saw the fear in the wide eyes of Ketil's men as they realised the risk of sinking, and there was a moment to make an escape.

Hundr leapt onto the deck of the Seaworm and cut the remaining rope that bound it to the

Windspear.

"Sigvarth, get over here, now!" he roared across the din of panicked men and creaking timbers. Sigvarth came backwards, but one man alongside him, Ingolfr, slipped in the water now rising beneath him, and Rollo killed him with a monstrous blow of his axe to the neck. Hundr's man fell to his knees with blood spurting from the terrible wound. "Get the sail up," Hundr said to his men, and they looked at him, gawping at his order to raise the sail in the middle of a battle. He set to it himself, working at the ropes, untying the reef ties. Men joined him then, and soon they were hauling on the yardarm as Sigvarth jumped onto the Seaworm's deck. The other man attempted the leap but fell short. He plunged into the widening gap between the ships and into the sea to sink to his death. Rollo appeared at the edge, snarling and shouting words Hundr could not hear above the clamour on the Seaworm's deck. "Push them away with the oars," he said, and his men pulled the oars from their callipers and poled away from the Windspear. Hundr heard a mighty roar and turned just in time to see Ketil Flatnose throw a spear at him. Hundr ducked, and it sailed over him, into the sea beyond.

"I will kill you, dog," Ketil shouted. But on the deck of the Windspear, Ketil faced a fight for his life. He was trapped on a sinking warship whose rigging had tangled into his own ship. And the Windspear would drag Ketil's ship down with it, drowning him and his warriors if he didn't act quickly.

"Einar, Einar," Hundr called, running to the prow of the Seaworm to get his old friend's attention on board the Sea-Stallion. "Cut the ropes and pole away from them. Get your sail up. Now is our chance to get away alive. Ketil's ships are fouled, and he can't come after us."

Einar turned to him; his face spattered with the blood of his enemies. The battle raged there as the men aboard the Sea-Stallion fought back the two ships Ketil had sent to attack from the flank. One of those ships was still drifting away, her crew finally getting oars to bear, but Ragnhild, Hildr and Sigrid poured arrows onto her deck to keep the crew panicked.

Einar nodded and gave the orders to his men. Hundr felt the Seaworm lurch beneath him as the sail came up and it caught the wind. He turned and pointed at Rollo, who stared at him from the chaos of the Windspear's deck. *Nearly, Rollo the Betrayer. You nearly killed me. But we will fight again.* Rollo pointed his axe at Hundr and brought it to his chest in salute.

"The Sea-Stallion is away, look!" Ragnhild exclaimed, running to join Hundr. Sure enough, Einar had got her sail up, and the Stallion slowly came away from Ketil's ship. Missiles flew between the boats, but the distance between them grew.

"We run on the wind," Hundr said, resting his hands on his knees to catch his breath. "Any direction, just follow the wind until we are away."

"I thought we were done for," said Ragnhild.

"We were. Luck fell in our favour today." Hundr watched as they put distance between them and Ketil's ship. He could not tell how they fared in freeing themselves from the Windspear, and Ketil's remaining ships came about slowly and moved towards their Jarl. Those ships should have pursued Hundr and his men and killed them off. But Hundr was thankful for his luck. Those men would wait for orders from their Jarl, giving Hundr time to get away. The Stallion sailed in their wake, and Hundr had lost his finest ship. The Windspear was a small price to pay for the lives of his men and a chance to live to fight another day.

They found an inlet off one of the many small islands off Norway's south coast. It was only midday, and the sun had burned away the morning fog. The inlet had a narrow beach filled with shale between two cliffs, and there were no inhabitants that Hundr could see on the small island as they circled it before beaching. Finally, the Seaworm crunched onto the beach, and the warriors jumped from the deck to fall onto the tiny stones. Shortly after, the Sea-Stallion followed their lead and drove her prow up the beach to pour her warriors ashore.

Hundr sat alone, watching as Ragnhild and others tended to the wounded. He had not yet received a count of how many men he had lost, but it had been a fierce fight, and many had fallen. More still had been injured, and the sound of the sea was lost amongst the cries and moans of the wounded. Soon, Einar came stalking up the beach towards Hundr, his fists clenched and his jaw set. Hundr rose to his feet and held out his hand to greet his old friend. Einar glared at the open hand and shook his head.

"We should have died back there," Einar said, his voice quiet and trembling.

"Indeed," Hundr agreed. "We should sacrifice to Odin for the luck he brought to us today."

"What would it have been for if we had all been killed by Ketil and that bastard Rollo?" Einar had raised his voice, and his bottom lip was shaking.

"We came to rescue the boy. He is safe, and we return to Harald. Ketil attacked us because we raided Orkney." Hundr raised an eyebrow.

Their aim was clear, he thought.

"We almost died because you wanted to fight for a king. You want to be the man to kill Jarl Kjotve. You want to add to your reputation, and we all must suffer the consequences. It was the same in Ireland. You wanted to fight for that bitch Queen Saoirse, and we all paid the price for it." Einar was shouting now, and he jabbed his finger at Hundr's chest. The men around fell quiet and stared at their two leaders.

"You are angry, old friend. But we survived. You have Finn; calm yourself." Hundr raised his arms and lifted his palms to show he only wanted peace with his friend.

"Calm? Sten died, Kolo died, Brownlegs, Hrist. All dead. What do we have to show for it?" Einar stopped himself and turned to walk away but changed his mind and turned back. "It was a dark day when I met you, a Loki day. Ever since that day, my life has been cursed. You stole my luck. I should have left you on that shit-stinking pier in Jutland where I found you."

"Careful," Hundr uttered. Einar's words stung him, but there was a ring of truth to what he said, and Hundr had always known it. It had remained unspoken between them, but it was there. Einar had been a Jarl then, serving Ivar and famed for his reputation. He had been a sea Jarl and close to becoming a landed Jarl. Since then, Hundr had risen from nothing to become a sea Jarl himself, whereas Einar's star had fallen.

"Careful? Don't threaten me, pup." Einar marched towards Hundr with his hand on his axe, but Bush jumped on him and held him back. Einar threw him off, roaring in anger, and more men came to pull the old fighter away. "Leave me, don't touch me," he shouted, shaking them off. "I am done with you. I will take the Stallion and go my own way."

"Go then, if that is your wish. Any man who wants to go with you is free of his oath to me. Begone, find your luck again if that is your desire," said Hundr, and he turned his back on Einar, the man who had taken him in when he was nothing. The man whose luck he had stolen all those years ago.

TWENTY-TWO

Hundr pushed the Seaworm crew west and north, and the drakkar limped rather than sailed on the Whale Road. The fight with Ketil Flatnose had left her scarred and wounded. The clash of ship-on-ship had ripped her caulking away in places, and blades had cut through the rigging. Hundr kept to himself, fighting with the tiller at the steerboard and keeping the ship on course. He had to get to Harald and win his war. He had to get the land that was promised. Einar's cruel words rang around his head like a thumping headache, and Hundr knew that if Harald lost his war, or if Hundr missed the battle with Kjotve, it would leave him with nothing but a ship and a crew of sullen warriors.

The mood amongst the men had fallen into palpable misery after Einar had split them. The old brawler had taken the Sea-Stallion, with Hildr, Finn, and more than half of the surviving crew. Ragnhild, Bush, Sigrid, Sigvarth, and Skapti had stayed with Hundr aboard the Seaworm with the remaining crew. Six of those men suffered from injuries inflicted in the fight with Ketil and huddled close to the steerboard. They were shivering and groaning, and Ragnhild tutted at the smell of their wounds. Some had taken spear thrusts to the torso, some had hacked limbs, and they served as a reminder of the terrible risks of Viking life. They drew scowls and sideways glances from the rest of the crew, any sympathy for their plight oppressed by the unwelcome and visceral warning of the dangers of battle. The sounds of that suffering added to the bleak thoughts in Hundr's head, and he felt like they sailed in darkness, even though the sun was in the sky.

Hundr steered a course in a wide berth around the southwest coast of Norway to avoid Agder, where he knew Kjotve's fleet would patrol the fjords and islands there. His dead eye socket pulsed and ached, and his good eye constantly scanned the horizon for any sign of Ketil's black sails. The crew were the same, and every so often, someone would point into the distance, swearing he saw dark sails in their wake, causing men to shout and panic. But the black sails never materialised. It was a race to get back to Harald, avoid Kjotve, and outrun Ketil in his murderous quest for vengeance.

The Seaworm sailed deep on the Whale Road, out of sight of the coast. Monsters of the great green would roll to look at the wounded ship as if the Loki brood sensed the ill luck which had befallen Hundr and his warriors. The sky was forever clouded, and more than once, Ragnhild had complained that she was worried they were lost at the edges of the world. Hundr knew they tracked the shore. Bush used his stones and experience to track the sun and stars, and soon enough, the cries of seagulls whining above them mingled with the groans of the injured men. Seagulls told of land close by, and if Hundr could hear their caws and did not see a black sail, he knew they were safe. Nobody dared to speak to him of Einar, and Hundr knew his mood was black. He had lost his oldest friend, and the pain of it cleaved at his heart like the claws of Fenris wolf.

The wind plagued him, too frequently blowing against them, and they spent most of the day at the oars. Hundr himself took his turn, pulling until his back was sore, and he prayed to Njorth for a friendly wind. When he wasn't rowing, Hundr kept the prow beast snarling northwards. Squalls of rain would wash over them from time to time, soaking their clothes and adding to the water in the bilge, which needed bailing constantly. The damaged caulking made her leaky, and the rains joined the seawater to fill the Seaworm's belly. It was brutally hard work, and Hundr could not remember a time when he had been as tired. They thumped and drove into the crashing sea, and Hundr's muscles burned like fire. Fear kept the crew going, the terror that Ketil would catch them and butcher them at sea, that they would be drowned and denied their place in Valhalla. They had only stopped rowing in the deep of night. That night had been sleepless. They had plugged the oar holes and let the ship heave and drift in the dark rolling blackness of the night sea. Hundr had lain, looking at the stars where they showed themselves between the rolling clouds. He had been exhausted and craved sleep, but it would not come. Einar haunted him, the truth of his words and losing his friendship worse than torture.

That morning the wind had come in Hundr's favour, and he whispered his thanks to Njorth as the men hoisted the heavy, wet sail. A bitter wind filled that sail and helped the Seaworm race northwards towards Harald and his war. The water rushed past the hull, hissing as white foam burst from the oak timbers. Hundr felt his dead eye socket pulsing, and the wind blew raw on his face. He clenched his teeth when he saw Sigrid approaching, using her hands to move from rope to rope across the deck towards him. She looked at him furtively as she walked carefully, making sure she didn't trip in front of the crew. He wanted her company but did not want to talk, for he knew she would ask him about Einar and how their friendship had now dissolved into enmity.

"The wind is with us today," she said, smiling. Her eyes were pale blue against the darkness of the ship and the sea, and her long hair flowed behind her like a golden mane.

"I don't think we could have rowed for another full day. The men are too tired," he said, barely moving his mouth and dragging the words from himself.

"My father will come for you again. I could see the hate in his face."

"Did he see you?"

She nodded and looked out at the rolling water.

"My brother was there, too. They are ashamed of me, no doubt."

"Would they forgive you if you went back to them?"

Sigrid thought about that for a moment, brushing a loose strand of hair behind her ear.

"I don't think so. My father is a proud man. Everything he has, he made for himself with his strength and his cunning. My decision to run from Thorir and my duty has shamed him."

"Do you believe that?"

"I believe it was my duty to marry Thorir. That is the lot of a Jarl's daughter—to marry the match chosen by her father, a match that will strengthen him and bring honour to his family. But I also listened to his stories by the fire when I was a girl, stories of the gods and their adventures. Stories of great Vikings, like Ragnar Lothbrok and Sten Sleggya. Such warriors did not do as they were told. They did not live a quiet life. They took to the seas and snatched glory, wealth, and reputation with their bravery and daring. That is how I want to live my life. I want to spend eternity in Odin's hall or in Thor's at Thruthvangar."

"What do you know of Thorir Haklag, the man who was to be your husband?"

"Not much, really. My father told me nothing about the man, only that he would be my husband. But I heard gossip from the warriors of my father's hall. Thorir's enemies give him that name, Haklag, to mock his harelip. But he is a monstrous man, a berserker famed for his fighting strength. He is all axe and blood, whereas his father, Kjotve, is all cunning and fine words. Thorir would be a hard man to fight, I think. He is a man destined for Valhalla but would not make a good husband. Kjotve wanted my father to marry me to his son, to show that a famous warrior was so confident of Kjotve's victory that he would pledge his own daughter to Thorir. That gives credibility to Kjotve and, he hopes, brings more warriors of reputation to his banner."

"Why did your father agree to the marriage?"

Sigrid shrugged.

"I should be married already. My father was looking for a good match for me, and Thorir is a famed warrior who would bring honour to my father as his son-in-law. And my father grew suspicious of Harald's ambition."

Unless Kjotve loses, and Harald kills Thorir. "Ragnhild and Hildr will go to Valhalla, and so will you if you fight as well as you did against your father's men."

"I think I hit some of his men with my arrows. They were my people, once. They were men I once knew, people I grew up with."

"They would have killed us had we lost."

"I know. The battle was terrible. I had always expected it to be more, well...glorious."

"There is the glory at the end of battle, but the fight itself is luck, skill, blood and the will to kill your enemy. It is difficult to kill a man. But we all know the risks when we go a'viking. If this is the life you have chosen, then you must accept those risks." Hundr saw her eyes glance at the huddle of injured men. Their faces were pale and strained from the pain of their wounds.

"I thought they would kill you when you fought them alone on that ship," she said, still staring at the wounded warriors.

"So did I," he replied, looking at the injured men. "The grievous wound that does not kill is a warrior's greatest fear. To be wounded like that but survive the fight is a cruel thing. The slow death, to be denied a place in Valhalla. Or, worse, to survive as a cripple and be unable to sail or fight."

"What happens to such men?"

Hundr shrugged.

"The only wealth a warrior at sea has is what they carry, in a purse beneath their armpit or hidden in a boot. Some, whose reputations protect it, put their silver in the chests below the masts. They spend the summer months at war, looking for wealth, and then in Winter, they return to their wives or their families' lands in the north and live a life on the land. A hard life, harder than a warrior's life."

"Have you ever been badly wounded?" she asked, and then her face flushed ruby red. "I'm sorry, I mean, other than your eye."

He raised his hand to cover the empty socket.

"Don't worry. I know how I look. Yes, I was shot by arrows in Northumbria. I was stabbed in the back and leg in Dublin. I've had many wounds, but I am lucky because Ragnhild and Hildr are healers worthy of the Aesir."

"Hildr is gone now, and Ragnhild will not talk of it."

"She had to go with Einar. They are as husband and wife. Ragnhild stayed with me, though I did not ask her to. She and Hildr were raised together. They love each other like sisters, and I love Einar like a brother. Einar once suffered a terrible gut wound at the end of Ivar the Boneless' sword. Hildr and Ragnhild sewed up his insides and saved his life.

"Did you really kill Ivar?"

"I did."

"What happened between you and Einar?"

Hundr sighed and pulled on the tiller to keep the ship on its northward course.

"I had not thought of it until he said it, but he believes I stole his luck. He also believes I have made some grave decisions."

"Did you steal his luck?"

"Who can say? When I met him, I was nothing. He took me in and gave me a chance. Since that day, his life has changed; there is no denying that. Ivar and his son Hakon betrayed him. He was terribly wounded; now I am Jarl, and he is not. I do not know where he will go. He is in as bad a situation as we are. I am not angry with Einar. I owe him my life many times over. I fear he hates me, which is a terrible burden. When this is over, I will find him and see if we can be brothers again."

"Why do you fight for King Harald?"

"Because if he is victorious and becomes King of all Norway, he will give me land and silver. My duty to my men is to fill their purses with silver and build their reputations through battle. They seek wealth and Valhalla and swore their oaths to me because I can give it to them."

"And what do you seek?"

Her eyes bore into his one eye, but he did not feel awkward under that stare. On the contrary, it was a warm feeling, one he had not felt since he was a child.

"I seek what they seek, silver and reputation. Like your father, we are Vikings."

"So, how is it that men like you and my father become famous? You are the champion of all Northmen. My father is Jarl of the Orkney Islands. Most warriors, not the sons of Lords, never rise above the rank of carl; it cannot be done. Or so men say."

Hundr felt his dead eye socket pulse and heard a name whisper on the wind, an old name. It was a name he had left behind long ago.

"I was born in the East, in a great city on a wide river. I am the bastard son of a Prince who had three legitimate sons. My father allowed me to learn weapons with my brothers, which he thought was a kindness to the son of a northern slave. It was not a kindness. My brothers were cruel to me. Every day I was told I was lower than the rats in the street, that the best I could hope for was the life of a slave or a peasant. My father always said I would join his warriors when I was old enough, but my brothers would promise that they would forbid that. They swore they would make my father rescind that promise and that I would be a slave, bringing their food and making their beds. A nithing. So, I left that place. I ran away and swore that I would become a warrior of reputation and return to show my brothers what the son of a northern slave could become. So, I will fight for Harald and kill his enemies. I will risk my life and the lives of my men, and Harald will make me rich. Then, I will sail past the land of the Svears and down the wide river to the land of my people and greet my brothers."

"Or you will die."

"Or I will die and go to Valhalla."

"Harald would drench Norway in blood to make himself King of it all," she said, looking again at the injured men where one man coughed and groaned in agony.

"I am sure your father split some skulls to become Jarl; that is the Viking way. Was not Ketil aligned with Harald at one time?"

"Harald came to my father, and they agreed my father would not oppose him. But then, Rollo Ganger came to Orkney to persuade my father to fight with Kjotve the Rich against Harald."

"Rollo was always Kjotve's man?" said Hundr.

"Yes. His father's lands were swallowed by Harald's war, and Rollo fights Harald at every turn. Men call him Ganger because he walks across Norway, finding men to fight against Harald Fairhair. He came to my father and spoke of fighting for freedom, a free Norway and to help Kjotve kill Harald. Rollo called the King a tyrant, saying that Kjotve was the last one who could stand against him. Rollo promised my father that Harald would come for Orkney once he had defeated Kjotve. He went too far and called my father a coward."

"So Ketil put him in chains?"

"Yes. To teach him a lesson and punish him for his impudence. My father and his men were not gentle with Rollo."

"So, Rollo fights for a dream?"

"Yes. Does that make him right and us wrong?"

"No. We honour the gods and sail and fight

for their pleasure. I will make Harald King of all Norway and kill his enemies. I will take their land and wealth with the strength of my sword. That is the Viking way. So tomorrow, we will find King Harald, and I hope we have not already missed the war."

Sigrid folded her arms across her chest, and Hundr noticed she had gooseflesh prickling her fair skin.

"Are you cold?" he asked her, and she nodded. Hundr bent to retrieve his heavy wool cloak from beneath the steerboard platform. It was dark green with a fox fur trim at the neck, and he wrapped it about her shoulders. He pulled it in tight so that it closed about her, and she smiled at the feel of the fur on her slender neck. Hundr left his arm about her shoulder tentatively, fearful that she would shrug him off and grimace at his scarred face and empty eye. But she leant her head on his chest, and he rested a cheek on the top of her head. The closeness warmed him, and Hundr felt the same relief flood his chest as though he had survived a Holmgang because Sigrid was beautiful, fierce and strong. Hundr held her close, and he thought about Harald and Kjotve. He thought of Thorir Haklag and Ketil Flatnose. Great men who brought armies together to fight for the lordship of all Norway. Hundr had to get to that fight and be a part of that battle. If Harald won, then he would enjoy the spoils of that victory. But to lose that battle would mean death for Harald and Rognvald and likely for Hundr himself, for he would surely fight where the battle raged to earn the gratitude of Harald Fairhair.

TWENTY-THREE

Although he searched for Harald, Hundr saw the first of Kjotve's ships as the Seaworm rowed past the island of Rott and along the coast of Tananger. He had not expected to find Kjotve's sails this far north. That first vessel had been a small karve warship, rowing lazily along the coast, travelling north and unaware of the Seaworm's approach behind them. It was a clear, still day, with barely a breeze across the tired, calm sea. Hundr ordered the men to trail the karve as it followed the coast, which was low-lying and dotted with villages beyond where occasional beaches broke through a coastline of rock and yellow-brown heather. As the land veered eastwards, Hundr brought the Seaworm about, turning her before curious enemy vessels spied them. Ships were thick on the water, as though Njorth had gathered all his worshippers into one place to hear their prayers. There were masts beyond count, and this surely was Kjotve's army who had come for their reckoning with King Harald. Hundr asked for a man amongst his crews who was familiar with this part of western Norway, and a wiry warrior came forwards, flanked by a larger man with a scar across his forehead.

"I was born here, lord," said the wiry man named Hekkr. He had lost part of an ear fighting for Hundr, and despite his short stature, he was renowned amongst the men for being a fine wrestler.

"Me too, lord," said the scarred man. "Hekkr and I took to the Whale Road from here. We didn't fancy a life of fish for every meal and a sea hag for a wife." He grinned, and the men around laughed.

"Kjotve is here. We can see that. Which means Harald is also here. So where is the most likely place the King will have his fleet and his army?" Hundr asked them.

"Hafrsfjord, lord," Hekkr answered. "There is a narrow entrance to a large fjord just north of here. Beyond that, there is an island between the two sides of the entrance channel, and then the water opens into a wide fjord, surrounded by towns. Harald must be in there somewhere. There is enough water for his ships, and the fjord is hidden from view of the sea, and the towns and villages will provide food for his warriors."

"Is the fjord wide enough for the King's fleet?"

"Yes, it is, lord," the scarred man piped up. "When you sail through the narrow corridor, it looks like a tiny fjord, but then it opens wider than Hekkr's mother's legs."

The men laughed again, and Hekkr rewarded him with a cuff around the head.

"If Kjotve wanted to, he could block the narrow passage to the fjord and trap Harald's ships," said Hekkr.

"How far is it from here to the shores of Hafrsfjord if we went overland?" asked Hundr.

The two men looked at each other, and Hekkr scratched his head.

"Not far, lord, not even a day's march," he said.

Hundr nodded and rewarded them both with a handful of hack silver from the purse beneath his jerkin. They went away laughing and clapping each other on the back. He watched the karve join the massed fleet and ordered his men to stop rowing. Hundr rubbed his thumb across the ivory face on his sword hilt and wondered what Harald and Kjotve were each planning.

Both had brought their forces to this place, and there must surely be a fight. Hundr had learned the importance of the land to war leaders—how hills, ditches, bogs and forests were as crucial to a leader as the strength of his warriors' blades.

"So, Kjotve means to trap Harald in the fjord?" said Ragnhild. She ambled across the deck and leaned on the side, shaking her head at the vast number of ships in the distance.

"Seems that way," Hundr nodded. "But Harald did not fight his way successfully across most of Norway by being foolish. So if they have trapped him in Hafrsfjord, it is because he wished it so."

"As dangerous as a bear with his foot in a snare."

"If we want to play our part in this war, we must get to Harald, and we can't sail through that," he said, pointing at Kjotve's fleet. "But maybe we can go overland."

"Maybe. If Hekkr is right, we could be there before nightfall. But we have injured men who can't make the march, and what of the Seaworm?" Ragnhild said, touching the spear amulet at her neck as she mentioned the injured warriors. Two had died since the fight with Ketil. One man had simply stopped breathing during the night, and Ragnhild had only cut the other man's throat yesterday. He had received a wound to the shoulder and one to the gut, and both had festered. Despite Ragnhild's best efforts, she had decided there was no way to save the man, so she had cut his throat as a kindness to spare him any further futile pain and suffering. She had made sure he held a blade in his shivering hand and uttered a prayer to Odin over his sweating face before sending him into the afterlife.

"We can moor the Seaworm on the coast here. If Hekkr knows the people, they will look after her for us."

"Can we really do anything to help Harald win with the few warriors we have here?"

"He has two of my crews already. Those men added to what we have here? Yes, we can help him win. And we have you, Ragnhild, and you are worth ten men, at least."

She puffed out her cheeks and hit him with a playful punch to the stomach.

Hekkr led them to an inlet south of Tananger, where a collection of small houses of faded silver birch huddled around a river which trickled into the sea through a narrow rock-strewn beach.

"Home," Hekkr had said with a shrug.

A gaggle of bent-backed fisherman and women with taut, wind-burned faces greeted him with toothless smiles and open arms. The crew hauled the Seaworm onto the beach, and Hundr winced as the stones scraped on her long, oak timbers. He left Hekkr and five men, along with the surviving injured warriors, to protect the ship and gave Hekkr's people the rest of the hack silver from his purse. Then, under high, scattered clouds, Hundr marched his warriors across a land of low hills and dark scrub until they saw the shining waters of Hafrsfjord glistening in the distance. It was late afternoon by then, and Hundr and Ragnhild knelt on the highest hilltop they could find to get a better look at their surroundings. The fjord swept away to the south and east, and beyond the low hills, hundreds of smoke trails twisted into the sky to make a thin fog snatched away by the soft wind.

"That must be Harald's force," said Hundr, jutting his chin towards the smoke. "We should be there before dark falls."

"Look there," said Ragnhild, pointing to the south. Hundr followed her finger, and the far horizon seemed to move like a serpent slithering over the shallow valleys, scales glinting here and there in the sun. "Kjotve also brings a land army to Harald's rear."

"So, Kjotve has his fleet to the north and his army to the south. The attack must surely come from the south. But why bring so many ships?"

The questions went unanswered, and the column moved on. Riders came to meet them as the sun went down and cast the sky into a pinkish hue. They brought Hundr and his men to a fortified town with a ditch and palisade, outside of which hundreds of men camped in small tents huddled next to campfires where the smell of cooking bacon and lamb was thick in the air. Hundr left his crew under Bush's command with orders to make camp and try to scrounge together a meal for the men. He and Ragnhild entered the fort and found Harald in a long hall, where a finely carved beast snarled from his roof posts and over the door. Guards went inside to ask Harald if he wanted to see the Man with the Dog's Name, and eventually, Ragnhild and Hundr walked into a small room. A fire crackled and spat at one end, making the room oppressive and close. Hundr wore his mail and pulled at his neck to breathe easier.

"Welcome, Hundr. You arrive just in time," came Harald's voice, and the man himself rose from a high-backed chair to offer a thin smile. His face was drawn, and his famously long hair fell in bedraggled plaits on either side of his shoulders. Rognvald rose from the seat opposite and raised a horn of ale in greeting.

"Did you get your Prince back?" asked Rognvald.

"We did but were then attacked by Ketil Flatnose. I lost a ship and many good men," said Hundr, noting the lack of surprise on both men's faces.

"It seems the Norns have turned against us both then, my friend." Harald sighed, and he took a long drink of ale from a deep mug.

"We saw a fleet of ships to the north of the fjord, King Harald, and an army approaching from the south," said Hundr. He carefully observed Harald's face as he barely flinched at the news, which meant it was not fresh news. Harald knew his business and would no doubt have scouts patrolling the land for miles around the fjord where his army now camped.

"Kjotve has been busy, and men have responded to his promises of silver. He is not called Kjotve the Rich for nothing," Rognvald commented. He turned to pick up a black poker and twisted it into the burning logs, sending sparks spitting into the grate.

"He has more men than when I saw his forces at Agder," Hundr remarked.

"Kjotve has risen the people of Rogaland, Agder, and Telemark against me. Men have risen who would have been kings but for my victories. And now they bring their resentment and their vengeance to Hafrsfjord. Eirik, who would be King of Hordaland; Sulke, the would-be King of Rogaland and Jarl Sote, his brother—all men I should have killed when I look back. Bavlos said it was so when he talked to his dark gods of the land and sky. I spared these men, and they swore oaths to serve me and acknowledge me as their King."

"Oath breakers all, nithings and cowards!" Rognvald sneered. "Hroald Hryg and his brother, Had the Hard, also come from Telemark to fight alongside Kjotve. They have more ships than us, and we think their warriors outnumber us by two to one."

"So, it comes down to a final battle," said Hundr. "I have also learned that lesson the hard way, King Harald. Pity and kindness have no place in this world of ours. The gods do not look well upon it. Pity is often returned to us with a knife in the back."

"Just so." Rognvald nodded, and he took another drink of his ale. "This will be the battle that decides the rule of Norway. There can be no mercy shown for the vanquished. This will be the greatest battle of our age."

"I just wish we had more men," Harald uttered, his voice quiet and his eyes searching the flames for help. The King had dark rings under his eyes, and Hundr thought he looked as though he had not slept for days.

"These men who come to fight you find strength in their numbers," said Ragnhild. "But most of them are whipped dogs, men you have already defeated in battle before. They are like the men who skulk at the rear of the shield wall, waiting for the enemy lines to break before they strike a blow with their spears." She took a step towards Harald, and the firelight flickered in the dark of her one eye, and the shadows danced across her hard, scarred face. Ragnhild raised her hand and clenched the fist tight, so her knuckles showed white. "We are not those men. We are the warriors who fight in the front where the battle is hardest, where the blades strike at the throat and chest. One of our warriors is worth two of theirs. You have allowed yourself to be trapped here, King Harald, so this final battle can be fought and won."

Harald turned to her and nodded slowly, and a mirthless grin split Rognvald's face.

"They come to trap you," Hundr added. "But the glory and heart-lifting victory will take place when an enemy thinks he has lured you into his trap and comes to kill you, yet realises that he has instead stumbled into your ploy, and his plans are turned to bloody ruin. You are Harald Fairhair, King of war, victor of countless battles. We are stuck in a wide fjord with a narrow entrance, and Kjotve will bring his ships in to block the way out. He plans to kill you with his army from the south and foil your only means of escape. How can we use this to our advantage?"

Harald paced the room, stroking one of his long plaits.

"Kjotve has committed most of his men to the landward fight. But what if we can bring the fight to the water, fight the battle in the fjord and deprive him of his numbers?" he contemplated, the tiredness slipping from his face like an old cloak, his eyes darting between Hundr, Ragnhild, and Rognvald.

"It could work, but it would be a grim fight," said Rognvald. "Our fleet against theirs, ship against ship. Armoured men who fall overboard will sink to their deaths, and we won't have much sight of how the battle goes once we are engaged."

"And we would need to be sure that Kjotve and the other leaders are aboard their ships rather than having joined their army in the south." Harald nodded.

"So, we invite them to parlay in the morning, before their army arrives," said Hundr.

"If we do it on the island in the fjord, Kjotve will come to crow. He must be so certain of his victory to commit his forces to this place," smiled Harald, and he laughed aloud. "We can win, and I will be King of all Norway."

"I will pray to Odin. We will need his favour. He is the god of war, battles and frenzy, and we will require all three, I think," said Ragnhild.

"Oh, we will bring the frenzy," retorted Rognvald with a wolfish grin. "Bavlos will help with that."

TWENTY-FOUR

Einar sat on the shore, whittling a piece of ash wood with a small knife. The carving was crude, but the bright wood beneath the bark began taking the form of a small ship. He shaved a golden slice from its tip and started work on the hull. It was a toy for Finn, and Einar wanted to make it look like the Seaworm, his beautiful old ship with her sleek lines and the familiar feel of her tiller. Einar carved another chip away from what would form the prow and allowed his mind to drift to the adventures he had seen as her captain. He had sailed east, south and west on that ship, spending most of his life at sea. Einar rolled his shoulders and stretched his back, the memories re-evoking the pain of old wounds, aching in his shoulder and throbbing in his stomach.

He had brought the Sea-Stallion as close to the

shore of the small island as he dared. One of the crew had leant over the hull with a length of rope to plumb the shallows, checking for high sandbanks or a hidden clutch of rock which would scupper the ship in the unfamiliar waters. Eventually, they had come ashore at a quiet inlet on Norway's southwest shore. Einar had let the Seaworm run with the wind when there was enough to catch the sails and blow them away from Ketil's ships, of which there had been no sign. When there had been no wind, the men had taken to the oars. They had searched for a spot such as this, unpopulated and away from eyes that would arouse suspicion and attention from armed locals. It was a mere spit of sand beneath opposing crags of brush and steel grey stone, too small for fisherfolk to inhabit and too deep below the hills to be noticed. Einar had sent men to look for a river or brook to fill skins with fresh water and hunt for whatever game they came across. The ship was low on ale and provisions, and in his rage at Hundr, he had thought little of provisions. His only concern had been to flee his curse, to separate his life from the man who had brought him nothing but woe.

The afternoon was swiftly turning to evening, and beyond where the Sea-Stallion rocked gently against her anchor rope, the sky had turned pink behind scattered clouds. Einar watched Hildr and Finn practising swordplay with two sticks that Hildr had fished out of the surf. She worked with the boy on basic lunge and parry practice, but it quickly dissolved in a bout of tickling and raucous laughter from the boy as he and Hildr tumbled on the sand. It was mere days since they had rescued Finn from Gorm and his men, and so far, the lad had shown little effect from his time as a prisoner. He looked a tad thin, and he certainly missed Father Darragh, but other than that, Finn was in good spirits. The laughter peeled out across the sand, and the sound made Einar smile. He lay down the wood and his whittling knife to run over to kneel in the sand and join Hildr in her tickle attack.

"Please, no more." Finn giggled, batting at Einar and Hildr's hands. Then, finally, they relented in their assault, and Finn got to his knees, smiling and ruffling the sand from his hair.

"Did anyone ever teach you the secrets of skimming stones?" Einar asked, cocking an eyebrow.

"No, what are they?" Finn replied.

"Watch," said Einar. He rose and searched the sands for a small flat stone washed up by the tide. He quickly found a grey one laced with white marble. Einar cocked his arm and threw the stone in a low, flat arc. It bounced four times on the sea surface, and Finn's young face widened with a look of pure fascination.

"How did you do that? Can you show me?"

"Of course. We need another flat stone." They searched and found a small thin pebble pocked with dark specks of orange. "You hold it between your forefinger and thumb. Get low and keep the throw flat."

"It didn't work," said Finn, crestfallen as the stone plopped into the water five feet away.

"Keep trying, look for more stones and throw it like I showed you."

Finn combed the beach and tried another. This time, it bounced once in the gentle surf and then sunk below the surface.

"I got one!" Finn cried out, and Hildr and Einar gave him an appreciative nod. Einar helped him find more stones until he had a little pile to practice with. Just as Einar was turning to talk to Hildr, Finn tugged at his sleeve.

"Einar?" he said.

"Yes?"

"Do you think Father Darragh is in heaven?"

"I think so. He was a good man, and his god will welcome him."

"Are there two heavens? One for Odin and one for God?"

"That is a tough question. But I think so, yes.

One heaven for us Northmen, and then one for the followers of the Christ God."

"Will I go to heaven or Valhalla?"

"Your father is in Valhalla, but it's up to you to decide which god you wish to follow."

"I never met my father. You will go to Valhalla, though?"

"I hope so. You will be welcome there, and I will save you a place at a feasting bench. But first, you must become a fearsome warrior," said Einar, and he ruffled Finn's hair.

"Like you and Hundr?"

"Yes." Einar nodded. He bent to pick up a skimming stone and showed Finn how to throw it once more. Then he left the boy with his pile of rocks and went to sit with Hildr. She sat cross-legged on the sand, watching him and Finn.

"I think he's grown taller," she said as Einar sat beside her, groaning at his creaking joints as he lowered himself to sit.

"He has," Einar replied. "He does not seem to miss his priest too much."

"Finn told me how Gorm killed the priest and threw him overboard. He has seen a lot of death for one so young. He is used to it. Finn has been surrounded by violence since his birth, more than most Northmen, even."

"It will harden him. I should teach him to fight properly. He is coming of age to learn."

"He would like that, I think." Hildr reached over and held Einar's hand. "Do you want to talk about it yet?"

"What?" he said, knowing full well what she was talking about but bristling at the thought of it.

"You and Hundr? We have lost our friends. Ragnhild, Bush, and the rest of the crew. I have known Ragnhild since I was a girl, Einar."

"He blindly leads us into fights, thinking only of himself and his reputation. We nearly died in Ireland, and we only just escaped Ketil Flatnose and his surprise attack. He says he wants land, but I don't believe him. He wants to be the Champion of the North, just like Ivar. They are more alike than he knows. He has become so like his great enemy. And he stole my luck. The thread of my life changed its weft the day I met him. The Norns wove my fate with his, and not for the better. I was a Jarl. Look at me now. I was Einar Rosti, a sea-Jarl, a warrior of Ivar Lothbroksson." Einar picked up a stone and threw it into the sea, remembering the days when he would sail into a Jarl's port on Ivar's business in Jutland or off Kattegat, and he would be greeted with respect and fear.

"You are still Einar the Brawler. You have as

much reputation now as ever."

"Men used to fear me. It was I who was destined to be a landed Jarl in those days. Now, when we meet with warriors or lords, they want only to talk to the Man with the Dog's Name, the man with the reputation. Not I."

"Did they fear you or Ivar?"

Einar shot his head around to look at her, anger rising in his chest. She took her hand from his and placed it on his rough cheek.

"I do not say that to insult you, my love. Just to make you think. What is it you want from life? Do you want to be feared by men you will never meet? We have left Hundr, and all we have now is this ship and its ageing crew. Where will we go, and what will we do?"

Hildr smiled at him, and his anger washed away like the tide. She was stern, hard, beautiful, and wise.

"They feared Ivar. You have the truth of it there. And I don't want to be feared. I did...when I was young. But that is what all men want: reputation, fear, strength and silver. Now, I want a home for you and me and young Finn."

The men who had left with Einar aboard the Sea-Stallion were the older members of Hundr's crews. That was also true. Most of them had been men sworn to Ivar and joined Hundr's boats when their Lord had died. Einar knew most of them from the old days; now, they were a grizzled, balding, heavy-paunched lot. All as tough as the nails in the ship's hull, and all they had to show for a lifetime at sea was what they carried with them.

"Would Ivar and his son have betrayed you if Hundr had been there or not?"

"Hakon was a turd, and he blamed me for breaking his father's command. He raided East Anglia, killing and raping. I took the blame and was cast out. You know all this."

"But it was not Hundr's fault."

"No, I suppose not." Einar shook his head and launched another stone into the lapping waves. "But he still leads us into fights that make no sense. With our victories, we should be as wealthy as kings by now."

"True," Hildr said, and she threw a stone herself. "But is that not why he wants to fight for King Harald, to get the land and silver we all deserve?"

"Maybe. But more so so that he can garner more fame, so more men will believe he is the champion of all the Northmen."

"You don't believe that. What if he wants to win the land because he thinks it's what you want? He loves you, Einar, like a brother. All you talk about is settling down, building a home, somewhere safe to raise Finn."

"That's not all I talk about." Einar shook his head. He watched Finn searching the beach for more skimming stones. He wanted Finn to be safe so he could raise him like a son. Raise him to be a warrior and reclaim his inheritance as King of Dublin.

"But it is what you want."

"Yes," Einar said wistfully, watching Finn laugh, and he cheered the boy on as one of his little stones skipped three times across the sea's surface.

"I want that too. I will never return to my order at Upsala, and I have made my peace with Odin. We can raise Finn together, as mother and father. Who better than us to teach him how to fight?"

Einar laughed.

"Who better than you, my fierce Valkyrie shieldmaiden?"

"So, what will we do?"

"What we always do. Fight and take what we want with the strength of our arms and the will in our hearts."

TWENTY-FIVE

Hundr stood on the prow of Harald's warship, staring across the fjord. A wooden island rose from the centre of the glassy water with pines of dark green covered in lichen, and its shore was ringed by jagged rock. Beyond that island, six of Kjotve's ships patrolled the waters at the northern end of the fjord, which was the only way out of the landlocked waterway. Harald stood next to Hundr with his arms folded across his chest, and Rognvald bade one man hold aloft the huge leafy branch he had cut fresh that morning to show Kjotve that they came in peace and to talk. The warship was larger than the Seaworm but was six rowing benches smaller than the Windspear. As he gazed across the fjord, the morning air cool on his neck, Hundr wondered if the Windspear was at the bottom of the sea or if Ketil had saved her. Wave-elk, Harald's ship was named, and they had removed her prow beast and all the shields from the sheer stake to reinforce that they came in peace to parlay.

All the Lords and Jarls of Harald's army had jostled and positioned themselves for a place at the historic parlay, a meeting on an island between the men who vied for the lordship of all Norway. Harald had refused most of them. He was the King, and he would talk to Kjotve alone. There had been some grumbling and more than one sly look cast in Hundr's direction, but he did not fear those men. They were the Jarls Harald had either defeated in battle or who came from his father's old kingdom. They were sworn to serve the King and would obey his command. Harald brought only a handful of men with him to the meeting and enough of his warriors to row the ship. Behind Hundr stood Rognvald and Valbrandr, silently staring across the calm water towards the enemy fleet. Valbrandr was huge and baleful; his cold flinty eyes stared with the pitiless emptiness of an animal.

"If you refused to bring the great and good of your kingdom, why am I here?" Hundr asked.

"Because Ketil hates you, as does this Rollo, who keeps appearing everywhere. Also, Kjotve will have heard of you. And I think you are lucky. So why not?" Harald shrugged, not taking his eyes off the enemy ships.

"Kjotve will be confident, with his army approaching in our rear and his fleet in front. Try not to anger him, King Harald. We must see out this day without fighting if we can."

They had spent much time overnight discussing what to do about Kjotve and his well-executed manoeuvres. Harald found himself outnumbered and trapped. To fight and win meant using war-cunning, risk, and gambling on the luck of the gods.

"Do you think our plan will work? You who have fought across the Whale Road and lived through many such situations?" Harald turned to him now, and Hundr saw a flicker of doubt in the King's eyes, and the corners of his mouth were slightly turned down.

"Later today, we will pray and sacrifice to Odin, and your Sami sorcerer will do the same to his gods. Of course, we will need luck and the enemy to do as we wish them to do." Hundr had thought a lot about luck since Einar had left. He supposed he had seen his fair share of it, but it had been mixed with an equal share of misfortune.

"A ship approaches the island," announced Harald, pointing northwards. "And another. Do you feel lucky today?"

"I think we make our own luck, King Harald. The gods want us to fight and seek glory, and the more we risk, the more Odin, Thor and Frey reward us with luck. The gods, or so I believe, also reward us for doing the hard things, the thing that must be done. I had a dream once where I vividly saw that day long ago when Frey and Thor tricked Fenris wolf and bound him with a magical fetter. Frey lost a hand that day, but he had to put his hand into the beast's maw to persuade the wolf to put the fetter on. Frey knew he would lose that hand when the wolf became enraged and the trap was sprung, but he did it anyway."

"So, you think we try to fetter Fenris wolf this day?"

"No. I think we must defeat men who hate you and who would grind your bones into the earth. We must fight a rich man who deployed all his wealth and influence to pull together an army to stop you from becoming King of all Norway. His numbers will make him confident, and that is our only hope. And your magic sword, of course."

Harald smiled and let his hand drop to the Yngling blade at his hip. Heavy rocks surrounded the island, and those boulders were also visible beneath the pale waters, so the crew dragged forth a faering they had towed behind the Wave-Elk and rowed ashore to the parlay. Harald brought Rognvald, Hundr and Valbrandr, and they clambered from the rocking rowboat up over the cold stone and onto the island's bright heather. On the other side, Kjotve came forth with a band of his lords and advisors. Hundr saw Rollo the Betrayer there, towering above all others, and the unmistakable figure of Ketil Flatnose, his long silver hair loose and framing his lined face. There were others Hundr did not recognise, but they wore brynjar mail coats or fine, well-tailored cloth. Hundr himself wore his mail, as did the others in Harald's party. The obvious risk of falling into the water and being dragged to its bottom was not a valid concern when weighed up with the aim of looking as warlike as possible before the enemy. Hundr saw the comparatively short and slight figure of Kjotve the Rich amongst the enormous, baleful warriors around him. The would-be king was dressed in a simple wool jerkin and trews, a long cloak of rich brown fabric fringed with fur, and he wore a silver circlet on his brow. A monstrously muscled warrior flanked him, stripped to the waist like one of Gorm's berserkers and wearing a bearskin on his back, its head and teeth sitting atop his head like a hood. Hundr recognised him from Agder; it was Thorir Haklag.

Kjotve the Rich stepped forward, strutting with his hands clasped behind his back so that his cape flowed behind him. He stood on a patch of lush grass beneath an immense pine tree which swayed in the breeze. The lords of his retinue followed but stopped five paces behind him. Harald marched forwards, and Hundr, Rognvald and Valbrandr followed and remained a few paces behind the King.

"The fjord is beautiful today," said Harald, smiling broadly and looking out across the vast expanse of calm water and away towards the gently rolling hills.

"We are not here to admire the sights of Rogaland," barked Kjotve, puffing out his chest and keeping his hands clasped behind his back.

"Why are we here, then?" asked Harald.

"I have brought an army of the freemen of Norway here to punish you for your greed and warmongery. You brought the branch of peace to this island. So, Harald, what do you wish to discuss?" Kjotve smiled thinly, and his tongue darted out across slender lips.

"I wanted to give you the chance to pay homage to me now, as your King. I thought you might wish to save your life and the lives of your merry band here." Harald fluttered his hand carelessly at Kjotve's retinue. "There is no need for men to die. If you acknowledge me as your King and King of all Norway, you can continue to rule Agder as Jarl, and your men can continue to rule their own lands. Except him." He pointed at Rollo. "He must pay for stealing the Yngling blade. The sword was forged for the gods and wielded by my ancestors. Only a king should hold this blade."

Kjotve shuffled his feet, his face flushing red across his cheeks. Hundr watched him intently as the man tried to master his emotions, the struggle for calm playing across his face in the flickering of his eyes and the turning in of his lips against his teeth.

"You can add graverobber to your long list of low acts, Harald, son of Halfdan the Black. You took that sword from the howe of a dead man with the same ease with which you burned and killed our people needlessly in a desperate power play. We are the good people of Norway, and we will stop you and bring peace to our lands. Rollo Ganger here is just another victim of your greed and bloodlust. His father was a Jarl close to this very place before you burned him out and put him to the sword for not bowing to your false claim to our homes..."

Harald yawned loudly, and Kjotve's jaw dropped mid-sentence.

"Sorry, have you finished? I lost track of what you were trying to say there for a moment. Continue, please."

"Surrender yourself for judgement, Harald Halfdansson, or we will kill you and your men in this place," Kjotve said, his hands now at his sides and his fists clenched.

"Judgement? Bloodlust? Are you a Christ-follower to talk this way? I am a Viking, as my father was before me, and I am the King of Vikings. We fight, and we die to honour the gods. We are drengr." Harald gestured behind him towards Hundr, Rognvald, and Valbrandr. "We take what we can with the strength of our arms and challenge men to stop us. I honour Odin, I hold the Yngling blade, and I will be King of all Norway."

"Drengr?" Kjotve scoffed. "Rognvald Eysteinsson. Some men say he is a berserker, but I have never met a man who has seen him fight. I assume this one-eyed marauder is the one they call the Man with the Dog's Name? An assassin and a thief who burned my hall. I do not recognise the other brute you bring to parlay. Where are the Lords and Jarls of your army and your lands? Is this the best you can muster, thieves and murderers?

"I prize warriors and men of reputation above Jarls, men who have been handed everything they own by virtue of their birth." Harald straightened his back and paused, looking across the faces of the men behind Kjotve. "You seem set on your path, and I mark you all now as my enemies. You Ketil, Jarl of Orkney, to whom I offered friendship, and you Eirik of Hordaland, Sulke of Rogaland, Hroald and Had of Telemark. All men who have sworn to submit to me as King.

You are oath breakers, and the gods will see you as such." The men behind Kjotve bristled, and more than one hand fell to axe haft or sword grip. "We are beyond peace now. Kjotve, you challenge my kingship, so you and I can settle this now. We can make the square here on this island and fight a Holmgang. You and me. The winner will be King."

The men behind Kjotve murmured between themselves, and Kjotve coughed and raised his hand.

"A good ploy from a cornered animal. But I do not need to fight you, Harald. You are outnumbered and trapped."

"You wear a crown and fancy yourself a king, so let us fight now you and me. The strongest shall rule. No champions, just me against you."

Kjotve chuckled mirthlessly and shook his head. "I thought you had invited us here to surrender, given the odds you face. But it seems you are intent on dying. This parlay is over. Prepare for war."

"I challenged, and you refused. You are a shit-eating coward who would rather watch good men die than hold a blade himself. I hope your men know what kind of man they follow, with your fine robes and that woman's circlet you wear on your head. I hope you take the field, Kjotve, for I will seek you there."

"And I will seek you, Harald Fairhair," growled Thorir Haklag, his speech slurred by his harelip. "I will take your head and march it across Norway as a warning to all tyrants and murderers. I will cut your long hair and make an arsewipe out of it. And you..." He pointed a muscled arm and finger at Hundr, "...you stole my wife. You will die slowly. I will cut you...."

"She came of her own will," said Hundr. "You repulse her. She wants to live her own life, to be free. Many have tried to kill me, Thorir Haklag, and they wait for me now in Odin's hall. I will send you to join them."

"Goat turd!" Thorir shouted. "Piss drinking whore-master!"

Hundr laughed and turned away. The parlay had taken up the morning, and it would be late afternoon before Kjotve could marshal his crews and get messages to his army to the south in Harald's rear. That meant there would be no fighting until the morning, and Hundr smiled to himself, for tomorrow he would make his men rich.

TWENTY-SIX

Hundr felt the ship move beneath his feet as more warriors came aboard. In the darkness, each footstep sounded like a drumbeat, and though the men talked in whispers, the collective sound of so many hundreds of hushed voices was like the sound of the sea, akin to a constant undulating sigh. A covering of cloud shielded the heavens, and Hundr could see no stars as he peered into the fjord and the hills beyond. The moon peeked from behind its cloud blanket for a moment, showing itself as a thin crescent before disappearing again into the darkness. Abruptly, a warrior coughed and was jostled by his shipmates and urged to keep quiet.

Hundr carefully picked his way across the deck, ducking under rigging and stepping between benches and stacked weapons. He came to rest in a crouch close to the prow, next to

Ragnhild and Bush.

"Your eyes look like piss holes in the snow," whispered Bush.

Hundr chuckled under his breath. There had been no sleep that night for any man of King Harald's army. Bush and Ragnhild looked pale and drawn in the darkness, and Bush's own eyes were small, with puffy bags beneath them.

"Are the men ready to fight?" Hundr asked, turning so his good eye could watch his warriors continue to board the boat. It was one of Harald's fleet. The ships Hundr had left with Harald under Asbjorn's command were further along the line, crammed with his warriors and preparing for the battle to come. This ship, however, had a task to complete, which was why Hundr led it and why Ragnhild and Bush were with him. He saw the broad shoulders of Valbrandr on the pier waiting to board. The battle depended on Hundr and his ship of fighters breaking the enemy line, so Harald had sent a force of chosen men with Hundr, where the fighting would be at its fiercest.

"They are ready," said Bush, rubbing his hands together and blowing onto them. "Why is it always us in the bloody thick of it?"

"Because the King needs the fiercest and most daring warriors if he is going to win this fight."

"And because most of what we do here is your

plan," Ragnhild added. She knelt, running her fingers across the smooth feathers at the top of the quiver full of arrows at her waist, her breath steaming in the chill air.

"True," said Hundr, and he smiled at her. "How is your arm?"

"There will be worse than that to come this day."

"Let's hope those fires do the trick," said Bush. Kjotve's army had made camp half a day's march south of Hafrsfjord, and Harald believed that with the rising sun, those men would attack his camp on the shore, and Kjotve would attack from the water. They would try to trap Harald, and Kjotve would use his larger number to crush Harald's forces and cut off his escape. Harald had taken some convincing, but Hundr devised a plan he hoped would win the day. The glow of hundreds of campfires flickered on the Hafrsfjord's southern shore. They were fires that Hundr hoped would trick Kjotve and his captains into believing that Harald's army was in camp and preparing to march and meet the landward forces marshalled against him.

"It won't be long before the sun comes up and Kjotve's men see that there are no warriors at those fires and that the shores are empty," said Ragnhild. She had burned her arm on a torch as they had moved from fire to fire, making sure they did the job properly and that each one truly looked like a morning campfire. Kjotve had to believe that his plan was working and that he would have Harald trapped.

Valbrandr greeted them with a nod and crouched alongside Hundr, his eyes as dark and glistening as the fjord's surface.

"Let's hope your plan works," he grumbled. "I don't fancy sinking to the bottom of the fjord." Valbrandr wore a brynjar mail coat with an axe looped at his belt, and he'd brought aboard an armful of short-hafted throwing axes, which he had laid within the prow's curve.

"Don't fall in then," quipped Bush, and he winked. Harald's man rewarded him with a frown.

"We must push off, get them moving," Hundr said, noting that the crew had still not made the oars ready. "We need to reach the island within the fjord before the sun comes up."

His plan relied on surprise and savagery; for that to work, they had to be at least halfway across the fjord before Kjotve noticed their movement. So, without hesitation, Valbrandr cuffed a stocky warrior around the ear and gestured at the men to get the ship moving. Drums beat on the shore, deep and thrumming, and a line of torches jerked and dipped as men danced and twirled to the beat. The men holding the torches were garbed in animal skins, and their faces glowed as though they were fetches of dead warriors, risen from the earth to cause terror amongst the living.

"What's the point of us keeping quiet if that lot is going to bloody sing and dance?" huffed Bush, shaking his head.

"What in Odin's name are they doing?" Hundr hissed. The men were making far too much noise, and Hundr feared Kjotve's scouts on the coast and aboard his ships would hear the din.

"Ulfheðnar," said Valbrandr, and he touched the Thor hammer amulet at his neck. "Or something worse."

"I've had my fill of berserkers," tutted Ragnhild, shaking her head. "Norway is full of them. A man who must pretend he is a bear or a wolf to pluck up the courage to fight is no drengr."

"It is the work of the little sorcerer, the Sami," Valbrandr said.

"Bavlos?"

"Aye," Valbrandr nodded, still holding his amulet and looking at the dark night sky. "He calls to his gods, beasts, trees, the sky and the moon. The things that live beneath the earth, below Midgard. He makes Rognvald and his men more than Ulfheðnar or berserkers. They drink his potion and become like madmen, stronger than a man, more ferocious. They don't feel pain; wounds cannot stop them. Only death or victory releases them from the frenzy."

"That little man can do all that?" said Bush.

"Aye, the far north is a strange place. Odin does not rule there."

"I wouldn't have taken Rognvald for a berserker, or Ulfheðnar, or whatever he is," Ragnhild remarked.

"He wins battles for the King with his head and his Sami magic. Cunning and brave is Rognvald," said Valbrandr.

The boat lurched forward with a slight jerk at first and then picked up speed as the oars bit into the water. Hundr sighed and let his hand rest on the cruel face of his ivory sword pommel. He closed his eyes, breathing slowly. His whole life had led to this moment. If Harald won the battle, he would reward Hundr with land and make him a Jarl of Norway. Hundr would make his crews rich and finally become what he set out to be years earlier when he had fled his eastern home as a boy. His hand tightened on Fenristooth's ivory. The forces Kjotve had brought to Hafrsfjord were much larger than Harald had expected. That much was apparent in the worry etched on the King's face. The chances of victory were small, and much of it hinged on the success of Hundr's battle plan. To lose was to die. There was no in-between. Kjotve had them penned in, and if he was victorious, then Hundr and all his men would be slain. The best they could hope for would be a warrior's death and a place in the halls of the gods.

Hear me, Odin. Hear my prayer. We risk our lives this day in a war of kings. We honour you with our bravery and our deeds. Bring me luck, bring me victory. Let my men live, and we will send you many brave souls for your Einherjar.

The oar blades cut the water with loud splashes, and Hundr looked across the bay and saw dozens of other ships leaving the port. Harald's warriors crammed the decks. Even in the darkness, Hundr could see their heads silhouetted against the warships' hulls. Men brought axes, swords, spears and shields to fight on the water at Hafrsfjord. Most of Harald's army were the men of Norway, armed in leather and carrying only a spear. They came to fight and die for their King in return for the land he granted them to farm. But the men who would do the real fighting were the Vikings, the men who fought for Harald for silver and glory, men like Hundr. Hard-baked leather breastplates protected these men, and they brought axes and shields aboard their ships. The fierce ones, the leaders and champions, wore brynjar mail coats and were armed with swords or finely crafted war axes. The island grew closer. It emerged from the darkness first as a shadow, and then the outlines of its trees and rocks began showing themselves grey and silver in the night.

Hundr clenched his teeth. He turned and let his eye wander over the familiar faces of his crew. Sigvarth, Skapti, and others. Good men, strong men. They were Vikings all, and they deserved victory. Hundr wanted it for them as much as for himself. They had sworn an oath to serve him, and now he had brought them to this battle at the edge of Norway, where they would risk their lives for the wealth they craved. Sigrid, too, was there, armed with a bow, her hair tied back from her face. Her eyes looked enormous in the darkness, wide and darting. She licked her lips, and he thought he saw her shiver, either from the chilly night air or from fear. He wanted to go to her, to tell her to stay at the back of the ship when the fighting started, but he could not. Maybe he should have left her in Agder, where she would be safe now, not sailing to her death amongst a crew of battle-hardened warriors.

"She can look after herself," said Ragnhild, reading Hundr's face like a book. "She can shoot well enough and use that axe she carries."

"I should not have brought her here," Hundr whispered. "Maybe Einar was right. I am reckless and think only of myself. You could all die here today, Ragnhild. Just so I can be a landed Jarl."

"Don't flatter yourself. She left Agder to join us for herself, not for you. Sigrid wants what you want, what all these men want. She wants to honour the gods and fight with bravery."

"You mean she is not here for me? Am I not handsome, Ragnhild?" He twisted his face into a grimace and winked with his good eye.

Ragnhild almost choked from laughing so hard and clapped Bush on the back, causing him to fall off balance onto the deck.

"You have even more scars than I," she spluttered between fits of laughter. "You have one eye whose cavernous pit you never cover, and you are as surly as a toothless grandfather."

"I don't think I have ever seen you laugh so much," Hundr said, and he laughed along with her.

"Why is it that the laughter and jokes come at the most dangerous times," Valbrandr remarked. "We could all die here today."

"We could, but there's no going back now. I plan to stay behind you, anyway. Your shoulders will keep the blades away nicely," quipped Bush, to more laughter.

Hundr looked to the east, where the sun showed a sliver of itself against the black shadow of distant hills beyond Hafrsfjord. Pale yellow crept above the peaks and cast a pallid brightness onto the underside of the dark clouds above. He closed his eye and felt a chill wind gust across the fjord, its cold penetrating into his empty eye so that a tear of fluid ran down his cheek. Briefly, Hundr took in the stillness of that moment, breathing in the crisp morning air. Then, decisively, he opened his good eye, walked to the sheer strake and dragged his sword free of his scabbard.

"King Harald Fairhair," he bellowed across the water. The sun was coming up, and it was time for speed and viciousness. "Are you ready to kill your enemies?"

"To war!" Harald's voice boomed across the water, and Hundr watched as countless ships filled the fjord. They now bristled with weapons, shaking and held aloft by warriors ready to fight and die. Hundr urged the crew to row harder, for their ship must be first. It must be him to break the line and drive panic in Kjotve's ships. All Harald's warriors were on the fjord aboard the King's fleet, beating their oars towards the enemy. The shore was abandoned. Kjotve's land army would find hundreds of campfires burning but no warriors to face them. Hundr had sent scouts throughout the hills surrounding Hafrsfjord to ensure Kjotve and his leaders did not march or sail to join their land army after the parlay on the island. No scout had reported movement, which meant that thus far, the plan was working, and Kjotve and his leaders were aboard their ships in the fjord.

Enemy ships came into view as Hundr's vessel glided past the parlay island. Beast heads and curving prows emerged from the gloom, and the glimpse of morning sun sneaked over the hills and cast a shimmering white reflection on the water. Shouting erupted from across the fjord, and a horn blew a long, mournful note. It alerted the enemy; the fight was about to begin. Hundr was ready to fight and die for his dream, and where Kjotve thought he would face an outnumbered and trapped foe now faced an attacking fleet teeming with warriors baying for his blood.

TWENTY-SEVEN

A prow raced alongside Hundr's ship. Its beast head was a snarling bear whose face they had daubed with dark blood. Its oars moved swiftly and in time, and at each pull, its crew shouted in unison. Each oar stroke was powerful, and the ship surged forward, almost leaping through the water like a sea creature. Her crew were the beast-men, the Ulfheðnar, and as she came alongside, Hundr saw Bavlos the Sami. He was naked, painted in bright white and red, and dancing on the deck like the gods possessed him. He pranced and frothed at the mouth, his face contorted and stretched in his god-drunkenness. The wild Ulfheðnar howled and bayed on the deck behind him, still draped in animal skins but otherwise naked from the waist up. An old woman went amongst them; her shoulders draped in a cloak sewn through with bird feathers. She gave each man a drink from a strangely painted gourd, and they gulped it down hungrily. Rognvald had climbed up onto the mast post and its rigging. He leaned from the post with one arm, and with his other, he brandished his axe. He shouted and roared like a wild animal, and the head and pelt of a silver wolf hung from his head and shoulders. Rognvald looked down at Hundr, and he did not look like the Rognvald that Hundr knew. This man was as feral as the original owner of the pelt he now wore.

"Sigrid, twenty strokes," said Ragnhild. She was readying her bow and bade the daughter of Ketil Flatnose to join her. They took up a position on either side of the prow, and each tested their weapon's pull. Hundr was breathing heavily, and he could see men on the enemy ships now, bodies moving frantically and oars dipping into the fjord as they formed their ships into a defensive line. Hundr smiled to himself. The plan was working. He imagined the panic among Kjotve's fleet as they realised the caged animal had sprung free. Their ships had drifted during the night, a night spent in confident slumber. Kjotve's boats had turned and twisted on their anchor ropes, the heavy stones keeping the warships in place, but each vessel was in a different direction, and now their crews tried desperately to make their fleet into a wall of ships to meet Harald's attack.

"There, look," called Bush. He held onto the bowline rope, leaning over the side to point ahead to Kjotve's ships. Bush was wearing his war helmet, his most prized possession, and his brynjar—to slip in that heavy war gear was to die beneath the water. Hundr looked to where Bush pointed and saw that three of Kjotve's ships had become entangled in their rush to form up and meet Harald's surprise attack. Their hulls were clashing, and their oar strokes spoiled against one another. Hundr could hear the roars of their captains as they frantically shouted orders above the din of Harald's ship army and its undulating war cries.

"Full speed, fast and hard, Bush, straight into them," said Hundr. He took a deep breath. Fifteen strokes away.

Bush strode along the deck, bellowing orders and clapping rowers on the back. They were red-faced and sweating, backs stretching and muscles straining as they picked up the pace.

"Fifteen more pulls, and we are amongst them, lads," Hundr shouted. "Fourteen more now. Fourteen pulls, and we bring death to Kjotve and his men. Glory will be ours! Odin wants you to pull harder, he wants you to kill, and he wants you all to become heroes!"

Their faces now became wide-eyed and savage. Each man roared at each long pull, and the ship raced forward, surpassing even Rognvald and his Sami drunk wolf-men.

"Brace yourselves," Ragnhild bellowed, and she loosed an arrow shot which sailed swiftly from view. The air around Hundr hissed, and he heard the splash of missiles hitting the water and the thud of arrow slamming into the deck. A man cried out, and Hundr turned to see a warrior shot in the neck by a white-feathered arrow. His hands clutched at the wound, and it oozed thick blood between his fingers. The man's oar was loose and fouling the strokes of the surrounding men. Bush dashed to the injured man and dragged him away from his rowing bench. Hundr cursed as the loose oar spoiled the rowing rhythm, and the ship veered off course. Hundr sheathed Fenristooth and leapt onto the rowing bench. He grabbed the oar, waited for the strokes behind and in front to hit the water and rise, and joined the rhythm. He twisted the oar blade, the timber smooth in his grip, and leant forward. Hundr raised his arms, allowing the weight of the oar to bring it down towards the water and let out a clipped roar as the oar blade dipped below the surface, and he hauled back, leaning into the stroke. The muscles between his shoulders stretched and pulled, and he brought the oar up again, concentrating on keeping time with the other oarsmen.

"Row for the Man with the Dog's Name!" shouted Bush.

"Hundr, Hundr, Hundr!" the men responded. Hundr felt his heart swell and saw Valbrandr take up the battle cry. He stood close to Ragnhild with his throwing axes ready at his feet. More missiles poured into the water around the racing ship, and more slammed into the deck. Another man cried out behind Hundr, beyond his sight. Harald's bowman, Unarr, had joined Ragnhild, and they loosed shaft after shaft towards the enemy. With each one they loosed, there was one less man to kill.

Hundr pulled and chanted with the men. The muscles in his back were screaming. The twang of Ragnhild, Unarr, and Sigrid's bows thrummed, and Valbrandr grunted as he launched the first of his throwing axes across the space between the ships. Hundr heard a sound like a monstrous bird swooping from above. He flinched and turned to look across the bows. A forest of arrows flew from the long line of Harald's ships, sailing in an arc across the sky. The arrows rose, and Hundr followed their flight over his shoulder, pulling again, his arms burning from the strain. There was a collective cry of pain and horror as the wave of missiles struck Kjotve's ships, and already another wave was in flight.

"Here we go, lads, brace yourselves," Bush called from somewhere aft. Hundr clenched his teeth and gripped his oar, knuckles showing white. A spear whipped past his shoulder, and Hundr held his breath. He dipped his oar, forcing himself to concentrate and keep time with his oar mates. Hundr was suddenly jolted forwards, thrown from his bench to cannon into the warrior in front of him. An ear-wrenching crunch filled the air, and the deck was a mess of fallen men and scattered weapons. He tried to rise but slipped backwards because the ship had titled upwards where it had slammed into an enemy vessel, and her prow rode high on that ship's deck. Hundr grabbed the sheer strake to steady himself, and he saw the men from the damaged ship falling, screaming, into the fjord as their boat canted, almost tipping over under the impact, before righting herself. Hundr stood. He left his sword in its scabbard, the blade too long for the close work he expected, and instead grabbed an axe from the deck. He rose to see Valbrandr still hurling his throwing axes across the space between the ships, and then the muscled warrior made the leap, throwing his last axe as he was in mid-air, and then he went beyond Hundr's sight. Leif Lokisword followed Valbrandr across the bows, sword in hand. Sigrid, Unarr, and Ragnhild poured shafts of death into the enemy. Shouting, screaming, and carnage filled the air.

Hundr looked over the side and saw more men had already made the jump across to the enemy ship, but she was slipping backwards, the prow sliding off the deck and back into the fjord.

"Keep her here," Hundr shouted back to Bush, and his old friend nodded and roared at the men to salvage some oars. Hundr ran towards the prow and leapt, axe in hand, towards the enemy. He landed heavily on the sheer strake of the enemy ship, clinging to the timbers, his feet barely above the waterline. A snarling man came at him with a knife, but Hundr chopped his axe into the man's foot, pinning him to the deck. He let go of the weapon, scrambled over the side to knee his attacker in the face, and yanked the axe free of his foot. A red-faced man with a broken nose came at him with a spear, and Hundr swayed aside to dodge the blow and cracked his axe blade across the attacker's forehead. The man's skull made a sickening crunch, and warm blood spattered onto Hundr's face.

More of his men piled onto the warship and moved along her deck. Many of her warriors had fallen over the side when she had rolled from the impact of his charging ship, and so the fight was over in moments. Hundr saw Valbrandr throw a warrior overboard and then hurl a spear across the water to pierce an enemy's chest onboard the next ship. Afkar Magnusson's mail was already sheeted in gore as he moved amongst Kjotve's men like a killer demon.

"Keep moving. Attack the next ship. Go!" Hundr shouted and moved to the ship's stern, his foot slipping in the blood of a fallen enemy. A man writhed beneath the tiller and grabbed at Hundr's ankle. Hundr slammed his axe into the injured man's face to send him to the afterlife. He looked athwart and saw more ships had joined the fight. As far as he could see across Hafrsfjord, ships came together, like great wooden bulls clashing in a watery field. His men poured over the side and onto the next of Kjotve's ships, and Hundr followed them. He put his hand on the sheer stake and made the jump where the two ships touched sides. As he landed, he saw Sigrid fighting with an enemy warrior, and she was hard-pressed as the man hacked at her with his axe. She was parrying the blows with her own weapon, but the man's size was pushing her back towards the water. Hundr dashed forward, and the man saw him coming. The warrior swept his axe with a snarl, but Hundr ducked below the wild swing and slammed his own axe blade into the man's stomach. He wore no armour, so the blow was like cutting into a side of meat. The brute doubled over, and Hundr left him to collapse, clutching at his terrible wound.

"Stay with Ragnhild," Hundr said, putting his hand on Sigrid's shoulder.

"I can fight for myself," she muttered, shaking

his hand loose.

"Then fight harder," he snapped. "This will be a brutal fight, strike to kill." He whipped Fenristooth free and left her. Hundr cared for Sigrid. He could tell her things he usually kept locked away inside him, the pain of his past and his hopes and dreams. He didn't want her to die, but she had chosen the path of the Viking, and she was right. She must fight for herself. Hundr saw Valbrandr kill a man with his axe, but a bald enemy plunged a knife into his back, and Valbrandr fell to one knee with the shock of it. Hundr ran to him and swept his sword in a reverse cut across the knifeman's throat, sending him spinning and spraying blood across the deck. He didn't stop to check Valbrandr but instead pushed forward across the deck, where he saw a big man struggling to pull in a brynjar mail coat. The man was bent over with his arms outstretched, trying to shake the heavy coat of interlinked iron circles over his head. Hundr laughed and rammed the point of his blade into the man's belly. He laughed because the ploy was working. He was breaking Kjotve's line of ships, and the battle joy was upon him, the feeling of alertness where men try to kill you, but you kill them first. Everything was heightened, the clang of iron weapons clashing, the crunch and moan of timbers as ships smashed together, and the screams and yells of the injured and dying.

A howling caused Hundr to spin around, and he saw the wolf-men, the Ulfheðnar, swarming the deck, making animal grunts and calls, their pelts sticky with blood and their chests sheeted with sweat. They moved like a pack of wolves amongst the enemy, chopping and hacking with brutal efficiency. Rognvald sawed a seax so hard into a man's neck that his head almost came off.

"Rognvald," Hundr shouted, and his head snapped up, soaked in blood with a feral look in his eye. "We must get to Kjotve. Have you seen his ship?" The key to Hundr's battle plan working was getting to Kjotve and killing him on the water. But if Kjotve escaped and joined his land army, he could continue the fight. The war must end with the battle on the waters of Hafrsfjord.

Rognvald's glazed eyes cleared for a moment, and his voice was strangely low, almost a growl.

"Kjotve is three ships along the line. Let's hunt him together." Rognvald barked an order, and his beast-men rallied around him, and they charged towards the next ship in line.

"We must get to Kjotve. His ships are forming up," said Ragnhild. She stopped beside Hundr and nocked an arrow to her bow, searching for a target.

"Three ships along. Follow Rognvald."

She nodded, released her shaft across the water and set off after Rognvald. The next ship fell to

Rognvald and his savage Ulfheðnar with rapid brutality, and Hundr followed close behind. He could see Kjotve's warship now only one more vessel along, his hawk banner fluttering from the mast. Hundr dashed forwards. To strike Kjotve down was to win the battle, and he saw that glory stretching in front of him like a vision from Odin. Suddenly, that vision was interrupted, and Hundr was thrown from his feet, landing on his back on top of another warrior. He scrambled to find his footing just in time to see a baleful figure with iron-grey hair surging from the deck of an enemy ship. He wore mail and a shining helmet, his sword was dazzling in the early morning light, and Hundr's guts twisted. Ketil Flatnose charged the deck. He had come for vengeance.

TWENTY-EIGHT

"I have you now, dog. No escape this time," Ketil snarled. The shining warlord swung his sword, and Hundr raised his Fenristooth to parry the blow. The power in the stroke jarred down Hundr's arm, and he punched the old warrior in the stomach, driving him backwards. "Bastard," Ketil snarled, and he came on again, swinging, but he was gasping for air, winded from the punch.

"You are old and fat, and I stole your silver," Hundr said.

The Jarl was a skilled fighter and had a lifetime of oar strength surging through him. As a boy, Hundr's weapons master had often reminded him that fury can be a warrior's greatest strength, but it must be controlled, or it can cause a man to forget his skill and resort to wild rage.

"Die!" Ketil roared and came on again. He gripped his sword in two hands, and Hundr was driven back by a powerful downward cut. Hundr danced around him, and his shoulder crashed into one of Ketil's men, who sliced an axe blade across his arm. The pain of the wound burned, and he headbutted that man hard in the nose, turning just in time to parry another tremendous stroke of Ketil's sword.

"This blade is Battle Fang, and she belonged to my father," Ketil's voice boomed above the din of the carnage. He was hammering at Hundr, each blow more powerful than the last. Hundr fell to one knee, bracing his sword in both hands against the onslaught. Ketil kicked him in the chest, sending him sprawling, and Hundr rolled on the deck. Another boot stamped on his thigh, and he heard voices screaming all around him. He pushed himself to his feet and saw Ketil trading blows with Harald's man, Leif Lokisword. Leif moved fast and struck out with his blade, but the Orkney Jarl moved with unnatural speed for a man his age. Ketil parried Leif's lunge and brought his own sword around in a monstrous cut. The blow carved through Leif's chest, smashing the rings of his brynjar and cleaving open his chest in a mess of innards and white bone. Ketil grimaced and came for Hundr again. Hundr ran towards him, and this time he unleashed a savage attack of his own, cutting and slashing with his sword. Ketil met each strike and grabbed Hundr's mail to pull him in close. Hundr resisted, and he could smell Ketil's sour breath as the Jarl leaned into him, his face scarred around his bulbous broken nose.

Hundr reached behind him, and before Ketil could drag him close, he drew his seax and stabbed it into Ketil's guts. It scraped across his mail, but the links held firm. Hundr shoved harder, and the blade slid downwards until it found Ketil's groin, biting into soft flesh. Ketil roared in agony and clutched at Hundr's face, but he shook himself free of the dying Jarl's grasp and cut his throat with a slash of his sword. Ketil dropped to his knees, and his sword clattered to the deck. Hundr crouched and grabbed the blade, forcing it into Ketil's hand. The Jarl sagged into Hundr's arms, his body heavy and quivering as his lifeblood pulsed from him.

"Go to Odin's hall, warlord. Save a place for me there," Hundr whispered, looking into the dying man's pale eyes and ashen face. The battle raged around them, and Hundr saw himself in Ketil— or the man he would be, perhaps. A man who had fought his whole life and forged a reputation respected across the North, with an island to rule as his own.

"Hundr, Kjotve's ship is moving," Ragnhild called.

Hundr grabbed Ketil's blade, Battle Fang, and ran to the stern, still gasping for breath from his fight with the famous Jarl and armed with two swords.

"Shit," blasted Hundr. Ketil's flagship had pulled away from the savage clamour of ships and dying men. His warriors had oars in the fjord, and the vessel was driving for open water. "Who is that?" he pointed at a long warship, its hull painted red, deep blood-red, and pounded its oars through the fjord, racing towards the mass of ships.

"Thorir Haklag and his berserkers, and they aim for King Harald," said Sigrid. "I saw his ship in Agder." Her face was drawn and pale, and her leather armour splashed with gore.

"Sigrid...I..."

"Father!" she cried before Hundr could tell her of her father's death. She ran to Ketil's bleeding corpse and collapsed onto his body, oblivious to the battle raging around her. Ketil's men had broken once their Lord had fallen, and Rognvald and his Ulfheðnar were amongst them in their unworldly fury. The deck of that ship was a welter of death, and blood sloshed thick in the bilge, men rolled and screamed in agony with terrible wounds, and more lay forever silent, rocking with the ebb of the fjord. Hundr saw Skapti sitting against the hull, shaking and holding the stump of his arm severed at the elbow. He was white as a fetch as he watched his lifeblood pump out onto the deck.

The horror of the death ship had Hundr transfixed, and Ragnhild shook him by the shoulder to snap him out of his terror-stricken daze. He looked at her and nodded his thanks, then took three strides to where Rognvald knelt on the chest of a fallen enemy, stabbing him repeatedly with a knife.

"Rognvald," he said, but the warrior ignored him, so intent was he in his murderous rage. Hundr pushed him off the man, and Rognvald turned to him, sheeted in blood and his eyes wide and white beneath the crimson covering his face. "The King is under attack, and we can't get to him in time."

Rognvald wiped a shaking hand across his face and looked across the water. His jaw dropped as he spotted Thorir Haklag bearing down on Harald's ship. Harald was engaged with another of Kjotve's warships, and Hundr could see weapons clashing as the King and his warriors fought to subdue their enemies.

"They will outnumber Harald. We must help him," Rognvald whispered. His shoulders sagged, and whatever power Bavlos had infused him with seeped away to join the blood of the fallen.

"This ship is lost. We can't get to him from

here," Hundr said, and he could feel his dream slipping away with each stroke of Thorir's oars. He searched the waters, thick with battling ships like a twisted forest of death. He could not decipher which ships were Kjotve's and which were Harald's. The battle had turned into a clash of ship's crew against ship's crew, and he could not tell who was winning.

"There," Rognvald pointed. "We need to cross six ships and get to that boat at the end of the line. We can free that ship and get to Harald."

"If he lives that long," Hundr said, seeing the furious fighting across each deck they must cross to get to the King.

"Just so."

"So, to save the King, we must cross six ships filled with warriors locked in a fight to the death, free the last of those boats and row it to Harald before Thorir Haklag butchers him and turns our dreams to ashes?" said Ragnhild.

"Yes." Rognvald nodded, and he dashed about the deck, shouting the order to his Ulfheðnar to prepare them for the charge.

Hundr nodded and wiped a sheen of sweat and blood from his face with his sleeve.

"Let's get about it," Ragnhild said. She hooked her bow across her back and picked up a fallen axe from the deck so that she held one in each hand. Valbrandr joined them, and together they formed a wedge, the Ulfheðnar in front, chests heaving and bodies glistening in the morning light.

"To the King," Rognvald roared, and they set off moving at a half-run, a wedge of fifteen warriors cutting and slashing as they went. They reached the bow and leapt onto the next vessel, facing a crew of Kjotve's warriors on a ship strewn with bodies, writhing in pain or dead. The men on that ship were a ragged band of ten warriors, bedraggled and huddled together at the prow. Hundr noted the look of horror on their faces as they watched the Ulfheðnar board their ship. In the dead and dying of the deck, Hundr saw a battle already fought and won, and these men were the survivors. Those war-weary men braced themselves to fight again, and Valbrandr hurled himself at them, a knife still stuck in the back of his shoulder. The Ulfheðnar followed him, howling like animals as they charged. The fight lasted only a few heartbeats. Kjotve's already exhausted men were cut down with ruthless efficiency.

"Come on, to the next ship," barked Ragnhild.

Hundr followed her through the dying warriors, and they leapt onto the next deck. Sigrid came alongside him. She looked at him with a face stained with tears running through the blood and filth of the battle. The look did not signal forgiveness for her father's death, but it showed no blame either, and that was enough. She nocked an arrow to her bow and knelt to shoot a low, powerful shot through the rigging and on into the throat of an enemy sailor. The crew on that ship saw the Ulfheðnar coming for them and turned with their hands raised.

"Don't attack; they are ours," Rognvald shouted. The men came towards the Ulfheðnar, grinning. Sigrid had killed one of them, thinking them enemy warriors, but they were Harald's men, making ready to board the next ship over, where the deck was crammed with warriors and flashing blades. Together, they charged towards the stern, and the ship tipped with the weight of their collective bodies. Fjord water rushed onto the deck, and Hundr splashed through it to launch himself onto the third ship, swinging his two swords as he jumped. Ragnhild was with him, and the two of them forced themselves into the battle. Something hit Hundr in the back, throwing him forward, and his foot slipped on the slick deck. Fighting men pinned him close, and he couldn't move. The deck of that ship was full of men, fighting in a space too small to hold them all. Hundr couldn't breathe, and he felt panic burning in his chest from the press of it. Across the melee, he saw Rollo, monstrously huge, hacking his axe into the chest of Unarr the Bowman.

"Thorir has reached the King," a man shouted.

Then, across the fjord, Hundr saw it for himself. The red hulled ship was alongside the King's own boat, and now, Harald was fighting two crews of enemy warriors.

"We have to get across this ship," Hundr bellowed, and he butted and kicked at the surrounding men, furiously trying to get himself free. Ragnhild sliced her axe through the face of a warrior, and blood sprayed across Hundr's cheek. He wriggled one arm free and punched the hilt of Battle Fang into an enemy, causing that man to recoil in pain, and Hundr pushed himself to join Ragnhild in a yard of space amongst the press of death.

"We won't make it in time," she said, grimacing from sheer exhaustion. "Look, they outnumber the King. He will die here on Hafrsfjord."

"We cannot allow that, Ragnhild. We will die with him. I must get us across two more ships, and then we can get to him. We must get to him."

"We don't just have to get to the ship. We must row it to Harald. It can't be done before Thorir kills him. There are too many of them."

"We can," said Hundr. But he saw no way across the deck. The Ulfheðnar were winning, they were cutting through the enemy, but they were also dying. There were only eight of them still fighting that Hundr could see. Rollo had disappeared in the furious skirmish. Hundr sheathed one sword and hauled himself up onto the sheer strake, holding the rigging for balance. He edged his way along the ridge of the boat. The ship sat low in the water from the sheer weight of the men on her deck, and Hundr saw a chance for speed.

"Shit," cursed Ragnhild, and she followed him. It was a foolish move; one slip and they would fall into the water and drown in their brynjars.

Hundr could see the next ship along, and its deck was empty, all her crew having poured onto the death ship he now tried to race along. Before he could take another step, a fist grabbed his brynjar at the neck and hauled him onto the deck. The man was powerful, and his face was a flat slab of hate beneath white-blonde hair.

"I am Had of Telemark," the strong warrior spat in Hundr's face, and he tried to bring a war axe to strike at Hundr, but the press of men fouled the blow. Hundr raised his sword arm at the elbow and dragged the blade underhand across Had's mail and then across his face, slicing open his nose and eyes in a terrible wound of dark blood and pink flesh. Had tried to cry in terror, but the sword was in his mouth, and he gurgled on his own blood.

"The King, the King!" a man shouted, and

there was a collective gasp of despair amongst the battling warriors.

Hundr's heart sank, believing the King had fallen, but he twisted away from Had, and with his good eye, he saw the fight still raged aboard the King's ship and prayed to Odin that Harald yet lived. Hundr could see the bare-chested berserkers were more than halfway along the deck of Harald's warship, and he knew there would be no time to get to him. All was lost, and the King would die. He looked back and could see none of his own men. Hundr had led his crews into another slaughter, and as he looked at the warriors clawing and biting at one other, washed with blood and gore, he saw his end. He and his men would all die on Hafrsfjord and be lost forever. Hundr would never return to his homeland as a Lord and never show his father and brothers his worth. He sagged, the fight fleeing from him. His arms fell to his sides, heavy and exhausted.

"Another ship," Rognvald called. "Heading for the King!"

Hundr's breath caught in his throat as he saw a dragon ship—its oars pounding at the water and racing across the fjord. A warrior was at its prow, a big man shaking his war axe and roaring his defiance to the heavens.

"I know that ship," Hundr whispered in

amazement. "It's the Sea-Stallion. It's Einar Rosti."

TWENTY-NINE

Einar thrust his axe high in the air. The Sea-Stallion rowed into the wind, whipping Einar's hair back beneath his helmet. His heart pounded in his chest as he raced towards the fight.

"Pull, men!" he shouted to his warriors. "Let's send some bastards to Valhalla." The crew cheered and hauled on their oars. Hafrsfjord was raging with the sounds of crashing timbers, the din of clashing weapons and the roar of warriors. Einar had never seen so many ships; drakkars and karves filled the fjord, locked together in a ferocious sea battle. He had brought the Sea-Stallion around the neck of the fjord's narrow peninsular and then through a high-sided corridor of rock which split opposing headlands before emerging from the calm waters and into Hafrsfjord itself. In the channel, ships had sailed past him. Men with ashen faces looked away as they rowed towards the sea, afar from the battle, faint-hearted men, fleeing, not prepared to die in the churning maelstrom of the battle of Hafrsfjord.

"It is the King. I see his wolf banner," said Hildr, pointing across the prow.

Sure enough, Harald's wolf flag flew high on his mast, and he was under attack from two of Kjotve's ships.

"Can you see any of our ships anywhere?" Einar asked. They had rowed around the eastern side of the battle, trying to spy one of Hundr's ships, but without success. It had been impossible for Einar to tell who was friend or foe. The green sails of Harald's fleet were furled as the sea battle raged, and it was a mess of crews killing crews. As the Sea-Stallion rowed into Hafrsfjord, there had been a moment of uncertainty as Einar struggled to decide where to attack.

"No," Hildr replied. "But King Harald will die if we don't sail to his aid."

"That's why we are here, to save a King."

"No regrets?"

"No regrets." One ship being attacked by two seemed like as good a place as any for Einar to join the battle, and the Norns had weaved Einar's fate in with King Harald's and led him to the King in his moment of peril. Once Einar had decided to return to Hundr, the Sea-Stallion had followed Norway's coastline until fishermen spoke of great fleets massing to the north. Einar had found the Seaworm along the coast, dragged ashore at a fishing village. The folk there spoke of the battle in the fjord, and some of Hundr's crew had remained with the Seaworm and told Einar where to find the Man with the Dog's Name. "Brace yourselves for impact." He shouted. The men rowed with their backs to the King's ship, and Einar did not intend to pull alongside the three fighting vessels gently.

"There are berserkers on that ship," noted Hildr as she nocked an arrow to her bow.

"I hate berserkers. Seems to me there are more of the bastards in Norway than there are normal warriors. Five more pulls, lads."

Hildr pulled and released her arrow and then immediately readied another.

"King Harald is at the stern. He doesn't have many warriors left around him," she said.

Einar sat down with his back to the prow and took a deep breath. He was old, and the Norns had turned the thread of his life sour in their home beneath the great tree, Yggdrasil. But he was Einar the Brawler, and he was here to fight for Hildr, Finn, and Hundr. The impact came with a crash to shake the gods in Asgard. Timber planking snapped and creaked. It threw men from their rowing benches, and Einar leapt to his feet, stumbling as the hull pitched to one side. He clambered up onto the prow and laughed as he stared along the deck of King Harald's warship. The Sea-Stallion had smashed into her keel, rolling her over and tipping every man onboard from his feet. She had righted herself in a wash of seawater in the bilge, and men roared in terror as they were thrown around the deck like weasels in a sack.

Einar jumped onto the deck and slammed his axe into the neck of a berserker, a man with red hair tumbling loose about his head and wearing no armour. The man did not even have the chance to see his killer. He was on all fours trying to rise when Einar's cold blade sliced open the back of his neck. The blade came up and flicked blood in an arc, and Einar kept the axe moving. He cut through a rigging line to send the mast spar loose and create more chaos. Through the mass of warriors struggling to get to their feet after the ship's impact, Einar could see a huddle of men at the ship's stern, crowded behind a shield wall four shields across. Before them, corpses were piled on the deck, like some grizzly sacrificial pyre to the gods. The deck was sloshing with seawater turned pink as it washed the blood from the fallen. Two men tried to rise before Einar, both with bare chests.

"Berserkers," Einar snarled, thinking of Black Gorm and Finn's abduction. He kicked one of them in the face and cracked his axe across the temple of the other. Einar drew his seax from its sheath at his back and trod carefully amongst the detritus. An enormous warrior rose before him with a blood-soaked face. The berserker opened his mouth, and the tendons in his neck bulged as though he were about to let out a war cry to shake the very heavens, but an arrow shaft slammed into the cavern of his maw. The warrior turned slowly, the arrow protruding from the back of his skull, and Einar kicked him in the chest to send him crashing into the fjord. Slowly, the berserkers rose to their feet, like puppets at a spring festival, dancing on a thread. One amongst them was muscled and smeared with dark gore, and his lip turned inwards at the centre. A harelip. A dozen warriors found their feet and faced Einar, but he smiled. The ship moved beneath his feet, pitching to port as his men joined him from the Sea-Stallion.

"I am Einar Rosti. I challenge you, Thorir Haklag, fight me here man against man," Einar shouted, holding his weapons wide.

"Haklag?" said Thorir, his face and left eye twitching at the mention of the insulting name. He barged his men out of the way, holding a sword in one hand and a bloody axe in the other.

Over Thorir's shoulder, Einar saw King Harald's

face appear above the top of the shield wall. The King was wide-eyed and pale, and his mouth was gaping. He nodded at Einar, and Einar smiled. He had come to fight and to earn the favour of the King.

Thorir was an enormous man, as tall as Einar himself but broader in the neck and shoulder. He was stripped to the waist, as were all his berserkers, and his torso was crisscrossed in cuts and wounds from the fierce fighting with Harald's bodyguards.

"You come to save your shit weasel of a King? He will die, but you can die first, old man," barked Thorir. He lunged forward with serpent-like speed, and the tip of his sword snaked out at Einar's face. Einar swayed away from the blow, forced the blade with his seax and drove himself forwards to allow Thorir's follow-up blow to foul on the shoulder of his brynjar mail. Einar was inside Thorir's reach, and he dragged his seax across Thorir's chest, cutting through his flesh as though it were a yuletide ham. Thorir grimaced at the pain and tried to headbutt Einar, but he lowered his chin, so Thorir's face smashed into his helmet. Thorir wheeled away and spat a gobbet of blood from his bloody nose and mouth. He swung his sword wildly, and Einar caught it in the beard of his axe and locked it. Then with a flick of his wrist, he sprang the sword out of Thorir's grasp, and it splashed into the water-filled bilge.

"Kill him, Einar!" the King roared, and his men took up the cheer.

The berserkers were staring open-mouthed as their famous leader was outmatched by the grey-haired warrior who had rammed their ship and halted their assault on King Harald. They began to stamp their feet on the hull and chant Thorir's name, the name of their leader and champion.

"Die, turd," Thorir rumbled, coming at Einar like a charging bull. He had let his axe drop and simply hurled himself across the deck. The sheer berserker madness of the attack surprised Einar. He couldn't raise his weapons in time, and Thorir smashed into him, driving him backwards against the sheer strake. For a horrifying moment, Einar thought they would both topple over the side, but the timbers held them. Thorir punched him in the face and clasped a meaty hand around his throat. With his other hand, Thorir held Einar tight to him with an iron grip. Einar couldn't breathe, and Thorir spat blood from his mouth into Einar's face. He felt darkness enveloping him, his strength pouring away like water. Einar saw Hildr with an arrow nocked to her bow, but a crewman waved her down. It was a fight to the death, and to shoot Thorir now would deny Einar his place in Valhalla with dishonour. But he was not ready for Valhalla yet. So, he released his own weapons from his hands and drove his thumb deep into Thorir's eye, gouging, twisting, and feeling the jelly give way beneath his nail. Then with his other hand, he grabbed Thorir between the legs and twisted savagely.

Thorir howled and released Einar's throat, and the two men fought brutally, hammering fists and forcing each other back and forth, slamming into the mast and twisting around rigging. Einar's face was a throbbing mass of pain, his ribs burned like a blacksmith's forge, and he feared one or more of his fingers were broken. Einar felt himself tiring, and Thorir felt as strong as ever as they beat, snarled and kicked at each other. Knowing he couldn't last much longer against the younger man, Einar hooked his foot behind Thorir's knee, and they fell together, splashing into the filthy sea water flooding the deck. Thorir rolled him as they fell, and Einar's heart thundered as Thorir forced his face below the water, leaning on him with the weight of his bulk. Einar scratched and beat at the berserker's arms, but they were as rods of iron, and he could not move them. He splashed his hands into the water and scrabbled around desperately, searching for anything he could grasp, knowing he was moments from death. Finally, Einar's right hand curled around something rough to the touch, and he yanked it upwards to clatter into Thorir's head. The berserker fell from Einar's chest, and Einar sucked in huge mouthfuls of air as his face broke through the water's surface. He kept moving and clawed his way onto Thorir's flailing body. Now it was Einar's turn to kneel on Thorir's chest. The thing he had grabbed in his death throes was an age-blackened wooden bucket, riveted together by rusty nails. Einar clutched it in both hands and beat Thorir to death with it, smashing his skull and face to an unrecognisable pulp of bone and gore.

"Your leader is dead, and the King's army has won. Surrender now and live," Einar shouted, between gasps of air. Thorir's berserkers looked at one other and then at King Harald. The shields before him lowered to allow the King to stride forwards. All fight went out of the enemy then. They looked across the fjord and watched as ships raced furiously away from the battle to row towards the channel and then on to the sea and survival. Einar could not tell whose ships they were, Harald's or Kjotve's. But it didn't matter. The berserkers dropped their weapons, and the King walked amongst them and came to place a hand on Einar's shoulder.

"You saved my life, Einar Rosti. I won't forget that," he said before addressing the others. "Drop your weapons, Thorir is dead, and I am King of all Norway. This is the Yngling blade, the sword of the gods and whoever wields it rules the north." He held the sword high, and the berserkers' eyes followed it skywards. They let their axes fall and looked at the King with open mouths. "Kill them all," Harald said softly and sheathed his sword. Hildr shot one man in the belly, and Einar's men joined Harald's survivors to hack into the forlorn berserkers who would die without their weapons and be denied eternity in Valhalla.

THIRTY

Hundr marched up the beach, clutching Fenristooth in one hand and Battle Fang in the other. His eyes were stinging and the muscles at his shoulders and arms burned from exhaustion. The Battle of Hafrsfjord had raged for most of the day. Fighting on the shifting and treacherous decks where ships had come together had been a perilous and murderous fight. Hundr had lost count of the men he had wounded and killed. As the day wore on, more and more of Kjotve's ships pulled away from the battle itself to flee the carnage and try to escape down the narrow channel from Hafrsfjord to the North Sea. Harald's fleet and Hundr's ships had hunted them whilst Kjotve's land army looked on helplessly from the south shore as they cut Kjotve's Lords and Jarls down before their eyes.

"Are you sure he is here?" Hundr barked at a

small, wiry man who came running up the beach towards him.

"He is, lord," grinned the man through a mouth of stubby brown teeth. "He is over that sandbank yonder. Four crews of them. Holed up in a fortress of the ancient folk."

"A fortress?" Hundr winced as he rolled his shoulders to loosen the muscles.

"Just raised banks of earth, lord, not a wall or palisade."

Hundr nodded his thanks and strode to the sandbank's top on the beach's fringe, where it fell away into a flat, open field beyond. The grass swayed under the wind in a sea of light green. Bush was there, his helmet and liner removed so that his bald head shone white under the sun.

"Is Kjotve behind there?" Hundr asked, pointing to a ridge of grass-covered earth that stretched for a hundred paces across the flatlands.

"He is. Rollo is there too," said Bush, and he grimaced and touched gingerly at a bloodstain on his thigh.

"Are you hurt badly?"

"No, some Norse bastard stabbed me from where he lay on the deck of a ship we crossed. I thought he was dead until he rose to stick his knife in me."

"Make sure Ragnhild or Hildr cleans and wraps it for you. More deaths happen from wounds like that rather than the actual fighting."

Bush nodded.

"Let's get this over with. There's been enough blood for one day," said Ragnhild as she strode past them and on down into the field.

"How many of our men have we lost?" Hundr asked.

Bush scratched his head and sucked at his teeth.

"Too many. Hard to say in all the confusion. That was a terrible place, an awful battle. I lost sight of most of the lads once we started crossing to the other boats. Old Einar saved the bloody day. Must have decided he still loves you after all." Bush chuckled.

"Here he comes now, with the King of all Norway," Hundr said, turning to watch the King's ship row through the surf and her hull rise from the water like a wooden sea beast. Harald jumped from the prow into the sand, Yngling blade in hand, followed by the survivors of his hearth troop and then by Einar, Hildr and their crew. Hundr raised a sword in greeting, and Harald returned the salute. Einar raised a hand, and Hundr smiled to see his old friend alive and well.

"Welcome, King Harald. Kjotve the Rich

and the last of his men are behind that embankment," Hundr announced as the King stalked up the beach. The sands and the grasslands beyond were littered with warriors who had come to the island in pursuit of Kjotve's ship.

"Your plan worked, my friend," said Harald. But, as he drew closer, Hundr saw the King's eyes were sunken, and the blood of the fallen crusted his armour and famous hair.

"The gods saw our daring and rewarded us with battle-luck, King Harald," said Hundr.

"Kjotve's army was impotent, and we trapped his leaders on the fjord."

"And now you are King of all Norway."

"We must kill Kjotve first," Harald sighed. "Many men lost their lives today, and Valhalla will teem with heroes."

"Four ships of them left?" asked Einar, nodding back towards the beach where Kjotve had abandoned four fine warships to bob on the tide.

"Four crew," said Bush, and then he winked at Einar. "Nice to have you back, Einar."

"I heard you were in it up to your bloody necks again, and I thought I would give you a hand."

"Thank you, Einar," said Hundr, and he stepped towards his old friend with his arm outstretched. Einar's hard slab face split into a broad smile, adding more lines to his already creased skin.

"It was luck, really. First, I came upon the Seaworm, and then when I sailed in Hafrsfjord, I couldn't find you, but I found the King." Einar grabbed Hundr's forearm in the warriors' grip, and they clasped each other warmly.

"You have always been lucky, Einar the Brawler." Hundr grinned, and Einar laughed. Then, he dragged Hundr into a bear-like embrace, and they held each other, slapping each other's backs, relieved to be friends again.

"Let's get this over with," said the King, and he marched through the field to finish the war with Kjotve the Rich.

The ridge of raised earth bristled with spear points, and the tops of helmets peeked over the rustling grass, their bright metal catching the late afternoon sun. Rognvald had marshalled a force of three crews of warriors, including his own Ulfheðnar crew. The warriors shuffled sideways to make a path for the King to approach, and Hundr marched just behind Harald, flanked by Ragnhild and Einar. The warriors were as bleary-eyed, bloodstained and bedraggled as Hundr felt. Harald held up the Yngling blade for the men to see, and Hundr saw the looks of awe on the warriors' faces as they watched not only their King march through their ranks but also a sword straight out of legend, a blade once held by the legendary kings of old and forged for the gods themselves.

Rognvald turned to meet the King with a nod and a grim smile. He raised his axe to the warriors and bellowed.

"A cheer for Harald, the first King of all Norway."

"Harald, Harald, Harald!" the warriors chanted, the noise of it rising at each call of his name.

"That ridge looks much higher up close. It will be a bastard to climb it whilst Kjotve's men try to kill us from above," Ragnhild uttered. Sigrid was with her, along with Hildr. Hundr caught Sigrid's eye, and she held his gaze. He could not detect any animosity there. In fact, she looked at him as warmly as she ever had, which relieved him, considering her father had fallen to his sword.

"There has been enough fighting today," said King Harald. "Enough of my people have died. So, who is there with him?"

"Kjotve himself, Sulke of Rogaland, and Rollo," Rognvald answered, glancing at Hundr as he mentioned Rollo's name.

Harald raised his hands and calmed the voices of his warriors. Then, he trudged towards the earthen rampart and stood alone, ten paces ahead of his front rank.

"Kjotve of Agder," Harald shouted towards the hill. "Your forces are routed, and your son is dead. Eirik of Hordaland is dead, and so are Hroald and Had of Telemark. I am King of all Norway and will give your men a chance to live. I will give you all a chance to leave this island of Ytraberget with your lives and your honour if you swear oaths to serve me as King."

There was silence, and Hundr could hear the rustle of the wind on the grass and the cawing of gulls above the beach as they all waited for a response. Then, finally, a figure stood on the ridge, a tall man armed with a spear and an axe.

"Rollo," hissed Einar. "Never trusted that bastard."

"Lord King," said Rollo. "You have won the day, and we have spilt enough Viking blood. Eirik of Hordaland is dead. He died here only moments ago from wounds taken fighting in Hafrsfjord. We fought for our people and for freedom, but our fight is over. We have a request of you, Lord King, a simple thing which can end this war here on this island."

A murmur rose from Harald's warriors, and the King raised his arm to quieten them again.

"What is your request, and where is Kjotve of Agder?"

"I ask for four ships, Lord King. The ships that brought us here to this island. Four ships to take my men and me away. We will swear to honour you as King if you guarantee our safety. Lord King, I will hand Kjotve over to you if you grant that request."

"When Rollo came to my father..." Sigrid said, "...he spoke of fighting for freedom, that Harald was a usurper and a tyrant, and he said Kjotve was his King. Yet now he would turn Kjotve over to save his own skin?"

"Seems to me Rollo breaks oaths and speaks fine words about whatever purpose serves him best. His loyalty is like a fart in the wind," tutted Bush.

"Four ships are a small price to pay to save the lives of the men on his island," said Harald.

"Just so," Rognvald agreed.

"I will grant your request. Now bring Kjotve forth," Harald shouted up to Rollo.

The big man turned and disappeared, and moments later, he returned holding a small man by the scruff of his neck as though he were a scolded child.

"Here is Kjotve, and I have met my end of our bargain," called Rollo. Then, with his free hand, he whipped a knife from his belt and dragged the blade across Kjotve's throat. The King of Agder clutched the gaping wound, and blood spurted through his fingers. He fell to his knees, and Rollo kicked him down the slope.

"So, it is done, and Rollo will live," said Hundr.

"He will live and have his four ships," nodded King Harald. "Rognvald will rule Rogaland, and Hundr, you will be Jarl of Vanylven, in recognition of your deeds in Hafrsfjord."

Hundr bowed his head and sighed. The King had granted what he had craved since he was a boy in Novgorod. His brothers, the princes, had taunted him relentlessly. Each day they had said he would be nothing, a slave and a nithing. Hundr had fought his way up to be the owner and commander of five ships and their crews, and the King of Norway had just made him Jarl of a fine port and all its lands. Hundr looked at Sigrid, and she smiled at him. He had killed her father, but Ketil was a Viking and would drink and fight in Valhalla for eternity. He had died as he had lived. Hundr saw much of himself in Ketil, and now that Harald lay the rule of Vanylven before him, he suddenly realised he did not want it. Hundr knew what he was; he was a Viking, a fighter, and a man of the Whale Road. He had only wanted land to rule to prove his brothers wrong, to show that he wasn't worthless. Now that he had won that land, he knew he could never settle on it and, therefore, never rule it.

"King Harald," he said. Harald turned to him, smiling. "Please allow Einar Rosti to be Jarl of Vanylven in my stead. My days a'viking are not yet over, and Einar will make a fine Jarl."

Harald frowned but then nodded at Einar.

"Einar Rosti, you saved my life when I thought Thorir Haklag would cut me down. You are a worthy Jarl. Will you swear an oath to serve me as Jarl of Vanylven?"

Einar looked at Hundr before closing his eyes. He nodded his thanks, knelt, and swore his oath to King Harald.

"Now, Rognvald, finally, you can cut off this fine head of hair," said Harald.

Harald's warriors cheered their king and made a path for Rollo and his men to march with bowed heads toward the beach. They were beaten men, bloodied and bruised, but alive. Only Rollo walked with his head held high, towering above the others.

"Rollo," Hundr called as he strode past. The big man stopped and smiled at Hundr.

"So, we both survive this day," he remarked and raised an eyebrow as he caught Einar's glare.

"You talked of tyrants and justice, yet you cut your King's throat to save your own life?" asked Hundr.

"I fought against Harald because he stole my

father's land. But I am like you. I fight for myself first. Now, I have four ships to command, so I am almost as wealthy as you, Hundr Dog's Name."

"Men will know you as a turncoat and a betrayer," growled Einar.

"Anyone who wants to challenge me can come and find me. I will be in Frankia, or on the Whale Road." Rollo smiled, and he strode away towards his ships.

"I hope we don't see that bastard again," Einar spat.

"Let him go, for we must sail for Vanylven to enjoy the hospitality of Jarl Einar," said Hundr, clapping his old friend on the shoulder. He watched Rollo disappear over the sandbank and then turned to see Harald walking amongst his men receiving their acclaim. Hundr smiled because they had won, and he could smell the sea in the breeze. Soon, it would be time to take to the Whale Road again and go a'viking once more.

THE VIKING BLOOD AND BLADE SAGA

If you like Bernard Cornwell, Conn Iggulden, Simon Scarrow, David Gemmell and Giles Kristian, you will love this epic Viking adventure, packed with battles, treachery, blood and gore.

Viking Blood And Blade

865 AD. The fierce Vikings stormed onto Saxon soil hungry for spoils, conquest, and vengeance for the death of Ragnar Lothbrok.

Hundr, a Northman with a dog's name... a crew of battle hardened warriors... and Ivar the Boneless.

Amidst the invasion of Saxon England by the sons of Ragnar Lothbrok, Hundr joins a crew of Viking warriors under the command of Einar the Brawler. Hundr fights to forge a warriors reputation under the glare of Ivar and his equally fearsome brothers, but to do that he must battle the Saxons and treachery from within the Viking army itself...

Hundr must navigate the invasion, survive

brutal attacks, and find his place in the vicious world of the Vikings.

The Wrath Of Ivar

866 AD. Saxon England burns under attack from the Great Heathen Army. Vicious Viking adventurers land on the coast of Frankia hungry for spoils, conquest and glory.

Hundr and the crew of the warship Seaworm are hunted by Ivar the Boneless, a pitiless warrior of incomparable fury and weapon skill.

Amidst the invasion of Brittany and war with the Franks, Hundr allies with the armies of Haesten and Bjorn Ironside, two of the greatest warriors of the Viking Age. Ivar the Boneless hunts Hundr, desperate to avenge the death of his son at Hundr's hand. To survive, Hundr must battle against fearsome Lords of Frankia, navigate treachery within the Viking Army itself, and become a warrior of reputation in his own right.

Axes For Valhalla

873 AD. The Viking Age grips Northern Europe. Seven years have passed since the ferocious sea battle with Ivar the Boneless, and Hundr is now a Viking war leader of reputation and wealth. A voice from the past calls to Hundr for aid,

and he must take his loyal crew and their feared warships across the Whale Road to Viking Dublin, in a vicious and brutal fight against Eystein Longaxe.

Hundr must fight against an implacable and powerful enemy, amidst brutal attacks, shield wall battles, and treachery. Will his skill and savagery be enough, and can Hundr and his crew survive? Find out in this unputdownable, fast paced adventure with memorable characters.

ABOUT THE AUTHOR

Peter Gibbons

Peter is an author from Warrington in the United Kingdom, now living in County Kildare, Ireland. Peter is a married father of three children, with a burning passion for history.

Peter grew up enjoying the novels of Bernard Cornwell and David Gemmell, and then the historical texts of Arrian, Xenophon, and Josephus. Peter was inspired by tales of knights, legends and heroes, and from reading the tales of Sharpe, Uhtred, Druss, Achilles, and Alexander, Peter developed a love for history and its heroes.

For news on upcoming releases visit Peter's website at www.petermgibbons.com

Printed in Great Britain
by Amazon

42793675R00229